Reckless Fate

Reckless Billionaires Series

Maxine Henri

"Every heart has its own skeletons."
Anna Karenina

Chapter One

Massi

This year will be the best year of my life. Everything I've ever wished for is at my fingertips, I just have to reach up and reap the benefits. If I don't fuck up. I've been there, done that. I'm not letting anything or anyone stop me from my dream this time.

I lick the bechamel off my finger and my taste buds tingle with pleasure.

"It's almost there, but adding saffron would get it to the next level." This is as much praise as I'm willing to bestow. I don't want this young, talented chef to stop working on his craft. I recognize potential when I see it. Or taste it.

"Yeah, I tried it before and it was too much." Richie continues whisking the sauce, but lowers the heat. He's at least ten years younger than me and I sometimes see myself in him. Well, to an extent, since we're complete opposites when it comes to temper. This young man with the quiet determination has great things ahead of him.

"The alchemy of cooking is not an exact science. You need to experiment. If it doesn't work the first time, try the second, the tenth, the hundredth, but don't give up." I pat his shoulder.

His wife, Manuela, comes in with a shot of espresso for me. "You look very smart today, Massi."

I was fine, but as soon as she mentions my clothes, the suit's constraining properties multiply. Fuck, it's like wearing barbed wire. I tug at the tie. "I have a thing later. How is the business?"

"We get enough reservations on weekends when many come to the market, but during the week it's hit or miss. Sometimes we are full and sometimes it's just at half capacity." She wipes the counter as she speaks.

Their small bistro is a family business. A couple's business, with the two of them covering all the parts of the operation.

"Come up with specials for Thursday evenings to begin with. Something that doesn't break the bank but attracts people." I shake Richie's hand and kiss Manuela's cheek. "Keep playing with saffron. I'll come and taste your bechamel next month."

Richie wraps his arm around his wife's shoulders. Once upon a time, I thought I'd run a family business. But then I became a lone wolf, which works just fine.

"Thank you, Massimo. For everything."

Some believe I'm supporting my competition, but there is plenty of room for excellent cuisine and dining experience in a metropolitan city like New York.

I walk the several long blocks to my business. My restaurant. Technically, only sixty percent mine, but it's my culinary mastery that brings people in. This popular place—and may I humbly say, one of the most popular—in Manhattan has been built on my sweat.

Casa Cassi has been named an epicurean gem in the middle of SoHo and I won't argue with that. This year I'll polish its reputation with a star. One that I lost early in my career, but not this time. This time, I'm focused and determined. This time my business partner, Phillip, will oversee the entire process, so my—some say horrible—temper won't interfere.

I waltz inside and two of my staff scatter away from the long, polished bar that lines the wall to the right of the entrance. Beside the mahogany and steel counter is the double door to my kingdom. I wave my greetings at the two employees, who suddenly get busy, and smile to myself.

I should know their names, but I don't. Not yet. I'm not sure if they share my vision, so I don't bother. Maybe I am an asshole like people say, but you have to earn my respect and many of these young servers just come to make money on the way somewhere else—college, other jobs—so why bother getting to know them?

And it's Phillip's domain to schmooze with the employees. That leaves me space to focus on the menu and the superb quality we offer here.

I make myself another espresso while the two servers wipe down the tables spread around eight hundred square feet of wood-like stone floor with the walls of exposed bricks and copper fixtures.

I love this place. Even in the dim lights of its last yawns before it awakens with crowds, orders, popped corks, clinking ice and clattering cutlery. This place has been my home for fifteen years.

I push through the double doors that lead to the kitchen. Today is Monday, my day off, but I can't stay away.

The room teems with activity, prepping is full speed ahead. The rich smell of a homemade meal whiffs my way, surprising me. Who dared to update the menu?

My sous-chef, Lena, Phillip's fiancée, greets me with a shy smile. She is slicing carrots on the stainless-steel counter in the middle of the kitchen. I wasn't particularly thrilled Phillip wanted her to work here, but it only took three days to see how capable she was.

"Morning," I grunt, because I don't like people in general.

The shift in mood upon my entry is palpable. Two cooks, who were chatting happily, are now focused on their tasks. They don't meet my eyes as they greet me back.

The only person holding my gaze is Lena. Phillip has said little about her, but it's been clear she has dealt with an asshole, or assholes, in the past and I don't scare her. That's the reason I like her. Within days she figured out my temper is motivated by my drive to create magic. Focus. Eyes on the result.

"Good morning to you too, boss," Lena says with a lingering smile. I swear to God she is mocking me with her attitude. And I like her for that even more. Phillip is a lucky bastard.

"You working on the soup?" I frown at the carrots that are perfectly shaped. Just like I taught her.

"Yes, and I took the liberty of preparing red sauce rigatoni for your mother." She gestures toward the oven, the source of the divine smell.

"How did you know I need a dish for my mother?" I snap.

"It's hard not to overhear your phone conversations. I hope rigatoni is okay for a wake." She returns to her slicing mastery.

She anticipated my needs. Lena the fucking Saint. And then I glimpse my expression in the mirror above the sink in the corner and I sigh. "Thank you, Lena, I appreciate your help."

To her credit, she only shrugs. I love people who don't gloat. Or who would do it inwardly.

I go to my office, check my emails and look over the reservation systems for the next two weeks. We are booked solid for the special menu I'm testing. Good. I'd go to get changed, but unfortunately my mother has other plans for my day off.

As she put it, spending a day off at work is not healthy. As if going to a wake is.

My phone buzzes in my pocket. Speak of the devil. I hate the days off.

"When will you be here?" Mother never starts a phone call with a greeting.

"In an hour or so." I dare to roll my eyes because she can't see me.

"Hurry. I don't want to be late. Are you bringing the lasagna?"

"Rigatoni." I stand up to leave my office.

"Rigatoni? You've never made rigatoni for a funeral. Usually we bring lasagna." Her voice is accusatory as if I've just broken our neighbor's window.

"What does it matter? You said bring *something*. Something, Mother. Not lasagna. Rigatoni is a perfectly respectable mourning dish." I slam the office door behind me.

"I just don't want the family to think we treat them differently."

Her response makes no sense.

"Mother, nobody remembers what you usually bring to a wake. Who died anyway?" I ask as I turn the corner.

Lena is ordering everyone around with efficiency and unnecessary kindness. The kitchen seems to run as smoothly as if I were working. Why does that annoy me?

"Just get here soon." Mom hangs up.

Somehow, as the oldest son, I became responsible for accompanying my mother to all the funerals. It might be my ability to bring the food, but for some reason Mother relies on my personal presence. I don't even know why, but I comply begrudgingly.

She hung up too quickly. God help me if there is an eligible freshly widowed woman involved.

I bark a few commands at Lena, who doesn't flinch

but continues to debone the fish of the day with expert proficiency.

"You don't want to be late, boss," she says, puts down the knife and hands me a large dish covered with foil. "Careful, it's hot."

Yes, I'm grouchier than usual. Perhaps. But I hate Mondays. I hate when people are trying to get rid of me. I hate not being here.

"Everyone, don't fuck up while I'm gone," I roar as Phillip ambles into the kitchen.

"I see you're your usual sunshine and all." He walks over and plants a kiss in Lena's hair. She hands him a bag with sandwiches that he picks up every day for a homeless person near his art studio.

"You know how he gets on Mondays," Lena deadpans.

"We agreed you have to take two days off for your own mental health, bro." Phillip pats my shoulder.

"Yeah, but we're only closed one of those days." I turn to get a hot box and place the chafing dish of rigatoni in it carefully. "Thank you for these, Lena."

"Look at you playing nice." Phillip snorts and someone else snickers behind me.

"Both of you, out of the kitchen now," Lena says and we obey. Before the door swings closed, I can almost hear the communal exhalation.

"Do you have time for coffee?" Phillip asks.

"The town car is picking me up in a few minutes."

He scratches the back of his neck, looking around the room. "I hired a consultant to help us get the house in order."

I raise my eyebrows and carefully place the box on the floor. "We need to get the house in order?"

"Okay, wrong choice of words, but you know what I mean. She operates on the West Coast, but she's going to be in New York for a few weeks and she's willing to advise us on potential improvements. She's worked with places that subsequently got a star."

I glower, but Phillip withstands it, unimpressed. "Michelin stars are awarded on the merits of exceptional culinary art. Some consultant is going to pump us for money to do what? Teach me to cook?" My voice echoes around the room, and for a moment even the kitchen behind me falls silent. The familiar quivering of muscles as my pulse speeds up reminds me to count my breaths.

"Don't be an asshole now. If it was the question of your culinary art, you'd have at least one star already."

His words placate me enough to remember the breathing. In. Out. In. Out.

"But they need to notice us first," he continues. "And that's where we may need some help. Give her one meeting, then you can decide. At the end of the day, this is your place and I'm only the silent *minority* partner." He raises his eyebrows, challenging me.

I stare at the floor, the ridges of the stone pattern twisting around as I see red, but eventually I pull myself together and look up. Phillip has been standing there, his hands in his pockets, waiting for my internal storm to pass. The fucker knows me well.

He showed up in my life when I was ready to close. My cuisine was exceptional, but I couldn't attract guests because, let's face it, my skills are in the kitchen. Phillip stumbled upon this place by accident and has never left.

"Okay. One meeting to see what she has to say." I pick up the hot box and leave without another word.

The drive to Riverdale takes almost an hour and Mother practically jumps into the car before we come to a full stop in the cul-de-sac in front of my childhood home.

"We're late. I'm sure your driver could continue for a few more blocks to get us there." She squeezes my hand as she slides into the leather seat next to me.

"He's not *my* driver—"

She gives him the address and I slump deeper into my seat.

"The service at the church was beautiful. It would have looked better if you were there." Bianca

Cassinetti is a master of the subtle art of the blame game. "You look stressed, Massi. Have you been sleeping well?" She narrows her eyes.

I straighten my tie and clear my throat. "I'm good."

"You need someone to take care of you, Massi." She squeezes my hand again.

Here we go. Sometimes it seems my mother, who raised eight children, is solely focused on marrying *me*.

"Is this again a plot to set me up, Mom?"

I stare out of the window on my side. We leave our neighborhood and the car's direction squeezes my stomach. I should have paid attention when she recited the address.

"Of course not, it's a wake, for God's sake." She pretends to be scandalized by my insinuation. If only I didn't have years of experience to prove I'm right.

"Yeah, as if that has ever stopped you." I raise my eyebrows and study her. She is clutching her black purse with vigor, as if... as if what?

The car pulls to the curb in front of a small house I've never seen before. I know this neighborhood well. Too well. At least it's not one of my former classmates. Women who are divorced and annoyingly eager.

Over the years, my mother has tried to set me up with completely unsuitable women. Sometimes I think she just needs me married off, regardless of who her future daughter-in-law would be, so she can move on and play matchmaker for my brothers and step-sisters.

We get out of the car on the deserted street.

"I told you we'd be late. Everyone is already inside." Mother picks lint from my lapel and pats me there in a reassuring gesture. To reassure me of what?

She starts toward the house and, as an afterthought, she says over her shoulder, "Gina will be there."

I stop dead in my tracks. So, a high school class-mate after all. One I haven't seen in almost two decades. Great.

Fuck. Fuck. Fuck.

Mother stops and whips around, beckoning me with her eyes. "What? It's her father's funeral, of course she's here."

I want to drop the box and leave. This meddling has to end. Me playing the role of my mother's plus one for dreadful community events has to end.

And then the door opens and my heart stops for a moment. She's changed. Her hair is in a sleek bob, hanging just below her ears. She's wearing thick-rimmed glasses and a navy-blue dress that hugs all her curves.

Those curves *haven't* changed. They matured like the best wine in the cellar, improving the vintage, making my mouth dry and my cock twitch in my pants. Fuck, she is beautiful.

But none of it matters, I remind myself, as I finally regain the ability to walk.

None of it matters because I'm not interested in a relationship.

Been there, done that.

Chapter Two

Massi

17 years ago

The best orgasm I'd ever had. Mind you, I'd only been with this one woman. The most beautiful girl in the world.

I didn't understand how it could have been better every time.

I didn't understand why my friends enjoyed playing around.

I didn't understand the need.

Being with the girl who was currently beaming at me by my side was too good to even test the waters elsewhere.

The afternoon sun played in her dark hair, splayed

across the pink pillow. We were so close my skin was practically glued to hers. I wasn't complaining about the twin bed, the girly covers or the threat of her parents catching us. But I'd give anything to have her all to myself.

Not to sneak around. Not to steal these wonderful moments when she let me claim her. When she was mine. When she broke through her shyness and allowed me to see her, be with her, share with her these amazing memories.

I loved her.

The first day I'd seen her I knew she was special. I didn't know how yet, but I'd known I had to discover more. Discover her. Sitting under the large chestnut, she had her nose buried in a book while her friends chirped away and giggled.

I couldn't turn away, and when she looked up my chest constricted in the most wonderful and painful way. I had never had issues asking girls out, but it took me three weeks of staring before I'd finally found the courage. And why this quiet, beautiful, smart girl had agreed I would never understand.

I was a nineteen-year-old lovesick puppy, and there was nothing better in the world than this feeling.

"Why are you staring?" She narrowed her dark blue eyes, the long lashes veiling them.

"I'm staring at the most beautiful woman in the

world, Blue." I kissed her, planning on a gentle peck, but that escalated quickly. I devoured her lips with a passion that burned me inside out and my cock saluted again.

How was she so perfect?

How was I so lucky?

A squeak on the stairs broke us apart.

"Oh my God, oh my God, oh my God, Massi, it's my mom." Blue dove for her T-shirt on the floor and kicked me off her bed. I landed with a thud and our eyes met for a second. The fear in her gaze hit me right in my stomach.

Fuck. I was causing her so much anxiety. She whipped around and scooped up all our clothes before throwing them in my direction. Lying between her bed and the window, I held her underwear to my nose and smiled. I was a lucky bastard.

"Mom, I was just changing," she said as the door swung open.

"Whatever for? There is enough laundry for an army to sort out. Come downstairs to help me with dinner. I've been calling you for half an hour. We should have never gotten you those headphones. Who goes around listening to music?" The last words were muted by the door closing and Blue's mom shuffling back downstairs.

Blue plopped on the bed, on her stomach, and

glared at me, her face a mixture of fear and relief. I couldn't help myself with this girl. I moved off the floor and claimed her mouth again. This time she pushed me away, half-heartedly, but still. Her mother had tainted the mood.

"Stop it, Massi. Now!" She swatted at me. "You need to leave. If my parents ever find out, my mom will send me to live with my aunt in Italy."

"Blue, it's not the fifties anymore." I hauled myself up to sit on the bed and pulled her to my lap.

The silky skin of her thighs caused a reaction in my briefs, but I tried to ignore it and stayed focused on calming her down. I cupped her neck and pulled her closer. As my forehead connected with hers, I was sure that my only mission in life was to make those deep blue eyes shine.

"It might not be the fifties anymore, but my mother's morals are stuck there. Massi, you can't be coming here anymore. She would send me away or force you to marry me to save my virtue." She shook her head slightly and rolled her eyes.

"Now that's an idea," I said and she jerked away. Two things happened at the same time. Blue tried to stifle her laugh, and my heart jumped in realization that I wasn't joking. Well, I was when I had said it, but the idea sounded too right. Too real. Too good.

She must have read my train of thought because

the amusement left her face. It disappeared slowly, and I could already feel the pain of rejection creeping in as her features rearranged into shock. Suddenly, she was lighter in my arms, as if part of her was already gone, suspended between my embrace and the need to flee.

"Massi," she breathed and the lightness of her voice gave me a ridiculous jolt of encouragement.

"I mean it, Blue. I want to spend the rest of my life with you."

"So you want to break up?" I paced around the small playground.

It was the middle of the night and Blue had sneaked out to meet me here. Somehow, the place that was normally full of children's laughter appeared sinister now, its slumber interrupted by the eerie creaks of the swings.

She threw her arms up. "Why are you being so dramatic? All I'm saying is we're so young—"

"Why does it matter? I want to be with you. Forever." I stopped and stared at her.

She stood near the sandpit, only a touch away, yet so far. Her face was obscured in the shadows of the night. Goddammit. Ever since the idea of marriage crossed my mind, I couldn't stop thinking about it.

"You don't know what forever means." She stepped closer, a thick line of stress marring her forehead.

We glared at each other, our chests heaving. The need to kiss the words away was too powerful. I clenched my fists.

"I know what *you* mean to me, but clearly you're just waiting for the next guy to woo you." I didn't even know what I was saying anymore. How could I feel so much rage and love at the same time? I wanted to shake her and make love to her in equal measure.

"You're such an asshole." Blue's voice quivered slightly and she turned away from me.

"Clearly." I rolled my eyes. *Why am I such an asshole?*

She whirled around and the fury in her face made me step back. The raging war in her stance, in her expression, was what I deserved, but I didn't care for it.

"What is that supposed to mean? You're being so unreasonable." Her voice carried across the playground and probably the entire neighborhood. Her breath came out in short, shallow bursts and her nostrils flared. God, she was beautiful.

Perhaps I was being a stubborn prick. Or perhaps I'd recognized we had something special and she just needed to catch up. But her fighting it made me desperate. Unable to judge right from wrong. Or reason.

"I love you, Massi." Her words were soft now and the vise around my heart tightened. "But we're nineteen. What's the rush? Besides, I don't think our parents would ever allow that."

I reached for her hand and she didn't recoil. Thank God. "They would come around. It's you who is against it. Is our age the only reason?" I struggled to keep my tone level and failed miserably. Frustration and need laced my every thought, and as a result my words.

"What's the fucking rush?" Her breath hitched. She bit her lower lip and a single tear escaped.

In that moment, I knew that if I lost her I'd regret it for the rest of my life. And I'd lose her if I continued pushing. Yet, I unloaded the truth—as desperate as I felt.

"I don't want to hide anymore. I love you, Blue. I know you're the one for me." I stepped closer and cupped her face in my palms. "I want to wake up beside you every morning. I want you to be there when I come home frustrated after a long day at work, because you make me forget, you make me feel better just by breathing the same air. You make me happy. Every smile or laugh I manage to elicit from you makes me happy.

"Every time your beautiful eyes go dark with worry I'm physically sick, and I'd move mountains to make them shine again. There is no doubt in my mind that we belong together, so why not be together?" I seized her lips, gently savoring the taste of her. Her shivers squeezed at my stomach.

With my mouth still on hers, I continued. "Blue, baby, you're the first thing on my mind when I wake up and the last whisper before I fall asleep." My heart was racing, faster than was healthy, for sure. I stepped back to regain control. Fat chance.

"Goddammit, you're the only subject of my dreams." My throat was coarse from shouting, but I was past any self-awareness. "Every single day you kill me and mend me back to life. That's how it feels. Like you're my poison and my antidote at the same time. You're it for me, Blue. However unreasonable, whatever the timing, regardless of the circumstances, you're it for me."

A loud sob broke through the midnight air. Blue's tear-stricken face was the most painful thing I'd ever seen, so I closed my eyes, still hoping my fucking stubbornness hadn't just killed our love. I pushed and pushed, and all I achieved was breaking two hearts at the same time.

The gravel crunching pulled at my heart. I was afraid to open my eyes. I couldn't watch her retreat. I couldn't watch the damage I'd caused. Every groan of the tiny pebbles pierced my heart with definitive sadness.

I'd always been partial to drama—the whole family was—but right now, without exaggeration, I knew I was on the edge of irrevocable suffering. I lost my father when I was younger, so the emptiness seeping into my heart felt too fucking familiar.

Until, just barely through the thumping in my temples, I felt more than heard footsteps crunching toward me. I opened my eyes at the same time as two hands wrapped around my neck and I was drowned in the smell of the summer's meadow I adored so much. Blue crushed her lips against mine and I stumbled, shocked by the attack.

Oh, but I'd take this attack any time. Her tongue thrust in and we danced with our mouths in a desperate choreography that screamed of our mutual hurt, frustration and passion.

"Damn you, Massi," she breathed, and I lost any awareness of time or space. Her voice, her sweet lips, her resilience and her love were more than I ever deserved.

I rushed my hands down her back, marveling at the feel of her against me. I cupped her round, perfect ass and lifted her.

She wrapped her legs around my waist without breaking the kiss. We staggered around like a pair of drunks. Blinded by our kiss but fueled by the desire to reach a destination, I stomped around to find a surface, any surface, to free my hands. Yet afraid to lose the contact.

Blue yelped as her back hit something. I ground my hips, something coarse chafing the top of my hand. I pushed harder against her, freeing my arm. However, we got there, Blue was pinned against a tree, warm and eager in my embrace.

I found the hem of her shirt quickly. As soon as my palm connected with the silky skin of her ribcage, my cock rose painfully inside my jeans.

I brushed the swell of her breast and we broke the kiss, both of us needing air and moaning at the same time. It was too dark, but somehow her eyes shone through, penetrating every cell in my body. This woman would be the death of me, and I'd be not only willing, but an eager participant.

"Massi," she whispered.

"I love you, Blue." I squeezed the hard bud under the lace of her bra and she sighed, tightening her hold on me in more ways than just the physical.

Her long fingers traced my back as she ground her hips against me. We needed to find a shelter, or at least a fucking shadow right now.

I dropped her down but held her close, afraid to break the spell. She grabbed my collar and yanked me to her, her mouth capturing mine again. Her teeth grazed hungrily over my lips.

"Ask me, Massi," she whispered.

I froze, at first seeking comprehension, but then afraid I understood what she was asking. Or misunderstood. *God help me.*

I searched her face. Washed by tears, but so resolute. Like someone who was ready to tackle the world. At my side.

She nodded and smiled. "Ask me, my love."

Fuck me. I held her so tight I could crack her rib, but I would not let go ever again. I cleared my throat, my gaze buried in the ocean of her eyes. "Will you marry me?"

I didn't think my words were audible because the emotions overwhelmed my ability to speak. But they must have been because Blue nodded frantically, and then came as close as possible to waking up the entire neighborhood when she screamed at the top of her lungs.

"Yes!"

I silenced her with my mouth, our joy and passion immediately clouding any sense of responsibility or propriety. Somehow I moved us to a bench and Blue straddled me. We fumbled with our zippers and buttons.

There was nothing sensual or gracious about it, just

two hungry people chasing release. No finesse. No patience. No foreplay. Just a raw confirmation of the commitment we'd just made.

I plunged into her and Blue whimpered or moaned or whatever the sound was, but it was the most beautiful sound. We struggled to find the rhythm, our lovemaking still very new, but we got there quickly.

We moved in unison, aware of the surroundings and unaware of them at the same time. She sank her teeth into my shoulder to muffle the sounds I loved to hear so much.

It was over as fast as it started. I tried to catch my breath, loving how Blue's body sagged in my arm. How we fit together.

"I love you, Massi."

"I love you, Blue."

Returning slowly to reality, holding her close to me, a wave of happiness splashed over me. Immediately followed by dread.

"Fuck, Blue, condom." I jerked back and met her gaze.

Her hair was now falling around her glowing face. Somewhere in the process, she'd lost the elastic.

She was radiant and so fucking beautiful, yet fear was the prevailing emotion roaming my blood.

She giggled and kissed my cheek. The scent of the

meadow usually calmed me, but my heart had decided to train for the rock and roll Olympics right now.

"We're getting married anyway, Massi."

She buried her face in the crook of my neck. Thank God for that, because if my face mirrored only a fragment of the horror seeping through me this relationship would be over.

Fuck me. I wanted to get married so badly, but not to burden our love with kids. We were only nineteen.

"I think our heartbeats have synchronized," Blue whispered with her palm on my chest.

I doubt that, I thought as I tightened my embrace, hoping that I hadn't pushed us head on into a crash we might not survive.

Chapter Three

Gina

I enter the busy bistro on 9th Avenue ten minutes early, but Mila is already waiting for me.

The open space gallery in the heart of the historic Meatpacking District is inviting if a little too busy for my taste. That's the problem with trendy places—they lack privacy. Something I value slightly more than the culinary experience itself.

But I have to admit this place is amazing. The designer has wed outdoor with indoor, combining glass walls and ceilings with shrubbery and trees planted inside. It's fresh, it's light and it's classy without being stuffy.

The hostess smiles at me and I wave at Mila who is bouncing in her seat. God, I love that girl. She is seven years younger than me but is my closest friend. Or really the only friend I have.

I've lived the life of a recluse of sorts, trying to avoid the spotlight despite working with influencers and trendsetters. I'm the one who stays behind the scenes. For all the good reasons. Some not so good, maybe.

"Oh my God, Gina, I'm so happy to see you," Mila squeals as I approach and several people turn our way. She jumps up and almost knocks the hostess down as she throws herself on me.

Enveloped in her tight embrace and lavender scent, I get strangely emotional and my eyes mist. I blink a few times. There goes my resolution to remain composed. "I missed you so much." Fuck, I sound teary. Well, I am teary.

"Oh, no, don't cry." She pulls me to our table and we take seats. "I'm so sorry about your father."

Oh yeah, and then there is that. My father. I hadn't spoken to him in seventeen years and now I won't anymore. "Fuck."

"Let's order drinks." Mila gestures to the server. She flails her arms around as if being served immediately is a question of life or death. All the while beaming. Her smile is so sweet and warm that even her occasionally outrageous behavior raises no eyebrows.

"Two gin and tonics," she announces without consulting me.

What the heck. I can have a drink or two after the hell of a week I've been having.

"Distract me, Mils. I can use some of your honey personality." I lean against the leather padded backrest and hope that nobody notices my spread legs. I don't have it in me to hold the form tonight. The tiny devil on my shoulder laughs. Falling apart already? Four days on the East Coast is all it takes?

"Well, since I left LA—"

"Since you've abandoned me..." I can't help but remind her of what I still consider a betrayal. Okay, not really, but I miss her badly.

Mila appeared in my life ten years ago when she was so young and inexperienced that only my inability to offer her a reasonable salary had qualified her for a job as my personal assistant. Lucky for me, her eagerness to stay in LA and partially her spontaneous nature made her accept my ridiculous offer.

And as it turned out, Mila was a godsend, and thanks to her knowledge and enjoyment of social media she helped me bring my business to a completely new level. We worked well together until six months ago, when she decided to move to New York. She broke up with her fiancé—a lovely man—and took off. She's never volunteered any details, so I don't pry.

"You're still bitter about it?" She tosses her long blond hair and I'm not sure if she is dismissing my comment or hiding her discomfort. "But now you're here and we can work together again," she chirps.

"Are you sure you can take on this one? I don't want to interfere with your current gigs. What are you up to anyway?"

The server brings our drinks and recites the specials before taking our order.

"I'm freelancing and you're lucky I'm available to take on your project." She wiggles her shoulders in delight.

"That's great. Until I sort things out with my mother I don't want to sit around. I need a distraction. We'll meet the client tomorrow and see what time commitment the project requires."

"Sounds great. How are things with your mom?"

The heavy sigh that escapes me says more about my feelings regarding this unexpected responsibility than I've been willing to admit to myself.

"Not so good. I need to find a home for her and put the house on the market. It may take days or weeks, but hopefully I can sort things out quickly before I'll be forced to fly back and forth."

"Everything okay back home? How is Sebastien?"

Mila plays with her straw, her eyes simultaneously on me and darting around. It's her superpower. She can be fully engaged in a conversation and absorb her surroundings at the same time. To others she might look distracted, but I know she's anything but.

"He's doing well, probably thrilled to have the place to himself." I pull my phone out to check if he called or texted and a wave of disappointment washes over me.

"Perhaps you should hook up with someone while you're here. That would cheer you up." She claps her hands, then grabs her phone, probably ready to call one of the available men who shower her with attention. Not even when she was wearing an engagement ring was she saved from unwanted flirting. She is beautiful and sexy, but it's her girl-next-door vibe that wins people around.

"I've just buried my father, lost control of my life on the West Coast by default, and found out that my parents' finances are in a less-than-ideal state. I've never found hook-ups attractive and I'm certainly not inclined to consider them now."

"Your loss. I met these two guys last month and the quality of orgasms is therapeutic. I'm sure they would be interested, and I don't mind sharing." She winks at me and for a moment I'm not sure if I envy her lack of inhibition or if her casual statement horrifies me.

My brain cycles through several parts of that statement. Sex with two men. Her willingness to share. And the therapeutic properties of an orgasm. I could use a handful of the last. Or at least one. It's been way too long. Not that my vibrator doesn't deliver, but still...

"You're sleeping with two men at the same time?" I whisper for some reason. "I can't imagine having sex with two men."

"Don't sound so scandalized." She takes a generous gulp of her drink. "Though to be honest the first time it was kind of stressful, but it got really amazing quickly after that." She bites her bottom lip, shrugging gleefully.

"You did it more than once?" Now it's my turn to down my drink. God, these are good. I wave to order another round. "I wouldn't be able to think what to do first, or next, for that matter." I chuckle.

"Think? Why would you think while having sex?" Mila shakes her head, laughing.

"I have a brain. I can't stop thinking."

The server brings our entrees and the aroma of thyme and lemon tickles my nose.

"And *that* is your problem."

I laugh. "And a threesome would solve that?"

"It just might." With her fork Mila spears a tomato from her salad and wiggles it in my direction before turning it playfully to her mouth, where her teeth slide it off as if it was the most decadent chocolate in the world.

That's the problem with having a younger, sexy, sensual and very graceful friend. You always feel less. Perhaps a threesome would solve some of my issues. My self-confidence would definitely get a boost... *if* it's really as good as she claims.

"You're insane." I say out loud to Mila, but it's a warning for me too.

"Okay, I mean it in the kindest way ever, but I'm certainly more satisfied and happier than you. All I'm saying is that sometimes you just need to let go. Stop trying to control everything."

"Where have you been? You know how late it is, young lady? Way past your curfew." My mom appears in the hallway.

I'm balancing on one foot, trying to take my shoes off without falling on my face. Okay, so I had a few more drinks than I should have, but I laughed so much. For a few precious moments, I felt free. Something I haven't felt in... well, in ages. If ever.

Mom, wearing a pink nylon bathrobe and rollers in her fine gray hair, stands at the bottom of the stairs and glares at me. I remember the menacing powers of that glare and shudder at its current version. She looks so fragile that I worry that even me speaking would blow her away.

"I'm sorry, Mom. Why don't we have some warm milk and go to bed?" I try to articulate clearly. It costs me more effort than it should. How much gin did I have?

"No warm milk for you, young lady. You were not here to help me out. Everything is up to me and your father..." Her gaze shifts slightly and her eyes widen as if the realization she's a widow crashes over her once more. As if remembering my father is gone comes in phases, shattering her world again and again.

"Your father isn't here to help anymore." Tears glisten in her eyes. She turns, the hunch of her shoulders even more pronounced as she shuffles toward the stairs.

I watch her carrying her sorrow and confusion up and I'm unable to move. To help her out. To share her grief. To be there for her in any useful way. The realization that the only reason I'm staying is a sense of responsibility hits me hard and I collapse onto the small bench.

Tears roll down my face and I'm not even sure why I'm crying. I hear Mom's bedroom door click open and then closed, followed by the creak of her bed. Only then do I allow a strangled sob to escape.

I sit there, sobbing quietly in the hallway, until physical discomfort brings me out of my reverie. There is no point in reminiscing about what could have been or what if. Those are stupid concepts that bring nothing good with them. Shit went down all those years ago, severing my relationship with many people, including my parents.

Looking back, I might understand their position. Faced with my mother's devastation when I arrived four days ago, I realized understanding is a useless notion, because it doesn't grant forgiveness. And to mend my connection with my home and my family, to mend my broken heart, forgiveness seems to be the necessary stepping stone.

That's what my therapist keeps saying, anyway.

I stand up and trudge to the guest room. Another surprise that waited for me here. This house. I had no idea my parents had downsized. Or when. This house isn't far from our old one, but it's small. Significantly smaller.

I get to the cold bed. The little stars glued to the ceiling—this must have been a child's bedroom—swirl as I keep staring at them for what might be minutes or hours. Every time I close my eyes, Mila's words haunt me.

Am I really a control freak? Perhaps a hidden one, but what other choice did I have? When one's life implodes, survival instincts kick in. And it's not my fault I survive by control.

Mila calls me a spreadsheet queen, but how else am I supposed to manage? Would a mindless fuck really help me? A therapeutic orgasm?

With a sigh—God, I've been doing that a lot lately—I get up and rummage through my carry-on to find my vibrator. I return to the bed and pull down my panties. My reliable toy works its magic and within minutes I stifle a scream, biting my forearm.

With a sigh, I sag into the mattress. Orgasm, yes. Therapeutic, definitely not. That's the problem with sex toys—they don't deliver the closeness of another person, a kiss, a hug or human intimacy. They leave me empty and lonely. Satisfaction that only intensifies the longing.

I throw the toy across the room. It lands with a thud and I cringe. Fuck. I hope I didn't break it. It might not be therapeutic, but it's the only O I've been getting. At the age of thirty-six, I can't decide if that's pathetic or normal.

I groan. An upgrade to the sighing—I really want to roll my eyes at myself. But my pity party is interrupted by a vibrating sound. I guess I didn't break the Womanizer after all.

I sit up and switch the bedside light on. Shit, there are two pink parts by the door. There go my future orgasms. But the sound buzzes somewhere by my feet. My bag is by the nightstand where I dropped it earlier.

Finally, the rest of my brain completes the picture and I dig my phone out. If I thought my week had been shitty so far, I was wrong. Seeing the caller ID, I decline the call, but I know I can't escape the caller.

Chapter Four

Massi

17 years ago

"You're so handsome, Massi." My mother held my face in her soft hands and planted a kiss on my forehead. "I still don't understand what the rush is, but I'm so happy for you."

"I'm happy too, Mom."

By sheer luck, Blue got her period shortly after our night of passion and the boulder of responsibility lifted from my chest. Slightly. The short engagement, the initial wrath of her parents, the wedding preparations and my work didn't allow for much reflection. But the heaviness of the responsibility—it's weighed on me daily ever since that night.

I fought her hard for something I wanted. Something I still wanted, just in a version that might not completely align with Blue's. She looked sad, finding out she wasn't pregnant. Or maybe I'd just been imagining things, but I was too freaked out to even broach the subject.

I wanted to be with her, but not with the burden of a family life. Not just yet.

The room around me lacked the same excitement that was missing from my mother's eyes. My brothers lingered around the suite, wearing their boy versions of tuxedos and utterly bored. Gio, at seventeen, had only one goal for today—to get laid. God help all the mothers at the wedding in protecting their daughters.

Andrea, at fifteen, might try to score a girl as well. Thirteen-year-old Baldo would stir up trouble just because he wanted to, and he could.

Gio was my best man and he couldn't be less thrilled about his role. He believed I was throwing my freedom away. It became a sore point during the bachelor party when part of me, the drunk me, admitted he might be right. An admission that sounded pathetic in light of my later howling about how much I adored my girl.

"I'd like to give you a wedding gift." Mom straightened the handkerchief in my breast pocket, her gaze stern on me as if she was contemplating something.

"Don't you want to wait for after the ceremony and give it to both of us?" I placed my hand over hers and studied her.

I couldn't decipher her expression. It certainly wasn't happiness. Nor was it sadness that her eldest son was leaving. In that moment she seemed torn, and the realization she wasn't completely on my side hit me harder that I cared to admit.

She was much shorter than me. It was a running joke in my family because she was the smallest of us all. Her tiny frame was really half of mine.

But regardless of her height, she ruled the family with an iron fist. And we might be large men, but none of us dared to challenge her. Well, maybe Baldo did. He was a spoiled brat because he was the youngest and he'd never known our father.

"This is for you. In *your* name and pre-wedding, so it's yours only. I wish you all the happiness, but just in case things don't go your way, I want to make sure your dreams aren't shattered."

I frowned. Was she predicting that we'd break up and Blue would rip me off? Of what exactly? It wasn't like I had much. My family was well-off, but I'd been an apprentice at Modigliani's, a popular restaurant in Manhattan, for a year now, but that was as much as I had to my name.

"Mom, are you saying my marriage will fail? Didn't

you just say you're happy for me? What the hell?" Irritation snaked around my insides as I tried to remain calm. Not something I was known for.

Mother swatted at me. "Don't be over-sensitive. I'm just protecting you. Open it." She nodded toward the envelope she'd pushed into my hands.

I ripped it open and the contents, really just one slip of paper, sent my heart pumping. My eyes darted between the check and my mother. Gio strolled toward us and craned his neck over my shoulder.

"Fuck me! I'm getting married tomorrow if this is the payout." He punched my shoulder.

"Language, Gio." Mother gave him one of her evil looks and he backed away. Her eyes landed on me and her expression was full of love and joy. This Dr. Jekyll-Mr. Hyde routine should be old by now, but it had always spooked me how she could change her behavior so swiftly.

"My dearest Massi," she said, "it's time you started working on your own restaurant. You can't work at Modigliani's forever, and now you'll have responsibilities for your own family." She swiped invisible lint from her perfectly pressed dress.

"The family you believe will rip me off." I couldn't shake off the bitterness from her earlier comment, or perhaps I was stuck on it because comprehension of the fortune that had just landed in my lap was too foreign.

"Oh, please, stop it. Just promise me this will go toward your business, your career." She patted my chest and waltzed away, berating my brothers in the process. Everyone except me exited the room.

Stunned was probably the closest description of my current state. I glanced at the six zeros on the check and shook my head.

Gio poked his head in the door and snapped his fingers. "Five minutes, bro. Are you sure you don't want me to wait by the back door? There is still time."

"Asshole. I'll be right out there."

Alone in the luxury suite of the hotel where, in a couple of hours, I'd start my honeymoon with the woman of my dreams, I couldn't stop thinking about my mother's prediction. Or her gift.

Our father left us a with a generous insurance policy and we lived comfortably. Even after my mother met Micah and he moved in with his four girls, my stepsisters, we never suffered from lack or need.

Eight children combined and six years later, my mother managed to save what must be millions because I doubted she'd just given me everything and left nothing for my brothers.

I put the check into my inside pocket and glanced at my reflection.

I'm getting married. I hoped it was the right decision.

* * *

"He was practically eating you with his eyes." I shrugged off my jacket and vest, then yanked at my tie and practically ripped off my collar, trying to open it up.

"For the love of God, Massi, it's not my fucking fault. It's not like I asked him to stare and salivate—"

"So you admit he was all over you?" I needed to break something.

"I admit? Admit? I have nothing to admit. I didn't encourage him."

As Blue pulled the veil off her hair, a strand got stuck in the small comb. She jerked it one more time and then gave up. The lacy fabric hung attached to the silky dark curl, falling down around her shoulder. She put her hands on her hips, the goddess of vengeance. *God, she was beautiful.*

"It's your boss, Massi. You think your boss hit on me at my own wedding, and somehow you're mad at me?"

Fuck. She was right. Fuck. I loved her. There wasn't much to say. This was our wedding night and I was being an asshole. Exhausted by my own jealousy and anger, I projected all my baggage onto her.

We glared at each other. Something we seemed to favor. And similar to the situation at the playground, our passion and attraction won, and this time it was me who pounced.

I ripped the bodice of her expensive gown in two and she shimmied the remains of the fabric from her shoulders and down her waist. The dress pooled around her ankles. I lifted her, and while I carried her to the bed she did a fast job of the buttons of my shirt.

Hungry. Desperate. Consumed. Both of us lost in the world of lust and need.

I dropped her onto the mattress, but Blue immediately bounced up and helped me take off my pants and briefs.

Overwhelmed by the raw need, I pushed her to the bed, and then I noticed that my bride, in line with the tradition, had been wearing something blue. I stopped, stunned. The bodice of her corset hugged her waist and pushed her breasts high, showing cleavage that was a naughty promise.

She wore a tiny thong that seemed useless given its lack of coverage. The innocent baby blue color of her lingerie contrasted with its sole purpose of seduction and I lost all reason. Like so many times with this woman who was now my wife.

I pulled down her panties and lowered myself, covering her with my body. I undid the top clasp of her corset. Blue hurried to help me with the rest of the clasps, but I grabbed her hand.

"Don't, baby, I want you wearing your something blue." My voice came out hoarse as if I'd been singing all night.

A blush spread over her face and my cock hardened more, if that was even possible. Seeing her shy and risqué at the same time was the best wedding gift ever.

I plunged into her without finesse and she yelped, her nails digging into the skin of my shoulders.

"You're too big, Massi." Her whisper both worried me and made me want to sing at the top of my lungs.

"Am I hurting you, baby?"

"It's the best pain ever." The only thing I heard was the praise. This woman made me feel like a king.

I gripped her thigh and hiked it higher to my waist, helping her adjust better. I sank deeper into her tight core and started moving at a slow pace. "Look at me, Blue."

Our eyes locked and I saw my soul mate in her irises.

My lover.

My partner.

My wife.

I dropped my forehead to hers, the closeness near suffocating and wonderfully scary. The energy shifted between us. An almost imperceptible rearrangement of feelings and trust. A new level of intimacy.

But the fear that came with such deep commitment freaked me out, and coward that I was, I sought validation.

"Who do you belong to? Are you mine?" I asked as I started losing control and plunged into her faster.

She nodded, wrapping her legs tighter around my waist and digging her heels into my ass.

"Say it, Blue." I cupped her chin.

Her hooded blue eyes seared through me with all the passion and love this woman had to give. "I'm yours, Massi. I'm only yours."

And with that, we chased the climax and sealed our union as a married couple.

"That's a lot of money, Massi." Blue stared at the check from my mother.

We were sprawled in our honeymoon suite. She was naked now because at one point the corset became uncomfortable and we both craved the skin-to-skin contact.

We lay on our backs, her head nestled in the crook

of my shoulder where she belonged. I couldn't stop kissing her dark, silky hair.

"It's enough for me to open my own restaurant." I rolled on to my side to see her face better.

She looked at me, a smile lingering on her face, her eyes tired. "And what would I do?"

"You have to finish your diploma. The business classes you're taking will be needed in our business." I traced her flushed cheeks.

"*Our* business." Her smile grew. "But I still have two years of classes."

"That's okay. We can start looking for a location and I'll still work for Frederick to learn as much as I can from the bastard. We'll work on a business plan together and start as soon as everything is ready. It might be busy, Blue"—I sat up, excitement filling my veins—"for a while juggling your classes and work at the restaurant, but we'll be building our dream. For us, for our family."

"For our family," she whispered and pulled me down for a kiss.

Chapter Five

Gina

"Oh my God, I never know which shade of blue suits you better, but this indigo dress kills it." Mila assesses my outfit.

After a sleepless night, I feel like a steamroller pressed me flat and then its engine died, parking it over my lungs. I'm glad that at least my outfit choice—a short-sleeved sheath dress hugging my curves—exudes confidence and some sort of control.

"But what's with the colorless face and bags under your eyes? We didn't drink that much last night." That kills any confidence her praise sparked.

"I couldn't sleep." I take a sip of my extra-large Americano and stifle a yawn.

We're sitting in a busy coffee shop across the street from Casa Cassi, my potential new client.

"Any particular reason?" Mila raises her eyebrows and slurps from her fancy drink that included at least ten words to explain the order.

"I broke my vibrator," I deadpan.

I won't explain it was a combination of her well-meant advice and an unanswered call from my ex-husband that kept me tossing and turning all night. Or staring at the ceiling.

"Where is the glow then?" She laughs, and I swear the entire male population in the visible radius turns and drools.

I frown to remind her of my position as her boss, but she just squeezes my hand, bites her lip and wiggles her shoulders as if our current situation is the most exciting adventure.

When I groan, she purses her lips and scrunches her mouth to the side, assessing me. For all the superficial flakiness she freely displays for the world to see, Mila is anything but. She is also discreet and won't pry if I don't offer any further details.

"Okay, then..." She pauses and narrows her eyes, giving me one last chance to explain. But when I respond with another sip of my coffee, she tosses her hair—and now I'm sure some men drool for real—and continues.

"I researched the restaurant. From what I could see, their reviews are stellar, the cuisine is exceptional, the only complaints ever relate to the staff being inexperienced. The chef has many awards, and a temper."

"Don't they all?" I don't tell her I know this particular temper more than I care to. My brain is floating. If only I could take the coffee intravenously.

"You're probably right. The thing is, by all readily available information, there is no reason the committee hasn't noticed them yet."

"What about their online presence? Are they booked out regularly? Word of mouth? Special menus?" Immersing myself in work momentarily relieves my anxiety and lifts my spirit slightly.

"I wasn't able to find out much last night, but yeah, we can definitely help them with social media and influencers. Generating enough concentrated buzz should spark the committee's interest."

She scrolls through her phone as she speaks. I used to hate that. I still do. How someone can talk to me and have their attention on the phone is beyond me. And it's rude, but Mila has always been taking notes on her phone, and when she talks she often consults them.

I learned to appreciate how much she has literally at her fingertips and I know she's not browsing while talking. But still, it's a strange habit.

"I skimmed the reviews and made a few calls when the owner called me. I agree with you, we need to generate interest and maybe look into the staff engagement. There doesn't seem to be an issue in the kitchen, but something is off. Let's call some of our friendly foodies and send them for dinner there." I look across the street at the inviting entrance. "We better go. We don't want to be late for the first meeting." I stand up and gulp the rest of my coffee.

We maneuver around traffic to cross the street. The front wall is tinted glass, only a few lights glimmering inside. Mila pushes the door open and we enter a dark interior. I like the evening mood and the modern industrial look. The bar on the right seems well stocked with offerings at different price ranges.

I'm wondering about the wine cellar when a tall, handsome man with a disarming smile approaches.

"Ms. Accardi? I'm Phillip Turner." He extends his hand.

"Call me Gina. Nice to meet you." God, he is handsome. We shake hands and I turn to Mila who is, of course, beaming as if she's just hit the jackpot.

"Mila Ward." She bats her lashes and I frown at her.

"Mila works with me, Mr. Turner," I explain.

"Of course." He seems immune to her charms. Ha! "And call me Phillip, Gina."

He ushers us farther into the dining room. "Can I offer you anything?"

"A tour, perhaps." I smile at him, pressing my tongue to my palate to stifle a yawn.

He clears his throat and licks his lips. "We should meet with the chef first. It's really his call on how this whole arrangement will work."

I might be wrong, but it feels like he's avoiding my gaze. What the hell?

"I wasn't aware this was an audition for the job," I snap and Mila winces. Not like me to lose my cool, but for fuck's sake don't mess with me when I'm tired. Or vulnerable. Or at the end of my rope due to current life circumstances.

The double door leading to the kitchen swings open and the three of us turn.

When Phillip Turner called me about this job and I realized who the chef was, I knew that taking on the project would be the most difficult thing I've ever done. As he called just when I realized how deep my parents' debts were, I pushed aside any animosity I harbored against the man I haven't seen in almost two decades and accepted.

Getting this job might expand my client base to the East Coast. And my mom needs me here right now. All logical reasons to work with the infamous Massimo Cassinetti, chef extraordinaire.

But nothing could have prepared me for this. His eyes are so dark I irrationally feel the lights fade around us. His hair hangs in messy curls around the face that could have been sculpted by a Renaissance artist. Simply perfect. And set by a vigor of grinding teeth.

If he is trying to scare us off, he's doing a pretty good job, considering my heart rate and the audible gasp Mila utters.

She turns to me. "He looks—"

"Shut up," I whisper, without looking at her because my attention is completely absorbed by the chef.

He strides toward us like a predator ready to pounce and the hair at the back of my neck bristles. The taut muscles under his white T-shirt expand wide. The tattoos on his arms draw me like sirens and I fight the urge to study the art.

He towers above us, not solely because of his height, but his personality, his overall presence that fills the generous space. And sucks all the air out.

As he gets close, I realize that accepting this job was the biggest mistake of my life. And I've made too many of those already.

Regardless of how removed or reasonable I can be in my mind, my body immediately reacts to his scent with intense yearning. The scent that evokes all the rotten memories of the teenage girl who pined after this man years ago.

Massi

There is no fucking way I'm working with Gina fucking Accardi. She's caused me too much suffering. I don't fucking trust her.

"I think we should hear your proposal, Gina, to see what you're bringing to the table, and then we can see how this collaboration could work." Fucking Phillip is almost physically trying to prevent a disaster, maneuvering around us as if we were rare artifacts. It's embarrassing. Well, he invited her without consulting me, so he can sweat over the consequences.

I was pissed about this before I knew the famous consultant was Gina, so I certainly won't welcome the help now when I know it's her.

"I'm Mila Ward, Chef Cassinetti. I can't wait to try your renowned grilled branzino with artichokes," an excited blond chirps and extends her hand.

I whip my eyes to her, all the while trying to count my breaths. "Massimo Cassinetti," I growl and shake her hand. She beams at me, untouched by my temper.

Gina stands to our left with her fists clenched. She

is not wearing glasses like at the wake, which brings out her blue eyes. One could drown in them. It's good that I know better. There should be a warning tattooed on her forehead.

But that dress. It's a tease and promise in one, wrapping her curves like a fucking present.

The neckline runs horizontally almost to her shoulder points, hiding her collarbones in a way that draws attention to them. I want to sink my teeth there.

The idea snaps me into even deeper resentment. Fuck.

"The branzino is regularly on rotation, so you're welcome to make a reservation anytime." I try to intimidate the blond—what was her name again?—with another glower. Shit, I need to get this boiling blood under control, or this place will reach a new milestone by hitting rock bottom rather than achieving perfection.

"So what is it you suppose you can do for us?" I turn to Gina, but focus my gaze above her shoulders, avoiding her eyes.

Inhale. One. Two. Exhale. Three. Four.

In the brief silence, she opens and closes her fists a few times. Phillip fidgets beside me and the blond darts her eyes between us as if she is following a tennis match. The air zaps with energy so foul I think the consommé I've just cooked is turning sour in the kitchen.

Gina lets out a long breath and raises her chin slightly, meeting my eyes. "While the criteria to receive a Michelin star are elusive, it's been recognized by industry leaders that it surrounds the quality of ingredients and products, the chef's mastery, taste of the food, value for money and the overall consistency of the food and dining experience."

Her voice wavers a bit at the beginning, but she quickly becomes very professional and clearly knowledgeable. "Some say it's a meticulously clean kitchen and staff that pay careful attention to detail. We believe that there is potential here to get noticed by the inspectors, but a few things might need improvement."

The sound of her accent, slightly singing some syllables, resonates in me like the most beautiful symphony, which only pisses me off more. Now I'm going to get a boner hearing a woman speak. Fuck me!

"I have a James Beard Award and a restaurant booked solid for weeks in advance. What else is there to improve?"

The blond jumps in. "Your restaurant needs to get noticed by the inspectors. This could be accelerated by strategic reputation building through a collaboration with bloggers, food writers and food publications. That is certainly an area we could help you with."

Phillips nods. "That sounds like something we have been neglecting, for sure."

"I don't need to schmooze some young selfie takers who don't know the difference between consommé and broth to prove myself." I spit the words so loudly my throat chafes.

Gina winces but recovers quickly. "Some believe the chef's personality in the cuisine is one of the criteria. To stand out, to be unique. It seems your personality could only poison the patrons."

Phillip sucks in the air and the blond steps backward, but Gina keeps her chin up, challenging me to argue with her. Miraculously, for the first time in my life, the fucking breath counting delivers and my heart rate regulates.

With the serenity of a monk, I look her up and down. "If that's your opinion of my culinary art, I don't think there is a point in discussing a collaboration."

I whip around and force myself to walk to the kitchen with grace, all the while wanting to scream.

"Come on, Massi, what the hell?" Phillip dashes in behind me.

"I fucking hate blue!"

Gina

Silence descends as the two men disappear into the kitchen. Before the door swings closed, Phillip gestures to us to wait with an apology, or imminent diarrhea, all over his handsome face.

I inhale, surprised I can breathe, but that is the only movement that I'm capable of. My body is paralyzed by the sheer amount of stress and the effort to act like a reasonably functioning adult for the past few minutes.

"Do you want to explain, or are we going to pretend this is all about you wearing what clearly is his least favorite color?"

Chair legs screech behind me and I turn as Mila sags into it.

"I don't know what his problem is." The intensity of his reaction leaves me confused. What is his problem? If I don't count the unfortunate wake, we haven't seen each other in ages. Holding a grudge for this long is ridiculous. Or telling. And the fact that my body aches for him is just plain annoying.

"But you forgot to mention you know him." Mila studies me, pursing her lips, and her eyes narrow as if she can see the truth in me by squinting.

"We went to the same high school."

And being the friend she is, she doesn't ask any

more. But judging by the gasp she uttered when she laid eyes on Massimo earlier, she gathered enough already. The truth is wilder than even her imagination could conjure though.

"Okay, well, the chef is an asshole, but that's not a first for us. The question is are you able to work with him, or are we walking out right now?" She stands up. Mila has always recovered quickly from stressful situations. It's another superpower of hers.

Before I open my mouth to respond, I consider my parents' account balance, the time it would take to find another client while I'm on the East Coast and all my clients back home who I can't bill my usual retainer because I'm not there. And that I'll go crazy if my only focus here is my mom. Or that this job could be my ticket to freedom. Or a semblance of it.

"Of course I can handle him." Shit. "I mean it. It. I can handle the job."

Mila raises her eyebrows. "At some point you'll have to tell me what the history is there, or why you want this job so badly, and if the two are related."

Fucking Mila. I love her. My carefully maintained composure crumbles under her words and tears threaten. "You're a good friend, Mila." But for the first time since I've known her, I'm not sure if her presence is a good idea. There are just too many secrets.

"Yes, but the woman I used to work with back in

LA didn't have *might* or *we believe* in her vocabulary. She'd say what she was going to do and name facts, not beliefs. So can you get your shit back to your A game while Prince Charming breathes down our necks?"

I nod, not sure if anything I could say would sound believable. Before Mila can press further, the kitchen door swooshes open again and we turn.

"I'm sorry we didn't start on the right foot." Phillip reappears and I'm equally relieved and disappointed he is alone. Disappointed? What the hell?

"Phillip." Mila steps in front of me and I'm grateful for her sensitivity. No bloody way I want them to see me with tears in my eyes. "If you think you can manage your Highness Mr. Cassinetti, we'll be happy to help you out with the awareness and reputation building campaign. We can also review the operation overall, focusing on the service, and suggest improvements, but that part of our services makes sense only if Mr. Cassinetti gets off his high horse."

Phillip clears his throat. "Why don't you prepare the reputation building plan and I'll see what I can do about Massi dismounting."

I can sense two pairs of eyes on me, but I'm unable to look away from the kitchen door. The two round nautical windows are in shadow, but somehow I know he's there, watching me. Part of me wants to march over and smash the doors into his face. Breaking his nose would be satisfying.

To my utter dismay, a part of me is strangely aroused by the idea of Massimo Cassinetti watching me through that small window. Heat rises to my cheeks and I finally will my eyes to refocus on Phillip and Mila.

"Phillip, I'll have to think about it all. If Massimo isn't on board with our involvement, it would be a waste of our time and your money." I sound like an automatic response on a voice mail. If the morning had a steamroller driving over me, I'm positively flat now. Deflated by everything.

My entire mind screams to abort, to go back home and back to Sebastien, because that's where I belong. But my stupid body, and if I'm honest, my heart, are both still peeking toward the small round windows. Hoping? Hope is a luxury I haven't allowed myself in a long time.

"I understand your concerns, Gina. Let me reassure you that Massi comes across like an ass, but he's the best chef in New York, and he's fair."

Why this makes me laugh, I don't know. Perhaps because I know it's true. Or because I know that once upon a time I stomped all over that sense of honor.

"What the hell? So you say you want to do it and then you decide to think about it the next minute?" At least Mila waited half a block before voicing her concern.

The whole time I've been marching one step ahead of her, mostly trying to rearrange my face into a normal countenance and blink away the tears. Tears of frustration. And of disappointment. Why I feel disappointed I don't know. What was I expecting would happen today?

Massimo stayed at my father's wake for all of five minutes. That's how badly he didn't want to be in my vicinity. So what did I think? I didn't. That's the problem.

I've been so bogged down by recent events that my perception of reality has been skewed. Yes, he's very attractive. The years have been kind to him. Massimo's presence has intensified with passing time.

The boy I used to know is all man now. And what a fine specimen of a man. Minus the bullfighting personality, which might be a side of him only I bring out. Who knows anymore?

I spot a coffee shop and barge in with Mila on my heels. "What do you want?"

"The truth." She cocks her head, studying me.

"Cappuccino then?" I quip.

She shakes her head and without a word leaves me by the counter and goes to find us seats. Shit. I should tell her the story, but I can't. I don't know how. I'm embarrassed. As if by never saying the words out loud they can be less true. Less painful. Less disturbing.

Also, I like Mila very much and I don't want her to think less of me. I've been holding it together for years thanks to therapy. Sebastien has been my only motivation.

Not even the expensive therapist could help me fix things. I've been too deep in betrayal to find my way out of it. So, I solidified myself by escaping. By pretending my life was under control.

The problem with running away is that things usually catch up with you. But they come back to bite you stronger, uglier, messier. I should have never come back or considered the job at Casa Cassi. It was so much easier to loathe myself for my choices when I wasn't confronted with the rubble I'd left in my wake.

I didn't have a choice back then. Well, that's what I truly believed. But making a terrible choice is one thing. Pretending it never happened doesn't fix the mistake.

I get our coffees and drag my feet over to the long bar table by the glass wall at the front of the shop where Mila is perched on a stool, studying me.

"Both of them are hot." She smiles at me as I sit beside her and I exhale. Maybe she'll let me off the hook.

"That they are." I take a sip of my coffee.

"Okay, boss, are we going to take the job or not?" She holds her cup between her hands as if she's cold. "And before you answer, I have a confession to make."

She has a confession? Mila takes a sip, then puts the cup down and fidgets in her seat. She bites her lip and I frown, concern rising inside me. She is clearly uncomfortable, which is so unlike Mila.

"I never told you why I left LA and I'm not ready to do that—just like you're not ready to tell me what happened in high school with the chef—but I really need this job. I've been pretending I'm doing well and working, but I'm not."

"You haven't been working all this time?" I'm shocked, to say the least, and immediately worried about my friend. Shit.

"Not really. I've picked up a small project here and there, but not enough. I'm running out of savings. Hell, since I'm confessing, I've run out of my savings already." She takes the cup again and sips, staring out the window as the silence descends on us and I wonder what to do.

"Why don't you pull out one of your disguises?" I smile as Mila's face lights up. *Thank you,* she mouths at me.

Every time we take on a new client, Mila books a table at their place under an alias and we dine there in disguise. A game we enjoy a lot. Mila mostly for the clothes and wigs. Me for the opportunity to be someone else for a couple of hours.

This time, I'm not sure if pretending to be someone else would bring me any joy. There is a lot that could go wrong here. At least one life, if not three, could be destroyed if I hang around Massimo for too long. Time will tell if I'm strong enough.

Chapter Six

Massi

17 years ago

"I brought you something." I opened a small bag and pulled out a smooth, transparent jar.

Blue's eyes widened in excitement as she picked up the glass. "You got me yogurt?"

She sat at the tiny kitchen table in our rented studio, books strewn all around.

Our place was the size of my closet back home. I hated it. The ad had said "cozy," which practically translated into dingy and disappointing in all sorts of ways. The only thing of worth here was my beautiful Blue.

We didn't want to use my mother's gift or any

further assistance she'd offered, so for the past four weeks, since the wedding, we'd been living in a shoebox apartment in Brooklyn.

"Yogurt?" I shook my head in a mock dismay. "I made you a panna cotta."

"I thought those are white." She popped the jar open and sniffed.

"This one is blue. For you." I smiled and turned to grab a small spoon from a drawer behind me. The kitchen corner was so cramped I didn't need to walk to get it.

She dug in and narrowed her eyes as the spoon connected with her tongue. She swallowed with a moan. "Oh my God, Massi, this is amazing. This is my favorite dessert from now on." She took another spoonful, closing her eyes and instigating several dirty thoughts in my mind. "Did you make only one?"

I grinned. "Greedy." I kissed the top of her head. As I straightened, I noticed she protected the jar with her hand and I laughed. "I've been perfecting it for weeks now. Tonight I finally felt it's worthy of you. Now that I know you approve, I'll make you one daily. If you promise not to pretend you like it more than me."

She jumped up and kissed me. "You've been creating a perfect dessert for me? I don't even know what to say." The corners of her eyes brimmed with tears.

I took the spoon from her and fed her another spoonful. She smiled, licking her lips. God, I loved her so much.

"I signed us up for tango lessons." Blue sucked on the spoon as if she could squeeze more cream out of it.

Shit.

"I can't take tango lessons." I wanted to refuse gently. Mostly because I wasn't interested in dancing, but the time commitment was another issue. That was the one I focused on, because my reaction immediately brought sadness to her eyes.

"Blue, baby, a line chef at Modigliani's has come down with something and I need to pick up his shifts. Plus, I took shifts at the Four Seasons. I'm stretched already as it is. We'll dance when we get old." I leaned down and kissed her forehead, stroking her hair with both my hands, overwhelmed by the emotions I felt for this woman. Everything felt better when I was with her, yet I seemed to constantly disappoint her.

"We barely see each other as it is. You work and I study. That's all we do. I want to live now, Massi, not when we get old." She stood up, leaving the unfinished glass on the table. She rose on her tiptoes to get a mug and filled it with water. As she drank, I wondered if it was just a ploy to hide her tears. Her profile seemed so fragile at that moment. Like she could crumble any minute.

"Baby, Four Seasons is a few months' gig. Jacques Froleau is a guest chef there currently. He's famous. Watching him work, helping him, is priceless for my career." I snaked my hands around her waist from behind, inhaling the scent of her. The scent of a meadow that had always brought peace to me.

She wiggled to turn around, her face rigid. "You know what's priceless for your marriage? Spending time with your wife."

I stepped back, her words hitting like a slap, hard enough to spark my temper. "I'm spending every fucking minute of my free time with you. That was the point of getting married."

"Yeah, convenient for you. At least before you made an effort to seek me out, to sneak a moment here and there. Now, you know I'll wait here for you, so you don't hurry anymore. Once a week tango lessons and you can't even give me that?"

With every word that came out of her mouth, my frustration rose, twisting at my guts. How could she not understand I was at the beginning of my career? How could she not understand I was doing it for our future family business? Fucking tango. Really?

"Before you continue accusing me, I gave notice to Frederick. Exactly for that reason. In two weeks, I'll only work at the Four Seasons and once that's over, we'll open our own place. But, baby, if we don't focus now, we won't succeed. We'll dance tango later, I promise." I wrapped her in a tight embrace. God help me.

Reluctantly, she curled her hands around my neck. Lifting to her toes, she kissed me. I captured her lips with all the passion, frustration and love cruising through my veins. After a moment, she relaxed in my arms and I finally felt like home.

I picked her up and she squealed, swatting at me gently, but clinging to me eagerly. I carried her to our bed, which really was only four steps away from the kitchenette, and we made love.

Loudly.

Voraciously.

Honestly.

Over the past month, our bed had become the only place where we seemed to communicate effortlessly. Without judgment, disappointment or disagreement. We would lose ourselves in each other's arms and everything made sense. At least for those few intimate moments, our marriage seemed like the best idea ever.

With every touch, with every moan, with every consuming sensation we reminded each other why we wanted this so much. All in, until we'd find release from our everyday reality.

And then, for a few moments, life was perfect.

"I'm late," Blue murmured, her breath hot in the crook of my neck as we lay spent, our bodies tangled. A veil of perspiration glued our skin together, and our legs intertwined as I turned to face her.

"Late for what? It's almost midnight." I stroked her head and sought her eyes.

"My period." She smiled tentatively, but my face must have shown the void my mind produced. "I missed my period by two weeks now."

"Jesus." I rolled onto my back, disconnecting from the bundle of love our bodies created. Immediately, my skin prickled with goosebumps.

"Jesus? That's your reaction?" She sat up, glaring at me.

"Well, the timing would suck, don't you think?" I jumped up and strode to the window.

The lights of the city across the river flickered with the excitement and adventure Manhattan served to everyone daily. Here, the walls of this fucking studio were closing in on me.

"First, we don't know I'm pregnant yet, but good to know you're so thrilled." Sheets rustled and footsteps retreated to our mini bathroom. The door slammed.

"Of course I'm not thrilled. A kid is the last thing we need right now," I yelled.

The door sprang open again and Blue, with the

expression of a warrior princess, marched up to me. "Well, I'm sorry if your fucking semen inconvenienced your plans."

"I thought those were *our* fucking plans. Our. Or were you just nodding without listening because your mind was already on nurseries and fucking baby showers?" I paced around, but within the minuscule square footage of this place it infuriated me even more.

"I'm right there with you and your plans, but I didn't make this baby all by myself, you asshole." She sobbed, the sound arrowing directly to my heart, squeezing at my chest painfully.

"Blue, for fuck's sake, we'll have time for kids later, but let's just first get the business running, get a bigger place. Where the fuck would we live if you're pregnant?"

"I don't know." She hiccupped her words now, tears streaming down her face. "We would figure it out. I thought you loved me. I thought you wanted to be with me. I thought we got married to become a family. Not only so you could fuck me at your convenience without my parents interfering." Her breath hitched.

And now I was pissed at myself. I didn't want her hurting, but how could she not see how having a child would set us back? I approached her slowly and cupped her tear-stricken face. The pain in her blue eyes stemmed from my attitude and reaction.

I wiped her cheeks with my thumbs. "Blue, I love you. I love you more than life itself, but somehow we're always on a different page of our book."

She lowered her head to my chest. "I love you too." Her voice was just a whisper, her breath warm against my heartbeat. "I understand it wouldn't be ideal, but if I'm pregnant, we'll have to figure things out. We're young. We could start the business later."

Her words sliced through me like a knife. Like a chainsaw. The wound left behind, deep and raw, started festering immediately with the realization she was right. And something died inside me.

Today was shaping up to be the worst day of my life. This morning, the blood test had confirmed Blue was pregnant, and now we were heading to Frederick's for my farewell dinner. Why the man had invited us was beyond me, but he was quite gracious about me leaving him, so the least I could do was suffer through a dinner with him.

Yesterday had been my last day at his place and I had my first day off in the longest time. And perhaps the last one too.

Instead of enjoying it with Blue, we had been tiptoeing around each other, barely speaking. The pregnancy had been hanging over our heads, making it difficult to focus, to be, to think.

I couldn't even look at her, because suddenly the woman that was my reason to breathe and wake up in the morning, the woman that made me the happiest man alive, represented the end of my dream. Or its inevitable delay.

I wanted to be the person who would just accept what life had dealt me. Take the consequences of my own insistence on this marriage—hell, who was to say she wouldn't have gotten pregnant if we didn't get married? But here I was, resenting her and myself. Hurting, and by default inflicting pain on her.

We walked to the subway, holding hands. The silence between us was so loud it gave me a headache. I clung to her hand as if my life depended on it. Because it did. My ability to function, which had always been tainted by my out-of-control temper, was directly connected to this girl.

I loved her with every fiber of my life. And I hated her right now with equal conviction, so I held her hand because I worried I would lose her. Because I was scared shitless that I'd fail her... Damn it, I probably already had.

Both of us were drowning in a sea of worries and disappointment, so we stopped talking about it. We took the train in silence and made our way to

Modigliani's in Tribeca connected by our damp hands, occasionally squeezing.

"Massi, so good to see you outside the kitchen." Frederick gave me a one-arm hug. "And your beautiful wife." He turned to Blue and kissed her knuckles, holding onto her a beat longer than necessary. Her other hand was still intertwined with mine and she squeezed it, digging her nails into my skin.

I wasn't sure if she was trying to stop me from reacting or sending me a distress signal, but as the images of Frederick's drooling at the wedding came back to me, I was pleased to finally have a target for my anger and frustration.

"Let's eat," I growled.

Frederick studied me for a moment and I thought his lip curled up slightly. Did he enjoy getting under my skin?

"I took the liberty of planning a menu for tonight." He led us to the back of the bright, busy bistro. When he pulled a chair out for Blue, I clenched my fists while he touched the small of her back to help her into the seat.

As we all settled at a small table in the corner of the dining room, he continued, "I'm testing a new menu and a new chef, since this guy has abandoned me." He gestured toward me and winked at Blue.

"It's very generous of you to host us under the

circumstances, Frederick." Blue smiled at him. "Though I'm afraid nobody can replace Massi." She gripped my thigh under the table and the slight gesture —and her praise—placated me enough to exhale.

"You might be right, which is definitely a loss for me." Frederick turned his head, studying me.

The man was a great restaurateur and an excellent chef. I had learned a lot from him, but I didn't trust him. I never had.

The server came to take our drink order, and soon after we were served the appetizers. To my dismay, it was delicious. The combination of the flavor and the presentation radiated with experience and culinary artistry, making me suddenly feel dispensable, questioning if last night's menu, prepared by me, measured up to this.

Distracted by the bout of self-doubt, I didn't realize what Blue and Frederick were talking about until I snapped out of it, hearing his words.

"I had no idea. Now that explains why a talented chef like your husband would go to a large production kitchen like the Four Seasons." Frederick tapped the white linen napkin at the corner of his mouth.

"But of course, it has always been the plan to open his own place." Blue smiled and squeezed my thigh again, as if reassuring me my dream still had validity. "*Our* own place," she added, beaming.

She was fucking proud of our dream and I should have focused on that, but I couldn't because I was too busy studying Frederick's reaction. I hadn't told him about my plans. No concrete evidence made me believe he would jeopardize my efforts, but I felt it was a possibility.

"Why haven't you told me about it? This is wonderful news, and I'm looking forward to having such fine competition." Frederick raised his glass and bowed his head briefly.

Blue smiled at me, the tension of the day still visible in her eyes, and my heart did some strange choreography that seemed way more important than anything else. I lifted her hand that rested on my leg and kissed it, trying to communicate with my eyes that we would figure things out.

She smiled again and the world seemed slightly better. I brushed her knuckles one more time with my lips and, for a moment, the world and its inevitable trouble ceased to exist. There was only me and her, the most important piece in the puzzle of my life.

Electricity zapped between us through that brief contact and I couldn't wait to be alone with her. Not only to make love to my beautiful wife, but to tell her how sorry I was about everything.

Frederick cleared his throat and we jerked away from each other.

"This is delicious." Blue recovered quickly and took a bite of her charred octopus.

"I'm glad you like it." Frederick watched her intently. "What would be your role in the new restaurant?"

"I'm taking business classes at college, so while there is very little I know about cooking, I'm hoping I could be useful in running the business side of things." She smiled at me again, but seeing Frederick's attention on her I buried my nose in my dish, hoping to survive dinner without causing a scene.

"Wonderful. Many skilled chefs fail because of the lack of business skills. Or they end up outside the kitchen for way too long, like me. The two of you are a winning duo."

"The school gives me the basis, and hopefully I'll figure out the rest with Massi's help. The restaurant business has specifics that I need to learn." Blue looked at me, her eyes full of hope.

"I've been looking for someone to help me manage this place. Maybe you can get your feet wet here while you're studying and learn the ropes, so to speak."

My fork clattered to my plate.

"Are you going to yell now?" Blue threw the keys onto the table.

Our return from dinner was just as silent as the trip to the restaurant. But this time, the silence was full of anger. The disappointment of the untimely pregnancy seemed unimportant.

We hadn't held hands. I'd tried to calm down during the ride home, but the thoughts had flown freely in my head, arresting any hope for reason.

"How could you?" I accused.

"How could I have accepted a generous offer to learn from the best in the business?" She folded her arms over her chest.

"He wants to get in your pants." I gritted my teeth so hard I feared I might lose my molars.

"No. That's fucking you. You married me to have guaranteed access to my pants and now you can't even face the consequences."

"I fucking love you, Blue." I stepped closer and cupped her jaw, forcing her to look at me, our noses only inches apart. "I love you. That's the reason I married you."

We breathed like racehorses for what could have been minutes or years. The anger and lust that consumed me sprouted fear. And that fucker coiled around my bones, lacing everything with poison.

"Trust me," Blue breathed. She raised her hands to

my chest, the contact snapping me out of my down-ward spiral for a moment. Her words and touch grounded me. That's why I needed her in my life.

I let go of her face, my arms limp at my side. I trusted her. I didn't trust Frederick, but I hadn't real-ized how my jealousy impacted her.

Spent from evil emotions, I sagged to my knees and wrapped my arms around her waist, holding on for dear life. "I trust you, Blue. I do."

Something unexpected happened and my eyes teared up. I hadn't cried since my father's wake, and this time it wasn't grief that brought on tears. It was fear. Somehow the train of my life had taken off too fast, and it was speeding ahead at a dangerous pace while simultaneously getting delayed. And I had a feeling that while I blamed Frederick or Blue or whoever else, it was me who would ultimately derail it.

She raked her fingers through my hair and leaned down to kiss the top of my head. "Let me learn from him, so we can take over Manhattan and get all the Michelin stars you deserve."

Blue dropped to the floor and raised her hands to hold my face. "Massi, the baby delays us by a few months, but we can use that time for research and preparation and then open up even stronger."

I lowered my head to hers and she wrapped me in an embrace. I snaked my hands around her slender back and pulled her as close as I could, hiding my tears in the crook of her neck.

However broken and vulnerable I felt, there was only one thing that I knew to be true at that moment. With Blue by my side, I would survive.

Chapter Seven

Massi

"Have you started a new workout routine? You look annoyingly buff." Phillip sips his espresso, leaning against the bar.

"Envy speaking." I snort. "Same routine, just more time at the gym. I have a lot of tension and anger I need to exorcise because of our temporary new team members."

"Come on, man, admit they've been doing a great job."

I stare at my reflection in the mirror behind the shelves of bottles. If I was a better man, I'd admit Gina and Mila added some much-needed attention from social media, and that they have some decent ideas about changes we should make. But...

"Particularly their suggestion that I can't keep staff and thus we lack in service."

A vacuum cleaner hums in the corner, but otherwise we enjoy a moment of stillness before I need to attack work with all my buzzing energy. Energy that has been consuming me over the past couple of weeks. Ever since that woman waltzed in and robbed me of my peace and reason.

I've been avoiding her like the plague, but just knowing she is around has been enough to make me feel all sorts of things. My initial anger—and I'm no longer sure if it's aimed at her or me—has great company. It fights for my sanity with regret, longing, fucking desire—the most annoying one—and lately melancholy. It all comes full circle to piss me off.

I draw a mindless pattern on the counter with unhealthy dedication, as if the prints I'm leaving on the polished surface are fascinating. It helps me focus. It helps me keep my temper at bay. Oh fuck, who am I kidding? It only aids me in avoiding the inevitable. Admitting my mistakes.

"Don't be so sensitive." Phillip punches me playfully in my arm. "Their assessment has its merits."

"Lena hasn't complained about my leadership skills, has she?"

"Somehow, Lena is the only person who can handle you. Probably because she's exhausted from the early morning visits to the market and she knows her gig here is temporary. As soon as she's ready I'm forcing her to take time off before she starts her own catering business."

I nod, because there isn't much I can say. Perhaps I've been more lenient with Lena because she's Phillip's fiancée, and maybe, just maybe, that led to her being better than anyone else. But then the woman seems to be resistant to stress.

"You work well with Lena and it shows in other areas. What about the rest of it? If you had a team of people equally dedicated to the success of this place as you are, we'd be one of the best restaurants in the world. And I'm not even exaggerating too much. People fear you. I take your temper at face value, but people don't want to be treated like a nuisance. Do you think you can try?"

I groan. Yes, I've been an asshole. But as my therapist pointed out, my anger is a safety net. One that I spread to cope with the other emotions. He believes I find the other emotions too weak and emasculating, so I resort to anger. But what does that prick know?

"I'll try if you think it would help." I'm mostly trying to get out of this conversation.

"Good. We can start easy. Perhaps try to thank people at the end of the day? Or point out when they do a good job instead of only when they fuck up? Give them the benefit of the doubt before you destroy them with your *well-meant* critique?"

"You don't have to fucking coach me. I'll make an effort." I shake my head because I find the whole idea of telling people they're good at their job preposterous. It's expected they're good at something they're getting paid for. Shouldn't they strive to excel at something when they spend twelve hours a day doing it?

"Good, glad to hear it. Perhaps start with Gina. You've been a mega asshole to her for no reason."

I slide down from the stool and start toward the kitchen without saying another word. God help me and get me the Michelin star so the woman stops coming here.

"Or is there a reason?" Phillip calls after me, and I —in a mature manner—flip him off before I kick the door open.

The kitchen welcomes me with the scent of thyme, boiling broth, fresh mangoes and something burning. So I pretend that the charred pan in the sink sets me off.

"It's not even ten o'clock and things are wasted already? We'll all smell like campers. It stinks in here. Why is the sink full of dishes? The mangoes should be shredded already." I address my frustration at Lena, who stands on the other side of the prep counter and is the only person brave enough to hold my gaze. The rest of my team scatters and gets busy.

"Where is the fish? Nothing gets done when I step out." I roll out my knife pouch then pull a cutting board from the shelf under the counter and drop it on the shiny surface with such a bang that Lena flinches. Fuck. So much for making an effort.

Even with the extra time at the gym lately, I can't control my mood. The longer Gina remains in my orbit, the more I have to fight. Fight with the rest of the world to compensate for losing the battle with my desires. I desired that woman once and it destroyed me. It destroyed all the hope, goodness and happiness I had in my life.

"My late husband was excellent at hiding his true feelings, his genuine needs." Lena's voice is soft as she runs her knife expertly around the middle of the mango, halving it.

I pause, my hand in midair as I reach for another piece of fruit. Not only is this the first time since I met her three months ago that she's spoken of anything personal, but also that she's mentioned anything other than work. And by the sound of it, she has an uncanny ability to hit the nail on its head. All I need right now is another woman who thinks she knows me.

"It didn't make him happy, but he still believed that by blaming me for his self-inflicted suffering it would get better. I endured his abuse for many selfish reasons, but he directed it at me because he was unhappy, and instead of fixing his problems he was sinking deeper into them."

I squeeze the fruit too tightly and the mango juice bleeds on to my board. I plunge my knife into the soft pulp. "These are too ripe," I growl and throw the smashed fruit into a large bin behind me.

"I think just that one was soft. I handpicked them all. Sorry, I shouldn't have shared that experience." She wipes her forehead with her forearm and hands me another mango. This one has an ideal softness, just like the previous one.

"Did your husband acknowledge his behavior and change?" I treat the fruit with more finesse this time.

"Unfortunately, no. He'd accepted his errors shortly before his death. He didn't get a chance to fully live his own truth."

"You think I'm hiding something?"

"Oh, I know you're hiding something. The question is how much is it poisoning you?"

I look up, but she is fully focused on her knife and the fruit. I stare at her, willing her to say more while refusing to ask her to explain what she really means. What she sees. Perceives. Why am I paying a therapist?

She meets my gaze and smiles softly. "It's not the

secrets you're keeping from others, it's the truth you're trying to ignore so desperately."

I leave Lena in charge after the lunch rush and make my way to my mother's house. The more I consider Lena's words on the ride over, the more agitated I get.

Mom opens the door, kisses me on both cheeks and says, "I need you to talk to Gio and Andrea. They haven't returned my calls." Then she strolls away.

I follow because Bianca Cassinetti has always commanded rooms with a simple gesture and sometimes just a thought. "I sacrificed my life to bring up decent human beings, or so I hoped, and they don't bother to talk to me."

Everything is always sprinkled with drama for my mother. She's wearing a beige designer suit and has golden jewelry dangling from her ears and wrists. She doesn't look like a suburban housewife. She never has.

We moved to this house shortly after my father passed, courtesy of his insurance policy. My mother has been a stay-at-home mom all her life. Sometimes I wonder how my father afforded so much life insurance, but I'm not complaining. Amid losing him, our wealth at least secured some sort of stability.

"Andrea is in Europe, Mom. What is it you need from them?"

I sit on the stool at the corner of the large rectangular kitchen island.

"What I need from them? Do I need a reason to talk to my sons? Have you spoken to Sydney lately? Is she dating someone?"

God help me. I was thirteen when my father died and I took on the role of head of the family—well, in my mind at least—and even after Micah moved in with his girls, I still feel the need to check on my mother.

She is more capable of living than I am, so these weekly check-ins with her are more habit than need. But every time I come I wonder why I'm willingly submitting myself to her inquisition.

"I'll have your peach iced tea, thank you for asking, Mom."

She sighs. "Don't be smart with me. Since all the other children are ignoring me, I have to get the information out of you."

I roll my eyes. "Gio is just busy with another takeover or a launch or whatever it is his holding is currently focusing on. Andrea is seeking a muse in Italy. I haven't spoken to anyone in a while, but last time I saw Sydney she was still single. Not a surprise there." I smirk, and somehow my mother manifests next to me—even though she was standing at the opposite side of the island—and slaps the back of my head.

"Really, Massi, you're old enough to be more serious. How did I end up with eight children combined and no grandchildren?" She closes her eyes and shakes her head. It's more for dramatic effect because I'm pretty sure Bianca wants grandchildren mainly to stop her friends at the club asking about it. In her mind, everyone thinks there is something wrong with us. There probably is.

"Mom, I'm sure Andrea has a child somewhere."

This earns me another smack before she walks to the fridge and pours me the tea.

"I was calling them because I'd like to organize a family get-together." She slides the glass toward me.

The last time we all got together was... well, I'm not even sure. Christmas four years ago? I'm close with most of my siblings, but there are too many of us to organize anything, and the younger ones probably endured so much in the large, loud household that they're happily staying as far away as possible.

"What's the occasion?" It's the middle of May, no birthdays in sight that I can remember. "And where is Micah, by the way?"

"The occasion is that we haven't been together for five years now. And Micah is in the city. Will you stay for dinner?"

She busies herself with a dishtowel, polishing the perfectly sparkling island top, and purses her lips. She seems uncomfortable and I can't decide if I want to find out why.

"I can't stay for dinner. I have to get back to the restaurant before the evening rush." I slide down from the stool and walk to her. I wrap an arm around her shoulders, take the towel from her hand and kiss the crown of her head. "Is everything okay?"

She dabs the corner of her eye and I think these might be real tears, not her usual drama queen reaction. "Everything is okay, I just want to have my family together for a few moments to create memories. Life is too short." She sniffles and raises her chin, the mask of iron Bianca back in its place.

"Okay, I'll talk to Gio and Andrea." I kiss her forehead. "I need to go now."

She walks me back to the door. "I hear you work with Gina."

Of course, she left the best for last. The woman must have hidden cameras in the restaurant. Probably even in my apartment. She knows shit about me even before I know it sometimes. Mother's intuition can't go this far.

I nod, hoping to remain as neutral as possible while trying to catch the wild horse of my heart. I clench my fists a few times. "Phillip hired her."

"How are you getting along? You couldn't get out of their house fast enough at the wake."

"I really have to go now, Mom." I open the door and wave at the driver who's been waiting for me as if my flailing arm could speed up the departure.

"I saw how you looked at her. You may pretend you hate her, but that's a lie."

Fuck.

"She'll be gone soon enough, so you don't need to analyze it much, Mom."

"And who will help you pick up the pieces this time?"

Chapter Eight

Massi

"For the next two weeks, Gina will manage the dining room," Phillip says, his eyes darting to me, coveting my support.

I protested this development half-heartedly already. I hate that I have no reasonable business argument against this decision, so I reluctantly accepted it. Or rather, swallowed my pride and decided not to sabotage it.

Our staff sits around the tables. Some of them gasp at Phillip's announcement. All of them move their gaze to me. Fifteen pairs of eyes are waiting for my outburst or signs of humiliation. Potentially for my approval.

Phillip clears his throat. Gina and Mila stand at his

side. The blond is beaming at me, as usual, completely unaffected by my temper. I'm good at spreading fear, but Mila is immune.

Gina is studying the faces of the team she's about to lead, clearly using the moment to read their reactions. For some reason this pisses me off, because it's exactly the right move on her part. While everyone is struggling with the announcement itself and focusing on my reaction, she is identifying her allies and potential troublemakers.

Damn her. With all her experience and all the right moves. Fuck.

Lena, who stands behind me, always finding her spot to shine in my shadow, touches my arm, trying to stop the silence from stretching to its already uncomfortable reality.

I know I'm expected to set the tone. To endorse Gina, but also to suggest I'm prepared to make the effort to create a better work environment. I'm not sure if Phillip or Gina really expect me to promise to these people I won't yell at them, but if they do, they've lost their minds.

I step forward. "I understand we have room for improvements here. I also understand Gina is the best to help us organize our processes and standards here on the floor of the dining room. I ask you to cooperate with her with the single objective of making this restaurant the best fucking experience on Earth."

Phillip claps and a few members of my kitchen staff nod.

"Now, some of you are stressed working with me. If that's the case, you should perhaps consider a different job."

Phillip groans beside me and I swear Lena chuckles.

"I have a temper, but let me ask you this: how many of you have I reprimanded for something?"

All of them raise their hands.

"How many of you feel you'd done nothing wrong when I yelled at you?" All hands go down except one. I look at the young man who started three weeks ago and has spent most of his time on smoke breaks. "Sorry for the misunderstanding. My money is on you not surviving the next two weeks under Gina's leadership, but if you do, I'll apologize for any wrongdoing toward you."

I would wipe the smug look from his face with a dirty dishtowel, but there is no need. He is hours away from getting fired without my intervention. I might not reward good work ethics with praise, but I know when someone is taking their paycheck for nothing.

"My only goal here is to provide the best experience possible for our patrons. It's my aim during my morning walk to the market to select the best ingredients. I think about that when I'm planning daily specials. It's on my mind when we're prepping the food or finalizing the dishes. It drives me and it should drive you, whether you want to be part of the success or just learn from the best before you move on. I won't promise not to yell because it would be a false promise, but I'll attempt to point out the good, not just the bad."

Everyone fidgets in their seats and someone claps. I raise my hand to stop them. "Okay, if you're here to make this place a success, stay, learn, follow, endure. If not, you can leave right now. Gina will work with all of you, and at the end of the next two weeks two of you will take over managing the floor and continue applying the changes we're about to implement."

Some nod, some straighten up, some move their attention to Gina. It's clear some of them won't be here in two weeks, but I'm okay with that. Gina will be gone too, which I'm more than okay with as well. And hopefully, in the wake of all the changes, we'll have better service.

"Don't fuck up," I holler just for the fun of it. "I'll let Gina address you now." I don't look at her.

I turn to sit on the stool behind me and catch Lena rolling her eyes. I frown at her and she rolls them again. I love that woman. I wish she'd stay on here because I won't find another sous-chef who can handle me as easily as she does. Most of her predecessors came to learn from me and moved on too fast.

"Casa Cassi serves excellent food in an inviting environment. The only three- or four-star reviews on most of the review sites are related to the service, and we'll change that over the next two weeks..."

Gina speaks with confidence, addressing the staff with authority and respect. The room is silent, everyone hanging on her every word. Including me.

Well, that's not true; her words are just grazing my attention. It's her grace, the melody of her voice, the charisma that captivates me, despite my efforts to ignore her.

She is wearing a light blue summer dress, one of those baggy styles that fits all sizes. Well, damn it, it fits her perfectly, hiding her curves in the most tantalizing way. As her words hum in the background of my mind, I imagine discovering what's under the flowy fabric, bending her over the table and... fuck. Fuck. Fuck.

I snap back and listen to her explaining the customer experience, from the moment someone calls in to reserve their table to the moment they leave. Why am I turned on by her poise and knowledge?

Her hair is in a short ponytail, exposing her long neck, the skin of her nape begging to be kissed. I snicker at the vision because I'm sure she would respond with her knee in my crotch. She whips around and all eyes follow. She raises her eyebrows. Fuck, I undermined her with my reaction to my own fucking depraved fantasies.

"I need to go debone the fish for lunch. Please continue." I beeline for the kitchen with a raging erection behind my apron.

Gina recovers her composure and picks up her speech before the door swooshes closed. I dash to my office and lean against the wall. Closing my eyes, I swear under my breath.

Silently being an idiot in my head is one thing, but doing it in public is getting out of hand. I can't hold it together any longer. Avoiding her while stealing glimpses of her is making me certifiably crazy.

I breathe heavily as if I've just finished a marathon. The woman is going to be the death of me. Why do I find her attractive when I know very well there is no chance there could ever be anything between us?

Or could there be? Fuck.

This is so fucked up. Why did she even take the job? Clearly she's stronger than me. Unaffected by memories, perfectly mature and past all the shit that went down all those years ago. Why is she even in New York this long? Last I heard she was happily married.

And here I am stupidly reacting to her essence, her presence, her allure. It's come to this—I'm hiding in my office while she commands my staff. Skulking in my own kitchen because the rhythm of her speech and her beautiful fucking nape give me a boner.

The clicking of heels alerts me. I try to regulate my breathing and regain my usual, grumpy composure.

I turn to block the doorway and face Mila's arched eyebrow. I'm not sure if she's trying to scare me or portray annoyance because on that sweet face her effort is kind of funny. I don't get to react, anyway.

"I don't know what the fucking deal is between the two of you—" she accuses.

Yeah, neither do I, frankly.

"Just do your job, okay?" I retort, knowing that won't help alleviate her suspicion or concern. And judging by the semi in my pants, she should be concerned.

"The job aside, I'm Gina's best friend, and I don't take it lightly when someone fucks around with my friends. The tension between the two of you is so palpable it may just burn the house down."

"I don't know what you're talking about." I know exactly what she is talking about and I dislike it as much as Mila does, if not more. I turn around and hunt through the drawers of my desk, opening and closing them with unnecessary force. I'm not looking for anything in particular, but I don't know what to do with my hands.

"Listen, Mr. Cassinetti, I need this job, and Gina took pity on me and agreed to work with you. You have a great restaurant here and we can bring it to the next level. But for that to happen, the two of you need to put aside whatever it is hanging over you." With every word, she swings her petite index finger as if it was a sword. "Or here is an idea, perhaps the two of you should fuck and get it over with."

Now that's an idea. While I can't believe she's just told me that, I kind of think she is onto something. Or my dick thinks that. Fuck.

I whip around and pull a card from the top drawer.

"Let's keep this professional, Ms. Ward, but if your colleague and *friend* needs to relieve tension, this might be therapeutic." I hand her the card.

"If someone needs therapy, it's you," she spits, but then it looks like she realizes she crossed a professional line. I don't mind, but it's kind of entertaining to watch her fight internally to recover.

Her face rearranges in quick succession, showing many emotions before she settles—perhaps under the influence of my words—on her professional, kind demeanor.

She grabs the card and glances at it, frowning. When she meets my eyes again, there is something else I detect. Suspicion? Epiphany? Well, she could ask her friend to elaborate.

She studies me for a moment and then turns on her heels and clicks away, but before she turns the corner, she looks back.

"As long as the two of you fight this, neither of you will win or feel better."

Chapter Nine

Gina

"**G**et out!" Massi's voice carries across the dining room. The bartender glances at me and then at the kitchen door.

The lounge music creates a pleasant backdrop to the fine dining experience, but it's not loud enough to drown out whatever is happening in the kitchen.

For the tiniest fraction of a second, everyone freezes. A few patrons at the tables closest to the bar look toward the kitchen. I slide down from the barstool where I have been sitting and taking notes about the floor management and I smile toward the guests, but really at no one in particular.

I walk casually toward the swinging doors, but my spine is rigid. My posture results from the tension that fills me any time I have to face Massi. It has just intensified tenfold because I fear what I find when I open the door. By the time I reach the door, the dining room exhales and resumes its normal beat.

Through the nautical window, I assess the situation. Nobody is coming out, so I take a moment to inhale and let out a long breath. It does shit for my composure. I put on the generic smile that I've worn around here all day and push through the door.

I stop a foot from the entrance, careful not to get run over by the servers coming and going. My eyes dart around, and as much as I'm trying to comprehend what has just happened, I can't figure it out.

The commotion in the kitchen resembles chaos. Well-orchestrated and probably quite logical for those performing the choreography. Still, it feels frantic. Lena is shouting orders. A pair of line cooks rush around the range, mixing, cutting, stirring. Other team members are all at their stations, bustling through their tasks.

Massi is finishing a plate at the plating counter. Holding a squirt bottle filled with an orange sauce, he's drawing curves on the plate, adding finishing touches to the presentation.

A dark curl escapes from his man bun and bounces across his forehead. I can't help but stare. Like an artist, he leans back for a brief second to assess his creation and immediately moves to the next plate.

A shadow of a smile lingers on his lips, and while there is a lot of activity around him he doesn't seem impacted by the pandemonium. He thrives in the hectic buzz of his kitchen, drawing energy from it. Drawing joy from it.

He's a tall man with impressive muscles, but he moves with a grace and elegance as if everything around him is sacred. If ever there was someone who'd found their true calling, it's Massimo. I feel strangely jealous of anyone around him. It's like working with a true master.

I shouldn't be this attracted to him. I shouldn't feel my chest tickled by butterflies and my core burning like I was sitting on the stove instead of standing at a safe distance. I shouldn't be staring at him. But I'm unable to control my feelings, my body's reaction or my thoughts.

He puts the squeeze bottle down and almost simultaneously dings the bell on the counter. It only takes a second before the door opens and a server comes to take the plates. New orders come in and Lena keeps everyone on task.

Before Massi leans over the next set of plates, he notices me. Our eyes lock and all the feelings flooding my system since I entered the kitchen engage in some weird tug-of-war.

I want to dash away, but his gaze captures me in a way I haven't felt in a long time about a man. About anybody, really.

I'm marginally aware that everything and everyone is still whirling around, but for me time and space cease to exist for a second. Or a year. Or an eternity. It's only me and him. His hooded eyes communicate so much, but I fear interpreting what it is.

Desire. Regret. Pain. Lust.

But it's not what he's saying with that look—it's what his silent look takes from me.

Reason. Resolve. Rationale.

All gone.

I'm turning into a mushy mess, wanting him to eliminate the distance between us and kiss me.

And while I'm not sure what his eyes are saying, when he licks his lips I'm sure at least a fraction of his thoughts match mine. Perhaps more than that, but I'm a pessimist. Or a realist. Scratch that. I'm clearly insane.

The door swooshes open with more force this time and I have to jump away, breaking the moment. A moment I probably just conjured in my head.

"Sorry, Gina," Sharon, one of the servers, says, but doesn't stop, her hands full of plates.

I should say something, act like a normal person, but I don't know how. I'm afraid to glance back at the plating station, so I just scurry through the kitchen, trying to avoid everyone, but mostly the dark eyes that still feel like scorching coals within me.

I shove the back door open and let out the breath stuck in my lungs. I lean against the brick wall, not minding the lingering smell of garbage.

I feel safer here. To a certain extent. Because I can escape Massi's gaze, but I can't escape my feelings. There is a lot of desire swarming through me, and some hope as well. A large red abort sign is flashing in my mind's eye, but there is a big part of me that wants to get to know this Massimo. How different is he from the high school boy?

But I made a decision seventeen years ago, and as much as I regret it I can't take it back. If Massi knew what I'd done, he'd be giving me a very different look. If he even cared to look at me again. He'd either resent me or be indifferent, and I don't know which one would kill me faster.

The door opens and the saucier steps out. She's on the phone, murmuring something. She stops when she sees me. Her eyes are red from crying and I want to ask her if she's okay, but she keeps the phone up, so I don't interrupt.

She nods a greeting and pushes around me. I watch

her disappear behind the corner into the alley that leads to the main street.

I check my watch. It's way too early for her to leave. And she was crying. I've completely forgotten why I stepped into the kitchen in the first place. Now I understand the shouting.

The bastard must have fired her. And then he decorated the fucking plates as if nothing happened.

I slept poorly again. It seems a theme of my stay on the East Coast. The few weekends in LA I squeezed in are not helping. I'm suspended in a perpetual jetlag and other feelings I don't want to address. At least, last night I spoke with Sebastien for almost half an hour. I miss him so much.

I shuffle downstairs and find my mom sitting on the sofa in the family room. She's wearing her robe. I don't think she's changed at all in the last few weeks. Perhaps since the funeral. Shit. I should spend more time with her, but we've never forged a bond.

I was a teenager when I left home, resenting everyone. More my father than her, but she missed out on all the milestones in my life and I don't really know her. Not as an adult woman who would want to share her life with her mom.

Seeing her like this, lost in her own world, adds to all the regrets I've been collecting through my life. And if I'm good at something, it's making stupid decisions—most of the time driven by circumstances, but still very poor choices—and then regretting them.

"Good morning, Mom." I lean in, my hands on the backrest of the sofa and I kiss the top of her head.

She reaches out to grab my hand and squeezes it. I think this is the first physical show of affection she's awarded me since I arrived and I don't know what to do with it. I circle the couch and sit down next to her.

She pats my thigh and leaves her hand there. It's warm, small and wrinkled. I don't know if her hands were always this small. I turn my head and study her profile. She still seems frozen in the moment. The lines on her face are more profound, as if the grief has wrinkled her up.

I wish I loved my father as much as she did. I wish I could forgive the way he treated me back then, but I know it won't change much. It wouldn't ease her suffering if we both grieved him the same way.

I want to tell her about Sebastien, share with her my joy and happiness, but some topics are hard to broach after so much time apart.

"I have to go to work, but let's spend Saturday together," I say instead, though I can't imagine what we'll do. "If you want to stay in your robe, we can have a pajama day together."

We used to have those when I was younger. She turns her head and her lips curl up slightly, softening her features. Her eyes flicker with recognition and I'm not sure if she's found the same memory as me or if she's just realized I was sitting next to her.

"I love you, Mom." I push the words out with more struggle than a daughter should. It's not like I've been saying them on a regular basis, but the difficulty comes from the realization of how much I really do love her. Regret sinks its teeth into my heart immediately, reminding me of all the lost time. Time we didn't share.

I lean over to kiss her cheek and squeeze her hand. "The nurse is coming shortly. Don't forget that Saturday is a pajama day." I grab my things and leave.

I get off the subway two stops early because I want to walk. Clear my mind, or maybe just delay my arrival. I should address Massi's behavior last night and I don't want to. While I don't approve of his leadership style, I need to accept that he's free to hire and fire anyone he wants.

I may wish he'd treat people with more respect, but who am I to judge? Part of my job in smoothing out the restaurant's image is to ensure that, under no circumstances, these episodes reach the dining room like last night. Massi won't listen to me though, so I need to talk to Phillip and Mila. That's probably for the best.

I can't face him again. Not after the moment we had last night. Was it even a moment? It got stomped all over when I saw the saucier. Good. I don't need to develop sympathy for him. Or any other feelings.

I walk the few blocks, thinking, but also admiring the streets. A lot has changed since I was a student, but a lot has remained the same. I haven't had a chance to appreciate how much I used to thrive off the energy of Manhattan. I didn't even realize I was missing it. But now, being here, a part of its pulsing energy, flurry of activity and the vibrant scene of art, culture and life, it's hitting me hard that I love the city.

Something I don't want to examine guides me to the back entrance. I turn into the alley, wondering if I'm detouring from my usual entrance to glimpse Massi or if I just feel more like a team member so I use the employee door. I tell the little devil on my shoulder it's the latter, but we don't get a chance to argue the point.

As I turn the corner I see the saucier, Massi and Lena by the door. The cook is sobbing and Massi is giving her two large bags and patting her on her shoulders. I stay rooted to my spot on the sidewalk, trying to comprehend what's happening.

"Thank you," the saucier says.

"See you soon," Massi replies and disappears inside.

The woman walks past me and smiles through her tears, balancing the two bags. We say hi and I watch her again walk down the alley.

"Good morning, Gina." Lena is propped against the wall, smiling at me.

"Good morning." I move closer to her, still stealing glances at the empty space behind me. "I thought he fired her last night."

She narrows her eyes and shakes her head. "Why would he fire her? She's fantastic at her job."

"But she left crying and all the patrons heard him yell 'get out.'" I keep stupidly looking back as if the saucier might reappear to collaborate the story.

"She has a sick child and her husband was in an accident last night, and she stubbornly refused to go because she needed the pay. Massi didn't have time to reason with her, so he yelled it." She shrugs lightly.

"What was in the bags?" This is why assumptions are bad. I evaluated the situation incorrectly, and completely misjudged what was happening.

"Massi stayed late last night and cooked meals for her. At least one burden off her plate."

My mind struggles to reconcile everything. Not only did I misread the situation and misconstrue Massi's actions, but I've just grown a new appreciation for the person he's become. Shit. I'm so charmed, I might have to quit this job because the emotional turmoil and the attraction is too much.

"You thought he just fired her because he's an asshole?" Lena reads into the confusion on my face.

I swallow, but I don't know what to say.

"Well, he acts like an asshole most of the time, but it's all bark. He's a fair man."

"What about that server he fired last week because he was drinking a glass of water before he picked up the order?" I had considered that another management mishap, but what if I was wrong then too?

"That dude was lazy and stealing from the register. I don't know why Massi does things the way he does, but they usually have a deeper root." She closes her eyes and lets the sun wash over her face. "I better go before he misses me." There is a smile lingering on her face as she pushes off the wall and walks in.

I stay outside for another beat, shaking my head and smiling. Then I take a deep breath and hope I can avoid Massi as much as he's been avoiding me.

And learn quickly that I can't. As I close the door and turn, Massi steps from his office. It's just to my left, across from the employee room.

We both stop. The short corridor is dim as it is, but with him blocking the way it seems even darker. I want to pass by him, but there isn't much space on either side. He stands there, his eyes roaming over me like I'm edible. He is not touching me, but his gaze raises goosebumps on my skin.

Our eyes lock like they did last night and I really want to look away, but it's impossible. How could I lose command of my sight? Massi, on the other hand, is perfectly capable of directing his eyes. He drops them to my mouth and my lips part.

These involuntary reactions are concerning. I need to leave this space that seems to have shrunk since I entered.

I take a step, lowering my foot gingerly as if the floor is laced with broken glass. If I get any closer to him, my body may explode.

With heat. With need. With desire.

This morning, I rediscovered how much I missed my mom and this city. How much I loved her and the streets of New York. I don't think my heart can take any more.

I wish to God Massi would just step aside, but he doesn't. He seems completely immersed in watching me. With the same intensity and dedication he gives his kitchen, he's devouring me with his eyes.

Or I'm misconstruing again. I don't know anymore. But I know his scent spreads warmth through my body, and his fierce presence is probably stealing my air because I'm acutely aware of my chest heaving up and down.

I want to turn and run away.

I want to tell him to let me pass.

I want to ask him to stop looking at me like this.

But most of all, I want him to kiss me.

He leans forward and his proximity drives me crazy with more questions. But I don't want to have questions anymore—I want answers. I want to know how he tastes, how his lips would feel against mine, if his kiss can mend the past and spring hope for the future.

He raises his palm and cups my cheek, just feathering my skin, but I'm sure he's leaving marks because the touch is scorching. He leans closer and then he blinks and jerks away.

We're both blinded by the outside light as Phillip saunters in with a cheerful greeting.

Chapter Ten

Gina

It's been six weeks since my father passed and I've been stuck in some sort of alternate universe. I'm strangely relieved I'm no longer in LA despite it being my home. Or it used to be. I don't know anymore. And here? I'm definitely not at home here, but I have this uncomfortable feeling of belonging.

It's surreal because I don't belong here. My father is no longer around to drive my need to please him while constantly disappointing him. My mother is drifting away slowly. I haven't found a place for her in a suitable home yet. We live together and she seems determined to remind me daily what a failure I've been. Her mind is lost in the past.

We had a few bright moments, including a pajama Saturday, but those snapshots of time only make the whole situation worse for me. I'm grateful I get to experience them, and then even more remorseful for what no longer is. And what we've missed for all those years I was gone.

My only friend here is Mila, and she is really tied more to my LA life than my past here. And then there is Massi who avoided me, and now... I don't know what's going on now.

After our moment in the corridor at the back entrance two weeks ago, we both somehow put on professional hats and have continued to float around each other, pretending nothing happened.

He went back to his glowering, which is for the best. I think. If only my heart could find a comfortable beat whenever I'm in his vicinity. Seriously, the man is going to give me an arrhythmia.

Last weekend I traveled to LA again to spend time with Sebastien and we planned for his visit here with me. I miss him so much, I practically want to run to the airport every evening. He has a break coming up in a few weeks and he'll spend it here with me.

I want to introduce him to my mom, though I know it might only stir up shit. I may need to consult her doctor to ensure her heart can handle it.

The work at Casa Cassi has—weirdly—been a welcome distraction. Aside from the proximity of the owner himself. After dining there several nights in a row, I agreed with Mila that he was indeed an artist. I've always known he was a talented chef, but the way his skills have matured over time caught me by surprise.

It was his pecan crusted halibut with Dijon sauce that left no doubt in my mind that he deserved the star. He deserves all the fame and recognition because he is amazing. The best.

His culinary artistry is probably the only part of him I'm not confused about. He comes up with enticing flavors and has the courage to experiment. He stands out, and I know that because over the years I've eaten food prepared by masters. And Massimo Cassinetti is one.

But what's surprised me even more is his ability to command respect. It's in a a very gruff, nearly violent way, but I've observed that people who care about their work don't fear him. They don't ridicule his behavior— he presents a full asshole package. They simply accept and respect him.

I've spent weeks pondering what draws them to him. Because his team's dedication isn't only driven by their need to learn from him. To get the best training and move on. And it isn't the pleasant work environment for sure. It is his fairness. What I see in his kitchen is fascinating.

Massi leads with a choleric energy, but he leads. He doesn't micromanage. He expects the highest dedication, but everyone on his team gets a chance to learn, an opportunity to grow. And also room to fail. He yells to command excellence, but not so much when someone screws up.

I find myself wanting the star for him more than is reasonable. Or healthy, for that matter.

"You think we could pull it off in two weeks?" Phillip scratches his beard, glancing at Lena. She exudes calm confidence and Phillip often consults with her. They seem like perfect partners, in business and I am sure in personal life as well.

We're standing by the bar. It's morning and she looks like she's been up for a while now, but she never complains. We all nurse a cup of coffee while the cleaning crew is polishing the tables, preparing to open.

"Massi and I can be ready, of course, but such an event requires more than an amazing menu." She looks at me.

I nod. "We can be ready. The shorter the lead time, the more hype we could create. It would be like a pop-up, one-time-only dining opportunity, which would create a sense of exclusivity. We have several bloggers and influencers lined up who are interested in such private dining experience.

"Now that we have a good team here covering the floor to meet the kitchen's excellence, I have more time to focus on the event. This would be a great opportunity to assess the new processes and put the team's skills to the test while I'm still here."

Mila has been working her ass off, eating here every day with a different influencer, expanding her reach beyond the typical food critics. Soon there will be features on several high-profile accounts highlighting the decor, the story of the restaurant and reviews of several dishes.

"Think of it as an opening event," Mila explains. "Only obviously we can't open an already opened and well-known restaurant, so we will create a private dining evening to get exposure on social media. And word of mouth. We need a high-profile guest list, so think of any socialite or business tycoon you could invite to increase the prestige of the event. But we have the basics covered."

"Okay, I'm in." Phillip smiles and stands up. "Discuss the details with Massi and prepare the menu." He kisses Lena's temple and she blushes.

"Could you also make sure Massi is in a reasonably good mood at ten o'clock? The editor from the *Sunday Times* is coming to interview him. Now, we got her here because she owed us a favor, but it doesn't guarantee she'll run the feature. It's Massi's job to make it happen." I bite my lip, searching Lena's face.

"I can't guarantee his best behavior, but Massi is not a stupid man. He understands the importance." With that, she plants a kiss on Phillip's cheek and ambles back to the kitchen.

"Great," he says, probably to us, but it's not clear since his eyes remain on Lena. The man practically worships the floor she walks on. Mila looks at me and fans herself.

"We'll prepare the list of invitees and get going on some creative invitations." She whirls around, typing on her phone.

"I think we should go with something more clandestine than an official invitation. Maybe we just text people, as if they didn't get on the official guest list, but we're making it possible to squeeze them in?" I'm getting excited about the event.

"Ooh, I love that. We can personalize every invite that way." Mila chews on the inside of her lip, something she does when she's thinking. I adore that she's already taken my idea and improved it.

"I'll leave you to it, ladies. Should I stay for the interview?" We both turn, having forgotten Phillip was still there.

"I think the fewer people hovering around, the

better. Has he done big interviews before?" Something tells me Massi wouldn't enjoy it.

"We had an invitation to a morning show and a few media requests, but Massi's always refused, claiming he belonged in the kitchen." Phillip rakes his hand through his hair.

"Mila, see if he's willing to get a briefing," I instruct and she sighs, but goes to the kitchen, with Phillip following.

I find myself alone in the middle of an empty restaurant, wishing I was the one talking to him. Helping him relax to ensure his genius will come across. But my presence would only spark the opposite, so I stay on the other side of the swinging door that seems more like an impenetrable fortress to me.

Alone.

Isolated.

Outcast.

Just what I deserve.

"Did you always dream about this?" Catira, the editor from the *Times*, asks.

She's leaning against the shiny counter, her phone next to her, recording. I position myself by the door, rationing my breathing—partially worried my presence might upset Massi and destroy the effortless, pleasant energy, and partially in awe.

When Catira arrived I briefed her on all the outstanding capabilities of the restaurant.

"I looked him up," she said. "Massimo Cassinetti is the only apprentice of Frederick Beaufort who has succeeded in this business."

Hearing the two names in one sentence formed a lump in my throat. "I didn't know that."

"Well, there was gossip before Beaufort moved to LA that he'd been purposely jeopardizing their careers. Probably just jealous rumors." She waved her hand, dismissing the comment. "Can I ask him about that?" But she was clearly interested in the *gossip*.

"I don't think they parted on good terms, but it's ancient history, Catira. Let's not add to the rumor mill unnecessarily."

Luckily, that did the trick and she abandoned the topic and moved on. As she asked me a few more questions, I couldn't help but watch Massi as he stood by the bar with Mila. She whispered in his ear, probably coaching him on how to answer the questions and remain civil.

He was still, his eyebrows slightly together, his jaw set, listening. He cocked his head slightly to hear better, while he kept looking at nothing in particular.

At that moment of complete concentration, I saw

the man I used to know. But I also saw the man he'd become, focused and dedicated to his craft, a successful businessman.

The small lines around his eyes that somehow made him look more attractive deepened as he squinted in concentration. He was relaxed, and it wasn't just in his visibly loosened shoulders, but the features of his face also seemed somehow playful.

The whole time I talked to Catira I kept stealing glimpses at him, hoping not to be discovered. That wouldn't be professional. Not that my body cared about being professional because it was reacting in all the inappropriate ways.

My heart pounded, my stomach twisted in nautical knots, and at one point I did spontaneous Kegel exercises.

Massi leaned in and whispered into Mila's ear, and a pang of jealousy and yearning swam through my bloodstream. And then something really extraordinary happened. Mila threw her head back and laughed, and he did too. It was a sound that did all sorts of things to me.

Unfortunately, the most prevalent was inciting regret. I wanted to be the one who laughed with him. Who talked to him about the interview. Hell, about many other things.

Even Catira turned to see what was going on. And

then our eyes met and Massi stopped laughing. But he didn't glower—a smile lingered on his lips and I might have just imagined it, but he nodded, acknowledging me. Our eyes locked, his searing through me with equal parts caress and curiosity.

I shivered, barely realizing how shallow my breathing became. I wanted to pull him aside and force him to listen. To explain my actions all those years ago. Or to just touch him, tell him without words how wonderful he was under all the bravado of an angry grump.

Mila interrupted our moment, possibly because neither of us sensed it was uncomfortable for her and Catira. She facilitated the introductions and Massi invited us all to his kitchen.

The plan had been to just let him talk to Catira this time. We wanted to invite her later for a private dinner to solidify her interest in the story, but Massi decided on a spontaneous dining experience. My eyes met Mila's and she shrugged.

But it's obvious now that being in the kitchen was the best plan ever. It's his domain, his territory, and if he was relaxed earlier, now he's nonchalant, graceful and charming.

"Not always. I wanted to be a fireman or a policeman like any other boy. When I was thirteen my father died, and it was hard on me. Later, when I turned fifteen, I got my first summer job in a kitchen."

He works with a small carving knife, shredding tuna steak into slivers, and I imagine this is how a sculptor creates art.

"I really didn't want to work there at first. I was young and stupid, not seeing the reason why I should have a dirty job." He chuckles at that. "We had money, but my mother made us all experience real life to build our work ethic, not allowing us to grow up spoiled brats with trust funds. The first day there I watched the chef working, and he reminded me of my father."

"Your father was a chef?" Catira asks, watching the knife work in fascination.

Massi turns and grabs a salt shaker, twisting it a few times above the shredded tuna. "No, but seeing the chef... I don't know. He was slicing vegetables—a simple task, but he took it seriously. After my father's death, I buried all the memories of him because it hurt. I replaced my grief with anger."

He glances my way and I'm caught in an avalanche of emotions. Is he telling me the story? Is he explaining himself to me? Why?

I never knew, never understood how his career and his behavior stemmed from the loss he experienced in his early teenage years.

"But there in that kitchen I remembered him. How

he always cooked Sunday dinner. It was a tradition in my house. And suddenly it was the most important thing that I learn how to cook. Somehow, through that, I felt I'd be connected to him."

From the corner of my eye, I see Mila cover her mouth with her hand, her eyes glistening. Catira, usually ready to challenge with a follow-up question, remains silent, observing Massi as he pours Parmesan batter into a sizzling pan.

I have to lean against the wall because my legs are weak. I have always admired his drive, but understanding the deep motivation behind it destroys me. It's much easier to live when Massi is just an arrogant, self-absorbed asshole.

He fries small Parmesan crusts and arranges them on three square plates. I focus on his hands, masterfully spooning the tuna tartare into each cheese nest. He garnishes the bite-size beauties and the plates with something, but my mind doesn't register the details, just the feelings. Watching him finishing the dish is like a symphony, dance and a theater production all in one.

Seeing it after his very human confession is so much more. More than I can cope with at the moment.

He pushes one plate to Catira and looks in mine and Mila's direction. Without hesitation Mila dashes closer, and Massi's eyes lock with mine yet again.

He is inviting me to taste. I take a step closer, wishing Mila didn't stand at the side of the counter because that leaves me with a spot right next to Massi.

He pushes the plate to me, and as I reach out our hands brush. It's almost imperceptible and I'm not even sure if he felt it, but the contact leaves me shaking. With nerves. With desire. With confusion. And, worst of all, with hope.

"Ladies, I hope you enjoy a little snack," he says, his eyes on me. I'm shaking so badly I have to grip the plate to ground myself.

Mila clears her throat, but Massi ignores her, staring at me, waiting. For what?

"Oh my God, this is amazing. I've had my share of tuna tartare, but this is divine." I register Catira's words and finally understand he is waiting for me to take a bite.

Picking up the fragile nest, heavy with the fish mixture, with my trembling hand is hard. Doing so with Massi's intense gaze on me makes the task impossible. I try to lift the delicate finger food with both my hands, my heart hammering in my chest.

"Massi, you're a genius," Mila squeals, and Massi darts his eyes to her for a moment long enough for me to throw the food into my mouth.

"I'm glad you're enjoying it. For me, cooking has

always been an art form, not mass production." He turns to me again.

The tartare is delicious, but I still almost choke on it. He stares and I chew, uncomfortable. In the background Catira and Mila chat, or at least I think that's what's happening through the pulse in my temples.

Massi expects my verdict, his eyes kind on me, but his fingers tapping on his thigh.

Inexplicably, I fear that accepting and liking his dish is so much more than simply eating a bite of food. It's as if he is trying to communicate words he's never gotten to say and now I'm left vulnerable and exposed, consuming the food and the heavy history between us.

I finally swallow, buried in the rarely visible kindness of his eyes.

His words earlier clicked in so many ways, explaining things I wish I still didn't understand. Along with his peace offering in the form of tuna tartare in a Parmesan nest, I feel like we've just taken a step in a new direction. The question is, will this path break me or will it mend me?

His face is full of need, but it's not just the need for approval or praise. It's more. So much more. Deep in my soul I know it's not my approval of the meal he's seeking.

The silence is loaded with years of unspoken tension, but also with something else.

The smell of lemon and fish mingles with Massi's natural musk, evoking memories. Awakening feelings I buried in the darkest crevices of my mind. His dark hazel eyes glint with an intensity that can set this kitchen on fire.

We stand there for seconds, or years, before I finally speak.

"Thank you."

His eyebrows jerk up briefly, he gives me a smile that I'm sure I'm imagining and before he turns back to Catira, he whispers so only I could hear.

"Anytime, Blue, anytime."

Chapter Eleven

Massi

17 years ago

"What do you mean you have to leave?" Jacques threw a towel across the room.

The fabric grazed over the stove and caught on fire. As soon as it landed by my feet, the busboy doused it with a spray of water from the hose at the dish-washing station. It all happened in a beat of a second, but in a well-rehearsed choreography because flying burning objects were a regular appearance in Jacques's kitchen.

"My wife was taken to the emergency room. I need to leave." My heart hammered inside my chest.

"You leave now, you don't have to come back. An

artist can't be distracted by everyday life. And you're very close to being an artist, Massimo. Don't let anyone stop you." He stood there, his stance screaming confidence and authority. With his chin raised, he stared at me down his aquiline nose, giving me an option.

To choose my fate. To rise or to fall. But both choices would only lead to a fall.

My chest heaved at an alarming speed.

"Honey glazed sea bass." A cook yelled beside me and my gaze moved to the stainless-steel plating table. The sauce sizzled in the pan. The dish was seconds from perfection and I snapped into action like a trained monkey.

"Veggies. Polenta," I ordered and two of my colleagues dashed to deliver what I needed.

I grabbed a polished plate from the warmer and arranged everything in the middle, spending mere seconds to create a culinary picture worth every penny of the money the dish cost at this place.

As soon as the plate left the station, I gestured to my second-in-command and strolled to the changing room. I pressed my head against the cold metal of the locker, Blue's eyes flashing in my mind. Our future. I opened the locker, pulled out my phone and called my sister.

"Hey, stranger. What do you need?"

Of course, Sydney would start by pointing out the

obvious. I only called when I needed something. As much as I loved all my step-siblings, Sydney and I had always had a weird relationship.

After they had moved into our house with their widowed father, I'd hated Sydney the most. For no good reason. But she was the same age as me and by default had stolen the status of the oldest from me.

"Blue is in the hospital."

"Shit, sorry. What can I do?"

"Syd, she's at Weill Cornell. Could you go be with her? I have to finish a few things. I'll get there as soon as I can."

"What is so important that you can't go there right now?" Fucking Sydney, being all reasonable.

"Could you do it for me?"

"Are you at work?"

Yes, yes, I'm fucking ten minutes' walk away.

"Syd, could you go be with her?"

"Of course I'll go. You better be there soon."

"Thank you." I hung up.

I typed out a text to Blue: *I love you, baby. I'll be there shortly. Syd is on her way.*

My finger hovered above the send button for a moment. I could keep this job or I could sit, helpless, in a waiting room. With the bitter aftertaste of betrayal, I sent the message.

"Good decision." Jacques patted my shoulder when I returned to my station.

If only it didn't feel like the worst one.

It had taken two more hours before I burst through the door, screamed at someone at the admission desk and reached Sydney in the waiting room. I froze immediately for two reasons that made my heart stop and restart in a violent way.

Sydney had cried. Her mascara was smeared under her eyes. That by itself twisted my stomach. But it was what was beside her that stopped me in my tracks. Or rather, who was beside her. Fucking Frederick stood up when he spotted me, a solemn veil over his smug face.

My mind backfired, spinning in all different directions. Reasonable remnants of myself argued Blue was at work when she'd fainted, so of course he was here. But that voice was too weak against all the guilt that I needed to channel somewhere. Or at someone.

I inhaled, pretty sure my nostrils doubled in their size, and stepped forward. Before I could do or say anything, Syd jumped up and threw herself at me, loud sobs echoing around the somber waiting room where several people waited for news with hope.

"I'm so sorry, Massi." The panic that gripped me with its cold, sobering touch made me forget everything around.

I grabbed Sydney's shoulders, jerked her away from me and tried to string words together. "What are you talking about? What the fuck happened to Blue?"

Sydney's voice hitched. "She is sleeping. She'll be fine, but the baby—" she wailed.

Time, space, my surroundings ceased to exist in those few brief moments as the words sank in at a painfully slow speed, unearthing all the dark corners of my soul.

"Is Blue okay?" The question scratched my throat.

"Yes, she is. I mean, she will be. They didn't want to tell us much. She was awfully quiet and they feared she was in shock. You should talk to the doctor." Sydney looked toward the nurses' station.

I nodded and she walked over with me. A very tired-looking nurse confirmed my identity and asked us to wait.

My skin prickled as I sensed Frederick's presence by my side.

"Massimo, I'm really sorry. Let me know if there is anything I can do." He patted me on the shoulder.

"Thank you. We're good. And thank you for bringing her over here." I said the words on autopilot, hating that he was there when I wasn't. Hating that he could leave his restaurant and I had to slave under an entitled French epicurean god.

If there was ever a time to start my own business, to be my own boss, it was now. So I could protect Blue and take care of her without depending on others.

"Of course, of course. Everything happens for a reason, Massi." He squeezed my shoulder. "I'll go now. All the best." He strode away.

"Mr. Cassinetti?" I whipped around to see a middle-aged woman in blue scrubs. I nod. "I'm sorry, your wife has suffered a miscarriage. My assessment is that it was one of those unfortunate, inexplicable occurrences and there is no worry about future fertility, but of course, her OBGYN will want to run more tests."

"Is she okay?" I should have been grieving, but I found the whole situation surreal. I hadn't had a chance to start looking forward to having a baby, or even acknowledge it was coming. I'd seen it as a reason for the delaying of my dreams. Right now, my only concern was Blue.

"Yes, physically she is okay. As soon as she wakes up, you can take her home. The nurse will give you information about support groups and other resources to help you both cope."

Cope? I couldn't help it, but the prevalent emotion

flooding my blood stream was relief. And guilt for feeling relief.

"Can I see her?" My palms were damp, sweat trickled down my spine, but I shivered as if we were standing in a freezer.

"You can go sit with her, but let her sleep." She turned and walked off to talk to another family.

"Do you want me to stay with you? To call Bianca?"

I shook my head. "Mom didn't know Blue was pregnant. We haven't told anyone."

Sydney sniffled and rubbed my arm. "I'll stay with you."

"Go home, you've done enough. Thank you, Syd."

"Listen, Massi, this might be the worst time to point it out, but you should have fucking been here." She bit her lower lip and stared at me, her green eyes a mixture of contempt and pity, and perhaps something else, but I didn't bother to decipher that. What for? She was right.

"Thanks again, Syd. Could you keep this to yourself? I don't know if Blue wants the attention. I need her to decide if and how we share this."

"Of course." She gave me a brief hug and assessed me with narrowed eyes. She opened her mouth, but then she changed her mind, turned and left.

I found Blue's bed and sat beside her. She looked pale and small, lost in a large pillow, her skin almost translucent. She was still the most beautiful thing I'd ever seen. Her chestnut hair, a little damp around her face, fanned across the white, sterile fabric. She resembled a sleeping princess. Her features relaxed and peaceful.

But that was only an illusion, a drug-induced calm. I wanted to believe that the miscarriage wouldn't change us. That we could simply move on from it without scars and dive back into our pre-pregnancy plans.

And as I sat there watching Blue sleep off her trauma, I started to believe that. With unreasonable, cold certainty, I concluded that things happened for a good reason.

If only I didn't voice my conviction when Blue woke up.

"What do you mean?" I yelled into the phone and several people turned my way.

I was livid, pacing circles in Central Park. I'd just finished my shift at the Four Seasons when my agent called me.

"I don't understand how this could have happened,

but someone seems to have pulled some strings because the place is gone."

"What do you mean gone? It's two thousand square feet of prime real estate in SoHo. It hasn't just disappeared. We reviewed and approved the paperwork. I'm coming to sign the documents now." I tried to control my voice, staring down the passers-by.

"I'll make some calls and see what can be done. Perhaps it's just a ploy to get you agree to a higher rent."

"I can't fucking pay higher rent. It's ridiculously high as it is. My projections don't allow for higher rent —the place doesn't have the capacity."

"Let me find out what's going on."

"You better, because I'll fucking look for a new agent." I snapped my phone closed and marched across the park to calm down a bit before I headed home.

I didn't even know if Blue was working. The last few weeks had been super busy and between her school and work, my shifts at the Four Seasons and the search for the location of my first restaurant, we barely had time to talk. Or perhaps we avoided talking to keep some topics unspoken.

I was painfully aware that unspoken equaled unresolved, but I hoped time would heal. Avoiding the elephant in the room was easier.

I was going to call her and see if we could grab a

meal together when my agent had contacted me to explain the situation with the property I'd lost. Or rather, that someone had stolen it out from under me.

The information pushed me into the first bar. Several vodka shots later, I stumbled into a cab and made my way to our stupid apartment in Brooklyn.

Blue yanked the door open after I dropped my keys several times and failed to behave like a reasonable neighbor. She pulled me inside.

"What the hell, Massi? Where have you been? I was worried."

I tripped and fell to my knees. Blue leaned down to help me, but I swatted her hands away. "Leave me alone."

"What's going on, Massi?" Her voice was calm, concerned. She wasn't even trying to pick a fight, she just wanted to help her drunk husband.

"Have you told Frederick about the place in SoHo?" I howled.

She blinked a few times, staring at me as if I spoke a foreign language. "What do you mean?"

"Answer the fucking question, Blue. How does he fucking know about the lease we were going to sign?"

"I mentioned it in passing. I was so happy we found the place. What do you mean *were* going to sign?"

I rocked a bit on the way to the chair and she dared to help me sit. I didn't want her help. Ever. Again.

"How many times have I told you not to trust that snake? He bought the fucking building. He bought it. It's off the market because he'll open a new location there soon."

Blue went pale, her hand flying to her mouth as she tried and failed to stifle a gasp. "Oh my God, Massi, I can't believe that. I didn't even tell him where it was. I just mentioned our plans were progressing nicely and we had found a place in SoHo."

"You ruined it all. Everything. Always. You ruined my dreams." I tried to stand, but the alcohol in my veins sat me back down. My stomach heaved.

"Massi," Blue whispered, her voice shaking with unshed tears.

"Just get out of here, Blue. I can't even look at you right now."

I ran to the bathroom and retched. When I finally made my way to our little pathetic room, Blue was gone.

For the first time we hadn't sought understanding in mutual embrace, through the language of our hearts and bodies. It was the first time we gave up on each other and chose pain over love.

Chapter Twelve

Gina

"What was *that*?" Mila is practically bouncing, unable to contain her energy. "He nailed that interview. Who knew he could be so charming and honest?" She plays with the paper umbrella in her moldy-looking blue cocktail. "I mean, he was honest, wasn't he? About his dad."

We're sitting in a corner at Casa Cassi, having drinks. Well, non-alcoholic ones, but pretending to be a part of the usual clientele. The floor is teeming with the evening crowd and I'm assessing where we can improve the customer experience without being too obvious about taking notes and making the staff feel they are being watched.

But I can't concentrate. Massi's interview, the revelation about his father and the delicious meal he not only prepared, but obsessively cared about my opinion on, are still reeling in my head. But it's him calling me Blue that shook me to the core.

Spoken softly, that name dived into the darkest corner of my soul to drill through any protective walls I've built. Simultaneously, my stomach tingled with awareness and apprehension. Lust and dread coiled around my bones, and I knew I wasn't strong enough to survive Massimo Cassinetti for the second time.

"His dad passed when he was thirteen, but I didn't know he started cooking to stay connected to him."

I watch tonight's maître d' interacting with a group of walk-ins, but it's just a cover, I don't really see what's going on. The war surging inside me prevents me from functioning like a normal human being. I'm a mess. Just pieces of shredded heart, festering soul and dark emotions that could effectively suck the life out of this room.

"Well, it sure made me look at him differently. All that glower and barking is just a wrapping with the fragile sticker. He's just as hurt and insecure as the rest of us."

Calling Massi insecure instead of an asshole would have made me laugh yesterday. Understanding that he is not only chasing fame, scratching his ego with the need for the elusive star, but rather creating culinary art to stay close to his late father, has shifted my perception of him.

The new light of comprehension is blinding me and I can't decide if this knowledge redeems him from the past or just makes everything far worse. We should have been this honest years ago.

"Are you going to finally explain what's going on, *Blue?*"

Shit. Mila overheard him earlier. Her inquiring gaze pierces me, and I swear the woman can probably read all the answers written in my eyes. Perhaps the answers I don't even know I have, the little witch.

"We were married once." Okay, guessing by her dropped jaw she didn't read this one. I chuckle. It's a tentative rumble in my chest, not really a joyous expression, but it feels good to let go a bit.

"And you didn't think of telling me this before? This is huge. Does he—"

"The day you and I came here to meet with them was the first time we'd spoken in seventeen years." The meeting we should have never taken. Desperate for money and something to keep me occupied, I'd naively believed I was stronger. Immune. No longer impacted. I've been wrong about many things in my life, but this one takes the gold medal.

Lesson of the day—it's impossible to build immunity against Massimo Cassinetti. There is no vaccine for the pull he holds over me. No immunization to neutralize his effect.

Not even the distance of time and space over nearly two decades doused the array of feelings I have. It's unnatural. Or perhaps the most natural thing ever, if only it was reciprocated.

"Okay and it seems his initial shock—or dismay—is wearing off, judging by today." She leans back and finally gives me a physical reprieve when she looks away, scanning the room. She makes a note on her phone. At least one of us is focused on the job.

I relax my shoulders a bit, hoping to mitigate the impending headache. God, I haven't even realized how tense I've been.

"What do you mean?" I frown at her.

She raises her finger and finishes her note. "I've been trying to figure out what's wrong at the entrance. The hostess isn't smiling. She smiles when greeting someone, but then turns back to her bored self." Mila puts the phone down and looks up. "What do I mean? Come on, he was talking and cooking for you the whole time."

"That's bullshit. I was standing in the shadows. He was fully focused on Catira." Why is my heart doing pirouettes?

"Sure, sure. Have you left your skill of observation in LA?" she deadpans.

"It makes no sense. He hates me. In his mind I left him all those years ago, and he's never forgiven me."

Dessert plates from a table beside us get cleared and I start a stopwatch on my phone to time how quickly the bill gets delivered. I need to do some work today. My half-assed dedication immediately goes out the window when a server places two small glass dishes in front of me and Mila.

"Lavender-infused panna cotta with blueberries from the chef, ladies." She smiles and waltzes away.

"A blue dessert for Blue... right, right, the chef hates you and expresses it with this delicious bowl of yum-yums." She sing-songs the words, conducting her gleeful melody with the spoon before she digs it into the creamy texture and tastes it.

I stare at the bowl. The presentation is beautiful. But it's all the memories that panna cotta represents. He remembers my favorite dessert. One that he perfected for me.

My brain and heart both forget what their vital functions are and the world around me disappears for a moment. From the corner of my eye, I see the numbers blinking on my screen, still timing the bill delivery. I tap the red button to stop the countdown and pick up the spoon with trepidation.

I'm afraid to have a taste. Not that I think it's poisoned for real, but figuratively it might as well be. If seeing the dessert circumvented my brain and heart, leaving me vulnerable, what would the actual flavor do to me? Am I willing to go down that road? There is a good reason I haven't had panna cotta for seventeen years.

"Oh my God, have a taste. This is divine. Not too sweet, perfectly creamy. Your Massi is a genius." Mila can't be more annoying right now.

"He's not *my* Massi," I bark.

"Sure, keep telling yourself that. Eat the freaking dessert. Give him a chance—"

I glare at her.

"I mean, give it a chance." She shrugs, the queen of innocence.

I take a spoonful and all the worries materialize. I have no right to feel longing, but I have missed Massi since the day I left all those years ago. The creamy texture carries my mind right into his arms.

All those moments when he made me feel beautiful, worshiped, the most important person in the world. All those moments I loved and was loved. Until I wasn't.

I wipe at a stupid tear.

"And while we're on the topic of him hating you, he gave me this a few weeks back. He said you may want to loosen up a bit." She pushes a card across the table.

Ballroom dancing in Chelsea.

The dam breaks, and I stand up and rush outside. The evening air hits my lungs but there isn't enough oxygen. I lean forward, supporting myself with my hands on my knees, and I pant, sobbing.

With a gentle touch on my shoulder, Mila helps me stand up. "Not here, darling. Let's take a walk." She rushes us away from the entrance to Casa Cassi, holding me, supporting, guiding us among the people while I'm blinded by long-overdue tears.

We find an empty, small kebab joint and she buys two waters, leaving them a twenty to let us sit in the back of the narrow space.

I bawl, the years of pent-up denial resurfacing in bursts of loud hiccups. Mila massages my back and keeps the space safe for my breakdown, staring down any poor passer-by who approaches.

When I have no tears left, I blow my nose and I tell her the story of my first marriage. It takes me what seems like the entire night, but probably it is just minutes. The story of love, pain, regret and guilt, all wrapped up in bouts of tears in the middle of Manhattan in an anonymous bistro with plastic chairs.

When I finish, we sit in silence. Traffic blinks and honks outside, reflecting a kaleidoscope of red, blue and yellow on the linoleum floor. A few people come for takeout, mostly ignoring us.

Telling her the story for the first time in my life, admitting my regrets, renders my limbs weak. I might need to sit here for days before I can move.

I tell her almost all of it, not yet ready to share the biggest secret, but I sense she might have picked up on that one already. If she has she doesn't push it, and I'm grateful.

"Maybe this is your second chance." Mila breaks the silence and my heart stops and restarts.

"It's too late for that." I sob again, the finality of the situation stabbing through me.

"I disagree, but it's not a decision for tonight. We left our things at the restaurant. Let me get you a taxi and I'll go back. Do you want me to stay with you tonight?" She strokes my head and kisses my temple.

"No, I'll be okay. Thank you for listening."

"Anytime, darling. Let's get going."

She hails me a cab and hugs me, holding me longer than usual. Before I get in, she whispers, "I say this with all my love—you shouldn't keep him in the dark, Gina."

"I'm not trying to get rid of you, Mom." I take a sip of my wine.

I don't want to be disrespectful or an ungrateful daughter, but dealing with my situation at home may turn me toward alcoholism. I love my mom. I hate that I've spent so little time with her. That I didn't know her dementia has progressed this far. That I wasn't here for my father.

Now it's as if the universe has come to cash out and I'm paying for all the moments I wasn't here.

"You want to move me to a loony house," Mom accuses me. She sits in a wingback chair in the living room's corner, a book folded in her lap. The book is upside down, which breaks my heart. She's trying so hard to prove how she has everything under control.

A deep red lamp shade above Mom's gray hair diffuses the light, forming shadows on her face. Bracketed by the wings of the tall backrest, wearing her pale pink bathrobe, she looks smaller. Insignificant. I wish we could talk about the past, catch up on time we lost, but instead, we're bickering, or I'm trying to guide her through elementary tasks.

She spent years taking care of me when I was a little baby and later a girl. It shouldn't be this difficult to return the favor. Yet I dread the responsibility. Maybe I'm just not a good person. Certainly there is a track record of decisions that would support that.

"It's not a loony house. Mom, you can't stay here alone, and my life is in California. I'm trying to find a home where you can be very independent, but also get all the help you may need. It'd be like an all-inclusive hotel, and you'll be around people your age."

"And who will pay for it?" She drops the book on the side table.

That's the question.

"Mom, why did you have to refinance the house and then downsize?" I've been here for weeks and yet I haven't found one good reason for the dire state of my parent's finances.

In one of those rare moments when she's really looking at me, she blinks a few times and then swats with her hand at nothing in particular as if she was trying to scare away a thought. She opens her mouth and then closes it again. A single, lonely tear rolls down her cheek.

"Your father was a proud man. He might have not been fair to you back then, but his beliefs were strong. They were too engraved in him to even admit he was wrong or forgive, let alone reach out. But he regretted how he spoke to you. How he'd driven you away from us. He never recovered from that guilt. So he coped in unhealthy ways."

She turns her head to the side, resting her cheek against the fabric of the chair, closing her eyes for a moment, absorbing the pain she'd suffered because of my failures. Because of my decisions. Because of my inability to fight for myself.

"That's the problem with forgiveness," she says. "It doesn't work unless we forgive ourselves. You can accept other people's reasons and behavior, but unless you accept your own and truly forgive yourself, the trauma festers."

Don't I know that. I've spent my all life trying to forgive people who might have wronged me back then, but forgiving myself? It was just easier to learn how to live with the guilt.

We sit in silence for what seems like a lifetime. I have so many questions, but right now I don't want to disturb the beautiful harmony formed between us. My mother hasn't been this open with me or this close to me... well, ever.

"The burden your father carried drew him to the gambling tables. Or perhaps I'm making excuses for him. I didn't want to bother you with that. And what have I achieved? Now you're burdened with an even bigger load."

So many things we can't change anymore. So many chances at happiness that we threw away for all the right reasons. Reasons that were so wrong.

"I wish you could stay with me. Now that he's

gone, you could live here." Her words are choked, lodged somewhere between her soul and my heart.

I wish the same. At least now, in this tender moment of clarity and intimacy between us, the idea of grasping at least the last memories we can create seems like the solution. But how would I deal with the debt?

"Thank you for telling me, Mom. I wish I'd known, but Dad made it clear he didn't want to have anything to do with me. I'm sorry I didn't reach out."

"Water under the bridge." She looks at me, her hands small in her lap. "It's what happens now that matters. That you have control over. That boy... Massi... still loves you."

And she's lost it again. If there was anyone more upset about me leaving than my father, it was Massi. The interview yesterday left me raw and unsettled.

He opened up a side that had been hidden, carefully curated to never come to the surface, and the broken-hearted girl in me wants to believe he did it for me, not for Catira, publicity or the prospect of a Michelin star.

But that is just wishful thinking. Or rather foolish thinking in an impossible direction. I can't contemplate anything related to Massi, but I like that we're moving past the animosity. Past the history. Then, perhaps, I'll be able to forgive myself. Because Mom is right—the guilt has been plaguing me for too long.

She stands up, heavily relying on the support of the chair, and shuffles slowly to the kitchen. "If you don't want to stay for me, you need to stay for him. You've been hiding from the truth for too long. And that boy is a part of your truth."

Tears build up behind my eyes and spill slowly in the aftermath of her words. I knew coming back would unearth deeply buried emotions, but the ride has been too taxing.

Too much. Too painful. Too real.

I wipe my cheeks and stand up, knowing that it can only get worse. Because I made choices seventeen years ago that are unforgivable.

Chapter Thirteen

Gina

I didn't plan on coming here, but I needed to get out of the house. There is a small part of me that would like to stay with my mom permanently. Well, actually it's not so small. But I can't take care of her full-time, so I still have to find help. If I sold the apartment in LA, I might be able to afford it. But that still leaves me with debts left behind by my father.

And would Sebastien want to move to New York? Would I even want to risk that? So many decisions to make. So many people to consider. So instead, I choose to take some time for myself. Selfishly.

Fortunately, this place holds a milonga each Monday. The restaurant is closed today, and I have nowhere else to hide from the depressing atmosphere of my parents' house, or unresolved plans for my future and the people in it.

My father was brought up by a generation who believed a woman does what she's told. I wasn't that woman, and he never recovered from the failure of my marriage. That's what I have been telling myself for years. Because I'm a coward and it was easier to believe that than to face the reality of my inability to stand up and speak for myself.

I made mistakes. I hurt people. I erred, believing I was protecting others. A false belief, but I didn't know that at the time. That's the problem with protecting others. When you choose to save someone, you act as if you're invincible, as if you know better. And too often, the only protection they need is from you. From your well-intended choices.

And now it's too late. I'm deep in the consequences of my actions, and if I could even find the courage to rectify the situation with those who are still alive, time has aggravated my betrayal. It's deeper now. More permanent. More irreversible.

I need to live, carry the burden and push through. And I need to avoid the downfall because it would cause too much pain again. At least now the parties are oblivious and I'm the only one suffering.

After I moved to California, I was heartbroken. But worse, I had left my sense of self-worth on the East

Coast. I left it in New York. I hated so much and so many, and most of all I hated myself, and so I sought attention. And attention I got. At a high price.

My therapist encouraged me to find a hobby, do something for myself. I immediately chose dancing, something I always enjoyed. Ballroom dancing helped me find something that was for me and about me only.

A form of expression that didn't require words. A way of life that seeks joy and lets everyone in, regardless of their past or circumstances. The weekly milonga helped me out of the state of despair.

It takes me almost an hour to get to the dance school. I don't know what to expect here, but I just want to get lost in the music, let myself flow and be led, relinquish control while creating something fluid and beautiful.

I don't want to think about the reasons Massi would even suggest to Mila this is what I need. That he would know. That he remembered.

I enter the building and take the steps to the second floor. The entry hall is nearly overwhelming with its array of colors on the walls, the floors, the square ottomans and seats and even on the shelves.

It's not a large space, but it sure is lively. I consider turning away because this looks like a hip-hop outlet.

"Hello." A cheerful voice intersects my need to

flee. A young woman appears behind the counter, startling me. "Are you here for our Monday milonga?"

"Hi. Yes." I look around for some kind of anchor because the colors are dizzying.

Familiar music drifts toward us from behind the corner. I latch on to it like a life preserver.

"Ah, it seems they've started. Just follow the music. You can pay at the end."

"Thank you."

I've never enjoyed entering unfamiliar places. New people and situations cause me an irrational amount of anxiety. But as I approach the glass double doors, the music takes over and my body is drawn forward, even though my mind is still steering me to pivot and run.

Another woman opens the door and gestures me in, and I accept there will be no escape at this point. She startles me with a kiss on my cheek. This room is a stark contrast to the reception area.

It looks bare, with windows on one side and chairs around the perimeter of the rectangular floor. The white walls are decorated with black and white photographs of dancers.

There are a few women sitting around the room and several couples are dancing. A shortage of men at these events is a constant problem. Watching people dance isn't as therapeutic as dancing itself, but as I glimpse a couple moving smoothly to the rhythm, I decide to stay for a few songs.

I strategize about the best seat, allowing me a good view but an opportunity to leave unnoticed if needed, when the door behind me opens again. I turn and freeze.

He wears a black vest over a white button-down shirt with its collar open. God, do I love a man in a vest. His hair is mussed, bouncing playfully. His rolled-up sleeves tone down the formality of his attire, but the casual touch only makes him hotter.

My heart is skipping beats as if it was its favorite pastime, completely ignoring my need to maintain life. Oxygen is in short supply suddenly, and as if my state of fluster wasn't enough, the music stops. People move around, switching partners, finding a seat or getting ready for the next round.

With the first beats of the next song, Massi steps forward and nods, extending his hand. He wants to dance with me.

Shit. Shit. Shit. He stands between me and the door. Combined with several pairs of eyes I sense on me, I don't think I can bolt.

I let out the air through my cheeks and accept his hand. The song is sensual and the mood is electric as I let Massi lead me. I try to focus on the beat, but my heart is pulsing in my ears, robbing me of reasonable awareness of my surroundings.

I tentatively place my hand on his shoulder because if I was to position it at his nape as expected I'd probably faint.

The problem with tango-style dance is that it speaks to our emotions. It's romantic but also extremely sensual, relying on the close contact of bodies. Massi leads me through the refined movements, improvising to the music. We pause on some beats and then speed up, allowing momentum to carry my legs into the air.

Slowing and pausing, turning, walking, rising and sinking, we glide through the staccato feel with drama and elegance. Soon even our breathing responds to the music and I surrender to the flow.

The melody rises and falls, it pulses through us. It gets quiet and then crescendos. Like feelings do in real life. And my emotions are screaming loudly in my soul right now. But I have no time to analyze that, because Massi steals all my attention.

He is an excellent dancer. He moves around in a cat-like manner with clear and alluring aim, drawing me into the magic of this transcendent experience. It's more than magic though. I came here to relax, but there is nothing relaxing about this dance anymore.

We're back in that hallway a couple of weeks ago,

observing and absorbing each other with fierce eyes. Our bodies communicate without words, and I find myself wishing tango was the background music of my life.

The connection is so intense that for a moment I forget about everyone else. It's just me and him. Fascinated by each other's closeness.

Playfully, he leads me into another step and I hook my leg around his. Our eyes project the desire that I feel deep in my bones. I step in the opposite direction, but our bodies are still so close the contact burns me.

With the music, we pause for a beat. Massi reaches, my hand still in his, and grazes his fingers down my cheek, dusting the corner of my mouth. Involuntarily, I part my lips, consumed by a need so strong it burns in my core.

The moment is brief but captivating, and so palpable I almost stumble as I sway my hips to cross around his leg, pulling away, but he steadies me and with a stealthy glide I step to face him again. My breasts brush his torso and my nipples immediately salute, craving attention.

I'm not the only one affected. Our pelvises and upper thighs are connected in the luscious flow, reflecting the song, and Massi's desire hardens between us. And it encourages me. The effect I have on him gives me confidence.

As we move around, I take every opportunity to

slide my leg up and down his, but it's not wanton. It's a natural mirroring of his moves. He dances with all he's got—brave, dynamic, frisky, but graceful and elegant. And I feel like a queen. Dancing with Massimo Cassinetti is as close to lovemaking as tango could ever come.

When the song stops, I'm breathless. And stunned. As the tones fade away, I crash back to reality, suddenly embarrassed that I allowed myself the freedom of this dance. Of his company.

"I didn't know you dance this well." My chest heaves as I try to collect my dignity and sound casual at the same time while his hooded eyes are studying me. I don't think I'm the only one impacted, which is great. And the worst possible scenario.

"I only regret I didn't start sooner. When I first had the chance." His words somehow have a direct line to my core. Or perhaps it's just a residual state post-dance. My legs go wobbly and I cling to him, worried I may fall.

What is happening? Why is he doing this? Our professional relationship has improved since that moment by the back entrance, and I forced myself to believe that the panna cotta was just a thoughtful gesture, but now I'm not so sure anymore.

The music starts again.

"I hope I can have another dance." He smiles at

me, and I'm irritated by the wonderfully tormenting effect it has on me.

I don't get to answer because he pulls me into the music. We dance and dance. Again, like the old times, communicating the best without words. We separate only to drink some water, then dive back into the tango.

These graceful, abrupt movements define our relationship. Just like the steps and intimate closeness to the beats of the slow music, we used to share the same intimacy and passion, and we danced through our marriage with equal ache... slow, slow, fast, slow, slow, fast. Moments of complete harmony used to take turns into explosions that burned us at the end.

"I think the ladies are very disappointed today, Massi," the woman at the door says when we are leaving. "You only danced with one partner the whole time." Her eye twitches as she tries to smile, the grimace as genuine as a corrupt politician. "Lucky you." She turns to me and the pretense in her smile intensifies.

I cringe inwardly but lace my arm through Massi's. Marking territory. One I have no claim to.

The city welcomes us with a light breeze and a sense of awkwardness. The list of confusion in my mind is growing, topped by the desire to spend more time with him. Which would be plain stupid, of course.

Yet I'm anxious, because what if he just says goodbye now? It would be smart. And disappointing. But for the best. And the worst.

"Are you hungry?" Massi asks and pats my hand. Realizing I'm still hanging onto him, I jerk my arm away. My foot slips from the curb and I almost tumble into oncoming traffic.

"Easy, Blue, I don't bite. There is a place at the Market with delicious food." He smiles, not mocking, just patiently letting me have a freak-out and ignoring it.

"Okay, I think I can eat." Why my voice sounds breathy is beyond me.

He points down the street and we fall into a stroll that would be pleasant and comfortable under normal circumstances. But nothing about these circumstances is normal. As much as my stupid body—and if I'm honest, my heart—thinks this is a great idea, I know we're going to end up hurt. And I'm afraid I will be the one causing it.

My mind is still fogged with the after-effects of our dancing, but as we walk, I recover remnants of reason. Grabbing food together will only lead to misunderstandings. And haven't we had enough of them?

How I wish we could clarify some of those from a long time ago. How I wish for a scenario where exploring what this is could be even remotely possible.

But then I remind myself of the reaction Massi had when he saw me at the wake—he practically ran away —how he lost it at the first meeting we had at the restaurant, and how he avoided me for weeks.

And frankly, just because he's suddenly started acting human, let me taste his food and danced with me like I was the most enticing woman in the world, that doesn't mean he is interested.

It probably just means Phillip and Mila got through to him finally and he's putting his best foot forward in the interest of his restaurant and our collaboration.

"I'm glad you came today," he says.

"Well, you gave Mila the card." See, this is just him making peace. But he remembered I wanted to dance way back when and he started dancing himself. Damn it. How could I ignore the gesture?

"I was really hoping you'd show up and we'd run into each other. I started with tango because of you." He shoves his hands into his pockets and it feels like he speeds up.

"You weren't interested all those years ago."

"I guess there is a right time for everything. Tango grounds me. I took lessons right after you left. I wanted to surprise you and take you dancing when you came back. I dropped it for a long time after... after you decided to stay in California. But I got back to it. It reminds me of what I've lost because I was stubborn and focused on the wrong thing. It keeps me in check."

His words turn in my stomach like poison and honey. He danced because of me. He still dances because of what the two of us destroyed. It's his source of reflection. Just like for me, dancing has become a lifeline. The painful memories resulted in joyful coping mechanisms.

Massi's confession, the sheer fact he allowed me to see this side of him, makes me want to tell him everything. But my shame at my choices is stronger, well-developed, since I've been nurturing it for years.

Then he asks a simple question, which in our universe of regret and lost chances is loaded, and I wish I didn't come to the milonga today.

"Are you happy, Blue?"

Chapter Fourteen

Gina

17 years ago

"My dear, you deserve better. That marriage has only brought you grief. A jealous man is the worst news. He's consumed by his need to prove himself and he blames you when things go wrong because of his own insecurities." Frederick wiped his hands on the hand towel attached to his apron.

It was my night off and I was leaving just as the dinner crowd started to arrive. Yet Frederick found the time to talk to me. To help me. Lately, it had seemed he was the only person on my side.

Part of me agreed with Frederick, but there was a

bigger part, a louder part, screaming with love for the man who kept hurting me.

When I had first laid eyes on Massimo Cassinetti, I was only fifteen years old. Not even five years later, the man had made me the happiest woman in the world and simultaneously broken my heart into a thousand pieces.

We hadn't spoken for two weeks now. Since the night he'd accused me of ruining him and his dreams. I knew the alcohol played a part in his harsh words, but I couldn't make excuses for him anymore. Frederick was right, I deserved better.

"Regardless of the situation, I still love him. I can't turn that off." I hated how needy I sounded.

"And where has he been the last two weeks? I'm a chef, just like he wants to be. Ten years ago, when I was starting, I was just like him. And you know what my only regret is?"

I shook my head. We stood by the back door. I was ready to leave, but I had nowhere to go. Staying with my parents the last few weeks had been a nightmare.

"That I married this job. Massi is full of passion. Look, he wanted you and he got you. But his true love is the kitchen. I recognize that calling because it takes one to know one. For your sake, Gina, because you deserve to be appreciated, I hope he realizes soon there is more to life than culinary art."

Frederick hugged me, his support helping only slightly. The lump that had lodged in my throat after that dreadful night in the hospital had only grown steadily in size. Under the influence of Frederick's words, it had now blocked my airways.

On my walk to the subway, tears pooled in my eyes. Frederick had denied any deliberate interference with the SoHo location and I had no reason to doubt him. He had been looking for a second location for a while.

I sat in a half-empty car moving through the underground of my home city and mulled over Frederick's words. He was right—Massi was passionate, but not only about his work. He was passionate in all areas of his life. And most of all when it came to us.

His love was all-consuming, burning, dangerous, but also rewarding and hot. Massimo made me feel like a queen. Like I mattered. Like I was the only woman in the world.

But was that enough? He equally made me feel small, insignificant, a burden. We seemed at odds more than we were in sync. And then there was the pregnancy.

As devastating as the miscarriage was for me, Massi was glad it had happened. I knew that it probably was for the best. We were so young and so lost, but that didn't mean I wasn't grieving.

Regardless of how I looked at the situation, the only conclusion was that we'd made a huge mistake rushing into this marriage. The thought broke my already shredded heart all over again. And still I couldn't articulate the solution to our problem.

Or rather, I didn't want to.

I opened the door to my parents' house, greeted with silence. My father had only spoken to me when he felt the need to express his disappointment in me. In my marriage.

"You got married young. Too soon. But that doesn't mean you can just give up at the first sign of trouble. You go back there and fix it," my father had said the night I came home sobbing after Massi's bitter words.

Though the house was quiet, a light shone from the kitchen, so I headed that way.

"Here you are." My mom leaned on the kitchen counter, her eyes red. She must have been crying. My father stood up from the table, his chest puffed out. Great. It was time to be subjected to another of his life lessons.

"You need to pack your things tonight."

I blinked a few times and glanced at my mother who was trying not to cry. And failing.

"You go back to your husband," my father said.

"He needs to come to me, Dad. He hurt me. He said horrible things to me."

"Well, I'm sure you deserved them. You need to leave. Go back to him or find somewhere else to live. You've embarrassed us enough. If you don't want to go back, then admit your failure to keep the man, but not under my roof!"

Before I could react, he stormed out of the room. As the door banged shut behind him, I stood paralyzed in the kitchen. My mother didn't try to soothe me, she just patted my shoulder and left.

I watched her climbing the stairs slowly. Her head down, her shoulders hunched. Her disappointment in me was too much to deal with.

I didn't know how long I stood there, considering all the ways I could salvage the ruin of my life, when the doorbell snapped me out of my misery.

I opened the door and my eyes met with Bianca Cassinetti's. The vise that had been squeezing at my chest for the past weeks tightened its jaws as Massi's mother stared at me with an unreadable expression.

"Perhaps we could go for a walk?" It might have been phrased as a question, but there was no room for an answer. Bianca turned and took the steps down, fully expecting I'd follow.

I exhaled heavily, hoping to find strength for another round of accusations, and trudged behind my mother-in-law.

"Massi is under the impression you've jeopardized

his dream." She laced her hand through my arm as if we were going for a friendly stroll.

"Is that what he told you?" I struggled to keep my voice even. Why was the only person on my side Frederick? Why did nobody want to see what had really happened?

"No, he hadn't really explained what's going on between you two. I like you, Gina, but you must know we were all surprised about the rush wedding. Sydney hinted at the likely reason for that and I'm sorry about the baby, I really am, but you both must know it was for the best. Massi needs to focus on his work now and you need to support him. You need to return to him if you want this marriage to work out."

We walked down our street and found a bench in the circular park that connected three streets in our neighborhood. The playground where Massi and I had sealed our commitment yawned empty behind us.

We sat there in silence. I considered explaining my pregnancy happened after the wedding, but what was the point? Everybody seemed set on the idea of what I needed to do. But I wasn't the only person in that relationship.

"We keep hurting each other. When we are together, we fight all the time. Massi said horrible things to me, and he hasn't reached out once in the past two weeks to talk. To apologize."

"My son is a proud man. Many times to his detriment, but you knew this, Gina, didn't you? Wasn't your attraction to him related to his ability to believe the world turned around him? Didn't you want to be a part of that world? Because if it wasn't, I'm afraid your union had no chance of success. But as much as Massi is as proud as a peacock, when he loves, he loves with every single fiber in his body. And perhaps, at times, the recipient of such attention might feel suffocated by the magnitude of his feelings, but in the long run, his love is very nurturing. You two are too young to appreciate that."

"Why hasn't he contacted me if he cares?" I sounded whiny, but I didn't care because that was how I felt. Disappointed. Hurt. Bare. And so fucking alone.

"Well, his pride comes with a side order of stupid. He'd been drinking and acting out, but that doesn't mean he doesn't long for you. Look, you two need to decide if you're staying together because the current situation is going to destroy him. And you, potentially."

"Frederick offered me a job in LA." I didn't even know why I told her because I wasn't considering taking it.

We sat in silence for a long time. Or perhaps just the heaviness of the conversation stretched too far.

"Gina, I don't want to see either of you suffer. I came to ask you to talk to Massi. It's not fair. You may think he needs to make the first step. And you might be right. Hell, knowing Massi, you are right. But, woman to woman, speaking from experience, you need to be the smart one this time." Bianca stood up. "Either fix what's broken, or perhaps Frederick's offer came at the right time."

Unable to move, I watched the proud figure of my mother-in-law walk away. Was she right? Had Frederick's offer come at the right time? Would time apart help us rekindle our relationship? Did we need to walk away to find each other again?

Massi opened the door and exhaled as if he had held his breath for two weeks. He looked ragged, disheveled. In a plain white T-shirt and running shorts, with a week-old stubble, he also looked beautiful and so vulnerable.

I had come determined to remain stern, to defend myself, to show him how poorly he treated me, but one look at him and all my resolve dissolved into an insignificant puddle at my feet.

"Blue," he rasped.

My heart hammered against my chest with a strange score of drums that echoed in my mind. All rational thought evaporated at the realization that however much I'd been hurting, seeing him suffer inflicted a new level of pain that skinned me raw and left me exposed to agony.

"I'm sorry," we both said at the same time.

Guided by pure instinct, Massi reached and pulled me in and our mouths fused. We stumbled inside, and he kicked the door closed then pushed me against the wall. Our tongues and lips danced in a frantic choreography of pain, lust, desire, suffering and torture, communicating all our feelings. The suppressed ones, and those that we had shouted at each other so many times.

The kiss was desperate, unforgiving and redeeming at the same time. I found the hem of his T-shirt, and when my hands touched his pecs a sound escaped me somewhere between a gasp and a sob. Coming from the deep, hidden part of my broken soul, the sound reverberated through both of us. A cry of our love. Of our desire.

I had come to talk, but my body overrode that goal immediately. I didn't even realize when or how my dress ended up on the floor, but when Massi raised my arms above my head and gripped my wrists with one of his large hands, the skin-on-skin contact sent all sort of signals into my center. Burning desire. Desperate need. Consuming obsession.

I was completely helpless when it came to this man. The love of my life.

Pinned by his solid body, my back cooled by the wall, I could not move, was absolutely dominated by the man who took so much from me. He grazed my jaw with his teeth, nipping and teasing and my breath hitched.

"Blue, baby, I can't live without you," he whispered against my skin, and this time I sobbed, tears streaming down my cheeks. He kissed them all away, whispering gentle words that were breaking my heart and gluing the pieces together at the same time.

My mind was blank, my body overcome by a need so strong I feared it would break me. But all the time the touch, the voice, the scent of Massimo Cassinetti, my husband, kept pulling me away from fear, closer to peace.

"I need you, my love," I whimpered, wiggling beneath his firm hold, grinding against him, desperate for a deeper connection.

He groaned. "Blue, my beautiful Blue." Our haunted eyes locked, and for a moment complete stillness descended, interrupted only by our heaving chests and thumping hearts.

He dropped his forehead to mine, and when I saw his tears something broke inside me. Something that tied me closer to him, for eternity, while at the same time warned me to run and save us both.

"Take me, Massi. I'm yours," I said, half-aware it was a mistake.

He stiffened, his dark eyes baring me to the last sliver of my soul, to its darkest corner. And while I didn't want to accept it yet, I could sense it, and he could probably feel the end of us there.

The shift in the energy palpable, I shook with lust and desire, with grief and fear, with love and agony.

"Blue," he groaned, and let go of any restraint. He ripped off my panties with his free hand, spread me with his knee, and I couldn't wait to find myself in him. He let go of my wrists to lift me and I wrapped my legs around his waist.

Fueled by the misery of the past weeks or months and by the feeling of finality, I guided his erection to my entrance and Massi impaled me with an urgent, almost violent thrust. And I met him with equal anguish.

We chased our release, bodies slapping against each other, skin covered with perspiration, the wall chafing my back, but none of it mattered. It was just me and him.

Me and the love of my life connecting on the deepest level. On the level where we had always created the most meaningful connection. Just not a lasting one.

Synced to the last fiber in our bodies, we went over the precipice together. The intensity of my orgasm shocked me to the core. I had never experienced such a tornado. A perfect storm and a blissful paradise in one.

Spent, I clung to Massi, my body wobbly. His breath on my shoulder was uneven, but so wonderfully familiar I wished we could just stay like this forever. I wanted to say something, but my mind was void of logic.

Massi stepped back slightly and scooped me up. He carried me to our bed and placed me down like precious, fragile cargo. He watched me for a moment, perhaps equally lacking words, or just not wanting to say them.

"You're beautiful," he said finally, and a wave of self-consciousness surprised me. I reached for the cover, suddenly feeling exposed.

"Don't." He stopped me and lay beside me. Turning me so my back molded into his chest, he held me tight.

We stayed like that for long moments, maybe centuries, unable to advance forward, unwilling to revisit the past, just suspended in the brittle cocoon of love that was threatening to burst if we moved.

"I'm going to LA. Frederick offered me a position

at his new restaurant there." I finally said what I'd come to say. I braced for the storm, for yelling and a fight. But none came.

Massi's body went rigid against mine. His breathing hastened and I could feel his heartbeat pulsing against my shoulder blade almost as fast as mine. But outwardly he didn't react, which scared me more than any of his outbursts.

I felt like the last five years of my life since I had first lain my eyes on him led to this moment. A moment of destruction.

"What does it mean for us?" His words came out strangled by an emotion I couldn't identify. Ache? Relief? Panic?

I turned to face him, but he used the opportunity to roll onto his back, his arm over his face.

"Is there still an us?" I put my hand on his chest, desperate to stay connected, to delay or avoid the inevitable.

"There wouldn't be if you leave."

The slight tremor under my palm brought tears to my heart.

"Or perhaps we could find us if we stay apart for a while."

"I was just apart from you for two weeks and I'm certain it's not what I want."

And once more we found ourselves at an impasse,

both trying to reach the same destination, but unable to walk together.

Gutted, I considered if staying might be the better option, but then Massi spoke, and all my hope was sucked into the vortex of eternal regret.

"That pregnancy, that miscarriage, broke us."

Chapter Fifteen

Massi

Are you happy? I'm not sure why I asked her because I don't want to hear that she's happy.

Of course, I want her to be happy, but at the same time, the idea of her happiness would eat at my ego, reminding me what I've lost.

I haven't been happy since I pushed her out of my life. Over the years I've found the way to be content, but happiness sailed away from me with Blue.

We're walking toward the Chelsea Market. The evening is warm and the street is alive with people. I don't remember the last time I strolled casually through the city, but I'm not in a hurry. In fact, I wouldn't mind slowing down even more. To explore the feelings stirred up by our tango.

I'm still dazed from our dance. While on the floor I was fully entranced by the music, the moves and the connection between us. I was sure she felt it, too. Now, I'm wondering if I was just imagining it, swayed by the passion of our dancing. Perhaps I misinterpreted the whole thing.

"That's a loaded question." Blue stares down, as if she were walking on an uneven surface, carefully choosing her steps.

"Is it?" Why I'm pushing this I'm not sure.

"My father just passed away..."

Shit. I'm an idiot. I forgot she came for the funeral.

Someone bumps into her from behind and she stumbles. I catch her arm to help her balance. The touch reverberates through my body and I fight an overwhelming need to pull her closer and hold her.

Our eyes meet and I don't know why, or how, after all the years, all the pain, all the heartbreak, but I see the girl I fell in love with and my heart jumps around my chest like a fucking pinball.

"I'm sorry about your dad." I won't tell her I'm also glad the unfortunate event brought her back. *For the time being*, I remind myself. And even on this coast, she's out of the reach.

"Me too. He hadn't spoken to me since..." She looks away. "Since I left."

That shocks me. It's been seventeen years. "Really? I didn't know that. I'm sorry."

"Yeah, well, I can't change that anymore. There is a pile of debt left that I need to address and I have to find a place for my mom to live, which seems to be an issue. And I miss..." She pauses as if weighing her words. "Home" is what she settles on.

A deep sense of regret grips my insides.

Who am I kidding? I missed my chance with this woman a long time ago. Her happiness is far away from here. With someone else.

"And to pass the time I took a job here and the client is a real pain in the ass." She looks at me sideways, the corner of her mouth quivering as she tries not to laugh.

"Yeah, I hear he's an asshole with a short temper." We smile at each other and I'm grateful she found a way to bring playfulness into our conversation.

"I wonder what's up with that." She pretends to admire a shop window, but I pull her back into the pedestrian traffic.

"I don't know. It's all the pressure of the engagement and wedding preparations." I walk on, avoiding her eyes, focused on the sidewalk. But even without looking I sense she stopped. I turn and shrug. "What? We are not talking about Phillip?"

Blue bows her head and covers her face. Her shoulders tremble with suppressed laughter, but then she lets go and laughs, looking at me and shaking her head. The sound of it is poetry, moving me without completely uncovering the meaning.

The small lines around her eyes deepen a bit with her laugh, and I mourn all the years I didn't witness her collecting them.

"Definitely not Phillip." She is still chuckling.

We arrive at the Market and I navigate among other diners and shoppers, holding her hand like it's a lifeline. She probably thinks it's just to ensure we won't get separated, but I'm enjoying it while it lasts, painfully aware it probably won't.

"Massi." The old fox greets me as we enter his watch shop in the corner of the Market.

"Alonso. Have you destroyed my favorite watch yet?" I shake his hand. "This is Gina."

He drops his eyeglass and smiles at her before he turns and shuffles in one of his drawers. Alonso is one of the last honest watchmakers in the city. Most of the shops similar to his have disappeared. He's too old for this fine work, but I appreciate his dedication.

"Here you go, and be more careful next time." He pats my shoulder.

"I will, but you wouldn't believe it. I need you to check this one as well." I put another watch on the counter.

He gives me shit like every other time. I pay him and he returns to his passion.

"What a quaint little shop. What was wrong with your watch?" Gina asks as we walk around the stalls and stands in the building.

"It fell into water at work." I don't want to lie to her, but this is something between me and Alonso, and it's a harmless lie anyway.

"I can't believe you'd be that careless." She stops and searches my face.

I shrug. "Okay, I bring him work because he's been struggling. People no longer use his craft the way they used to."

"So you deliberately damage your watches? Massi..." She breathes and stares at me wide-eyed. "I remember when you started your collection with your grandfather and your dad's watches. You loved those. I can't believe you would tinker with them just to—"

"Help someone? It's not a big deal. My collection has grown." I wink at her, grab her hand and start leading her to the other side of the Market. "I hope you're starving."

"Where are we going?"

"Just wait and see. You're going to have the best

burrito in New York, possibly in America. Hell, in the world."

I'm trying to focus on the conversation and the task of getting her to Richie & Manuela's, but my mind is swirling, analyzing what it means that she's letting me hold her hand.

We get to the small bistro in the corner of the Market.

Manuela smiles at me. "Massi, Richie is busy in the kitchen, but I'll tell him you're here."

We get our food and I choose a table in the back, granting us some privacy.

"This is amazing," Blue says after her first bite. She is craning her neck, making sure the rice and beans don't end up in her lap, and for some outlandish reason I find it incredibly sexy. Fuck, I need to get a grip.

"I told you." I don't take a bite, allowing myself a few more moments of perfection, sharing a meal with this woman. For a brief beat of time, we're just two people having a casual dinner.

"How did you even find this place?"

"Richie, the chef, used to work for me."

Manuela is wiping down the table beside us and *tsks* me. "And he helped us open this place, investing." She beams. "We wouldn't be here without him."

"Really? That's..." Blue shakes her head and studies me with interest.

Those tiny lines around her eyes are less profound now when she's not laughing. They add to her sophistication and allure. Who knew that the older she got, the more attractive she'd become. I wish it wasn't the case.

She licks her lips and I fight the tension behind my jean's zipper. I shouldn't be staring at her mouth. She's not free. And I want to kiss her.

"I heard you have a son." Desperate for self-preservation I venture into a new topic, to draw a boundary and remind myself she's out of reach.

Unfortunately, it also leads to the area of what could have been. But I deserve that. Judging by Blue's change of expression, she's shocked by the topic. Or annoyed. I'm not sure.

"Yes, Sebastien. I miss him very much. It's hard to be away. He's coming to visit though and I'm hoping I can return home with him."

Of course she does. I should have just kept ignoring her or arguing with her. It would have been painful, but this was like pouring acid into an open wound.

"Is he with—"

"Our neighbor, Danielle, steps in every time I need to travel. When we moved to that building he adopted her as his grandmother."

I find it odd she felt the need to jump in, avoiding

his name. Is she trying to draw the line as well? Are we just two fools smitten with memories? And regret?

Clearly, my rational thinking took a day off. She has nothing to regret. She moved on quickly and got all she ever wanted. A family I wasn't willing to give her at the time.

"You're not eating." She looks at the unwrapped roll in front of me.

I puff the air out of my cheeks and fidget with the foil. We eat in silence. I should use this moment to apologize for all the disappointment she suffered because of me. But I need to do it without letting on how much I miss her, because she doesn't need my neediness in her life. Or any complications. She's clearly sad about being away from home. She has her family.

I look up and our eyes meet. It's like looking into the mirror, her eyes reflecting my feelings. I might be just making it up, but this is a familiar situation. I know Blue understands me without words. It has happened before, so I know we used to have that connection. Oh, how much pain I caused her.

I open my mouth to speak, though I'm not sure I can find the right words, but Blue beats me to it and her words shut me up.

"Frederick and I divorced five years ago."

She looks away as if coping with a painful memory,

and I feel like a jerk because my broken heart rejoices. She's available. She's free. Hope blooms in my mind at the slightest chance that she could ever forgive me for the past, or our lives could coincide on the same coast.

I put down my burrito and take hers from her hands. I lean closer and cup her face, and before I can reason with myself or she can protest, I capture her lips.

Her entire body tenses and I freeze, not yet pulling away, but not really kissing her either. Fuck. Fuck. Fuck. What was I thinking? There is no way to recover from this, so I just have to suck it up.

As I disconnect the awkward touch of our lips, scrambling for something dignified to say, Blue runs her hands over her dress, straightening and dusting her skirt.

"I'm sorry," I rasp. "I-I crossed the line."

"Could you just walk me to the subway please?"

Though the words are meant for me, she addresses the corner of the table, avoiding my eyes.

"Of course." My throat is hoarse, the words like sandpaper, grinding through.

I'm pretty sure that my body is going into some sort of prelude to a heart attack, but I don't mind that because imminent death would be better than this.

Now I know I deserve this sort of humiliation, but my go-to defense mechanism kicks in and my shoulders spasm with a familiar tension that always comes with a quickened pulse and pounding in my ears. I'm angry. And I'm not fucking willing to count my breaths.

I march away, not even decent enough to check if Blue follows.

"Massi," I hear my name, but I can't stop.

The walls are closing in on me. The sushi chef on the left is smiling at me through his rotten teeth. The vendor on the left pours fresh juice into a plastic cup. A man is buying flowers and a group of women laugh over their cocktails.

Shrieking chairs, loud voices, disjointed conversations mingle with the smell of basil, fresh pastries, chocolate and cheese. The entire Market conspires to poke into my senses and I find the scene obnoxious, the complete opposite of the typical buzzing energy I often seek.

I finally make it out, almost knocking someone down. I stop and breathe, the air reaching only the top of my lungs, lacking in supply. I want to tilt my head back and scream, but even I'm not that crazy. Yet.

I need to find an outlet for the adrenaline. I need to get out of here and go to the gym, because that's the only way to physically destroy myself enough to tame the anger. That and the breathing exercises my therapist recommends, but those fucking never work anyway.

I don't even know why I am angry. And I don't want Blue to see me like this.

A light touch warms my arm, halting the passage of time. I pant, but the need to jump out of my skin recedes. Blue's scent of meadow reaches me as she steps closer. Her presence behind me, simply breathing, provides a measure of peace.

Her effect on me is therapeutic. She doesn't speak or move. She doesn't offer words or gestures of comfort —and I don't deserve them from her, anyway. But Blue somehow creates a space for me to find balance. Not yet feel calm, but to reach normalcy. Whatever that may look like.

I don't know how long we stand there. Longer than needed. I've become a reasonable human being again, but I'm unwilling to break the connection. She senses the storm has changed into a drizzle and slides her hand down, grazing my skin and sending all sorts of conflicting signals.

"You caught me by surprise. I didn't know you felt this way about me." She sounds apologetic, as if she was at fault here.

Fuck me. This is so hard. I just need to walk her to the subway and hide for the rest of her stay, and then I can go back to being my usual grump. I turn to face her, careful not to touch her. Her jaw is set and her eyes are full of kindness. Or pity more likely. Fuck.

"I'm sorry. I shouldn't have. It was stupid."

"No. That's not what I'm saying, I'm just... confused." She reaches out and slides her fingers under mine, not really grabbing my hand, just placing it into position, giving me the option to close.

And I do, I clasp her fingers and squeeze, equally reassuring her things are okay between us—a lie—while grasping for straws like a drowning man.

Her face contorts as the air between us pollutes with tension, hope, desire and regret. Deposits of mistakes, broken promises, disappointments are resurfacing as we both try to bury them deeper.

"There is a part of me," Blue continues, squeezing my hand gently. "A huge part of me that wants to explore this. But the two of us, the past—I won't survive the pain again. I don't want us to hurt each other again."

A sliver of hope encourages me to speak. "We were young and stupid. I know I was. It doesn't have to be that way."

She shakes her head and the sliver shreds into a crumb. "I don't know if I can believe that. Trust you. Trust myself."

What can I say to that? She is right, and I wish it was all different. But it's not.

"Don't look at me like that, Massi."

"Like what?"

"Like I've just punched you. I never wanted to hurt you, Massi. But I will. I know I will."

"Don't, Blue, don't go there. We killed our love before, but you can't deny the connection. Damn it. I've burned steaks in the last few weeks like a beginner, knowing you were on the other side of the door. I can't think. I can barely breathe. I haven't slept well since you opened the door at your father's wake."

Her breath hitches and she shivers, biting her lip as tears pool in the corners of her eyes.

"I don't know," she whispers.

"Blue, remember the night you left that fucking apartment seventeen years ago?" She nods. "Since that moment, I've regretted what I've done to us. Tell me you don't feel there is something left? Look me in the eye and tell me I'm making it up."

She doesn't speak. She holds my eyes, and even without words it's clear she can't deny the connection.

"When it comes to you I've regretted so much, and I don't want another regret, Blue. I don't want to regret never even exploring if there is a chance for the two of us."

She opens her mouth and then closes it again. She whimpers and then breathes deeply, the struggle within her palpable, adorable and fucking threatening at the same time. I could almost read the pros and cons as they fight in her mind.

"Blue, you're here for a few more weeks and then you're gone. We're both suffering already trying to fight this. Let me make you dinner. Let's have one date."

I don't care about pride anymore. I'll get to my knees and beg her.

"Can I think about it?"

I exhale audibly and run my hand through my hair, disappointed and relieved at the same time.

"Let me walk you to the subway."

She weaves her fingers through mine and I take it as a promise. I only hope we'll survive this time.

Chapter Sixteen

Gina

I check my lipstick in the compact. I've changed several times and now I'm thinking the dress is a bit too much. Too suggestive. Too sexy. It's a royal blue halter dress, tight around my chest and waist and flaring around my legs, falling just above my knees. It's classically elegant, yet casual enough. Or is it?

I can't change again since I'm in a town car Massi sent for me, already approaching Manhattan. What's up with the town cars anyway? I suppose he's done well enough for himself, and I know his mother has money. Nevertheless, this kind of service is expensive.

I check my appearance again. Jesus, I've been as nervous as if I was going on a first date with a stranger. I'm annoyed by how much I want this to go well. It's like I need to prove to myself I can have this man. Like a good evening with him could negate the past. Erase my self-doubt when it comes to relationships.

It's been a week since he took me to the Market. Massi has been working every evening and Mila and I are up to our elbows in preparing for the private event.

The energy in the restaurant has shifted into a more collaborative, pleasant atmosphere. The lack of glowering and snarling is conspicuous in the best way.

Massi's temper still flies high with all the tension and stress of operating the kitchen, especially during rush hours. But he's making an effort toward the staff. Especially after I requested that Phillip fire two of the least engaged servers.

I quickly realized that one key problem here is that Phillip—with his other business and personal interests —doesn't spend enough time on the floor to truly see the potential or lack of it in his front-of-house staff.

And Massi, a subscriber to passive aggressive behavior, yells at the bad apples until they fall off naturally. This unhealthy communication balance was creating unnecessary tension for all employees.

Phillip and the staff appreciated my direct approach to people management, leaving everyone more relaxed and more productive. It's still early days, but we've seen increased recognition at several customer review sites, praising Casa Cassi for the ultimate dining experience.

I think everyone believes that it's my—and Mila's—contribution that has settled the atmosphere. But I know it has something to do with the dancing and holding hands that happened last week.

I've been walking in a daze for the last few days, feeling his burning gaze on me at every opportunity. Every time I looked in Massi's direction, those dark hooded eyes seared through me, sprouting goosebumps all over my skin.

I don't think I've blushed this much in all my life. It's quite ridiculous, frankly. I'm thirty-six years old, a twice divorced woman, and I'm on the verge of giggling when in his vicinity. It's as if we put the past behind us —not a good basis for anything new—and have allowed ourselves to discover something that is familiar, but fresh at the same time.

I know we're heading toward disaster, but I'm so giddy with anticipation of the good that I stubbornly ignore the bad. The bad that is way too realistic in our scenario.

I will regret it, but I've decided to enjoy even the briefest second chance with this man, rather than suffer never seeing, talking, being with him. It's selfish and self-destructive, but I'm high on Massi.

The car pulls to the curb on the Upper East Side,

Central Park just across the street. I look outside where a uniformed doorman stands. A beige carpet leads from the car to the entrance flanked by two large cement flowerpots with mini cedar trees.

"We're here, ma'am." The driver turns and smiles at me.

I frown and look at the entrance again. "Are you sure?" Did Massi rent a place for the night with me? Perhaps this is one of those membership-only hotels?

"I've been driving Mr. Cassinetti for years now, I'm sure this is where he lives, and he asked me to get you here."

"Thank you." I feel like I should say something else, but the doorman pulls the door open, startling me. I mumble my farewells and step outside.

"Welcome, Miss Accardi. My name is George. Mr. Cassinetti is waiting for you upstairs. Let me show you the elevator."

I smile at him tentatively and look around as though I'll understand what's happening by making eye contact with strangers. Strangers wearing designer clothes with pedigree dogs on brand-named leashes. I exhale, stepping inside the marble foyer.

Everything, including the elevator, is wrapped in an understated elegance that shines through the beige and chrome materials. I'm slightly dazzled and have to force myself not to stare or gasp. My heels are inappropriately loud, but George doesn't cringe, so maybe I'm fine.

He swipes a card and presses a button on the console, nods and steps outside, leaving me alone as the door closes. I was nervous about this dinner date but now I don't know, I'm half excited and half freaked out. Why didn't I know Massi was rich? Really rich by the looks of it.

I realize there are no floor numbers blinking above the door as we ascend. There is only *one* button. P. Freaking penthouse? A private elevator?

The door opens and that's when I do gasp. It's not because I step out into a large open concept living room with polished stone floors and minimalistic yet homey decor. It's not because of the breathtaking view of Central Park from the floor-to-ceiling windows that make up the entire wall.

It's the immediate view of the owner himself, casually waiting for me, leaning against a pillar—yes, the room is so huge it needs pillars to support the ceiling— wearing a white T-shirt and jeans. His hair is damp as if he's just taken a shower, the curls framing his beautiful face. And his feet are bare. For some reason I find that so sexy, my knees buckle.

I stumble forward, mentally checking to confirm my jaw isn't slack. Jesus, that's what I call an entrance. All awkward on my part and all hot on his.

"Are you okay?" Massi frowns.

"The view behind you gives you an unfair advantage." I speak harshly because I'm flustered, so I add more softly, "You look great."

"It's just the view behind me, Blue. You, on the other hand, would look amazing even if you were in the middle of a swamp." He winks and steps closer to me.

A bit too close because his scent robs me of what little reason I have left. He leans down and kisses my cheeks and I have to grip his shoulder to remain standing. I'm thrilled and disappointed by the greeting.

"I'd show you around, but this is it." He turns, and with his hand on the small of my back he ushers me forward. Oh, but what does that touch do to me. "I mean, there is a bedroom as well, but I don't want to presume by leading you there right now."

I make a sound somewhere between choking, gasping and giggling. It takes me three deep breaths before I regain my dignity and speak normally. "So, this is just a simple one-bedroom."

Massi chuckles. "Okay, there is a guest room and a library."

"Oh, I see, just the bare minimum." I narrow my eyes now, teasing.

"And a gym and rooftop terrace."

"You're right, it doesn't deserve a tour," I deadpan.

He gazes at me through his thick eyelashes, looking

so handsome and nonchalant I want to jump at him and never let go.

"I'm happy to show you around. But why don't I offer you a drink first?" But he doesn't move, studying me intently.

He seems completely at ease, eating me with his eyes, while I struggle to compose myself. The energy in the room is zapping with tension, and if he doesn't kiss the hell out of me within the next few minutes I might just burst into flames.

"I'll have a glass of wine. Not sure what we're eating, so I'll let you choose." I turn to the window, pretending to soak in the green colors of the park below us, but really just trying to get my shit together.

Seriously, what's wrong with me? I know the man. I've slept with the man. I've argued with him. We've been there, we've done it all so to speak, so why am I such a mess?

"I'm making lamb, so I opened Sierra Cantabria, Rioja." He startles me, his words warm on my skin. How can he walk so quietly? Like a jaguar. There is no doubt in my mind, Massi is a predator tonight. The question is how long he plans to toy with me. And will I be a worthy opponent?

He steps away. I know because he takes the heat with him. Before I get enough air into my lungs, he's back. He snakes his hand around me, offering me the glass of red. His mouth is so close to my ear, his breath grazes my skin, erupting goosebumps on my nape. He's not yet touching me and my underwear is soaked, my core tingling with the need.

For crying out loud! I need to snap out of it.

It's the involuntary abstinence that has me this wound up. What else could it be? Well, if I'm honest, there is no other man in the world my body responds to the way it does to Massi. It's like we were born to mate. If only our hearts and brains would align so perfectly.

"You're splurging on me." The fact he owns such an expensive wine surprises me less than the significance of him casually opening it for me. "Do you dazzle all your lady guests with pricey wines?"

His body tenses behind me. "I assure you, Blue, you're my first lady friend in this apartment. Besides my mom and sisters. Actually, I think only Syd and Paris have been here."

I turn to face him. "Did you just move in?"

He flinches. "No, Blue." The annoyance in his voice is barely hidden. "I've lived here for seven years now, but you're the first woman I've invited here." His chest heaves with shallow breaths. Here we are again, my insecurity winding him up.

"This view is breathtaking." My trembling belies the casual attitude I want to portray. I take a gulp of the wine. Way more than this wine deserves because it should be savored. *Get your shit together.*

"I agree." He bites his lips, his eyes on me.

Screw it. I can't do this. "Massi, I'm really nervous." There. We've never tried honesty. Perhaps it's time to start.

"Me too."

My eyes widen. "You don't seem nervous at all."

"I've been biting my nails since this morning. I changed tonight's menu three times. Hell, I changed my T-shirt a few times, which is a considerable achievement since I only own white or black ones."

He takes my hand and leads me to the corner—definitely the heart of his home—an amazing white, polished kitchen. He puts my wine on the counter and cups my face.

"We shouldn't be this nervous," I whisper.

"Oh, but we care too much."

"You care?" I sound needy, but my fragile self-confidence needs all the proof.

"I've never stopped caring, Blue."

A sob chokes me, but it's swallowed by Massi's lips crashing onto mine with desire so strong I have to grip his shoulders to stay upright. He takes my mouth as if it has always belonged to him. And it has. I part my lips and our tongues move in a rhythm of released tension.

His kiss is loving and playful, but also possessive

and commanding. No room for negotiation. Massi Cassinetti leads us into a new stage of this date, my silly trepidations and self-control losing their power.

"Blue, I better get the dinner started," he whispers against my lips, but doesn't pull away.

"Hm," I moan, unable to string together anything more intelligible.

"Thank you for telling me you were nervous. When do we learn to speak about our feelings?" He chuckles.

"Let's start tonight."

We finally pull away, but stay close, our eyes locked.

"That's a great idea."

Comfortable silence stretches while we stare at each other, smiles lingering on our faces. I'm overwhelmed by joy, and if this will be my only night with this man I'm going to get all I can from him.

"Okay, woman, let me cook for you." He kisses the crown of my head and strolls around the counter.

I climb onto the stool and watch him create, fascinated by the simple elegance of his dance around the kitchen. Something I've observed countless times, yet it's never ceased to amaze me how Massi carries himself in his work space. His movements are calculated yet performed with ease.

It's like watching a tango. I smile at the realization.

That's it—Massimo Cassinetti has been tangoing since he first took a carving knife in his hands.

"So, this place is really yours," I say, trying to distract myself from the tattoos on his forearm calling me to touch them as he whisks something in a small bowl.

He throws his head back and laughs. It's the most beautiful thing to see and hear. God, I'm getting sappy.

"No, I borrowed it for tonight, to impress you."

"It didn't work at all," I tease. "But really, not to be crass, but I didn't know a chef, even as amazing as you"—I pause and his chests puffs up, which pleases me more than it should—"makes this much money."

"I've done okay for myself, but it's not just the restaurant. Phillip helped me invest my money and the man is pretty good at spotting opportunities, so I increased my earnings thanks to him."

"So you're a millionaire now?" I giggle, but then freeze when he looks at me, shrugging. "Billionaire?" I gasp.

"I've kept my wealth under the radar and I like it that way. Does it matter to you?" He moves around the counter, adding spices to the bowl.

"It surprises me. I'm impressed you've done this well."

"I make way more than I can use, so I reinvest. Mostly with young, promising chefs. I have shares in several restaurants in the city. Well, in the country really."

"You're helping young chefs open their own restaurants?" I recall Richie and Manuela from the Market.

"In a nutshell, yes, but it's not that simple. They have to work with me and they have to have good business acumen and plan for their own place. And Phillip gets involved too, making sure they follow through. Obviously I'm too busy in my kitchen, so I'm more of a silent partner after the initial investment."

"Why are you doing it? There must be more passive ways to invest."

Oh, but I'm falling deep and fast right now. The casual way he speaks about helping others. I know, he gets his profit share at the end, but the idea of him succeeding beyond his own kitchen is so hot.

And unexpected. This man is more complex than the boy I used to know. And there is so much more to him than the temper most people know him for.

"I'd have had an easy start with my mom's seed money. Not everyone has a rich mother though." He shrugs and throws something into the pan and the oil sizzles loudly, forcing my eyes away from him.

"This is a great PR story. You should talk about it with Catira, or we can call a few other leads—"

"Blue, this is a date, not a work meeting. And I don't want people to know. This is something that grows organically when I meet someone who deserves a chance. I don't want a bunch of wannabees to beg me for money. And I don't want the fuss."

I nod. I understand where he's coming from, but I also want to shout this from the rooftops, so that everyone who only sees the angry energy in his kitchen can learn about the real man behind the frenzy.

"Ready to eat, Blue?" He plates the vegetables and the lamb and drizzles them with mint dressing, explaining it all to me as he takes his time to design the perfect plate.

"It smells amazing, and it looks like an art piece." I stand up and follow him to a glass dining table by the window.

I didn't notice it before, as it's smartly hidden between a large plant and a tall cabinet. It's a small space, but with the park at our fingertips it doesn't feel cramped at all.

"Well, let's hope the taste measures up." He puts down the plates and pulls the chair our for me.

I take my seat, but Massi doesn't move to take his. He stands beside me, observing me.

"Sit down." I laugh.

He's clenching his fists and there is something wild in his eyes that I don't recognize.

"Have a bite." His words come out hoarse. I don't know what's happening, but I pick my fork. The lamb is so tender I don't need the knife. I put a slice in my mouth, too aware of his tight fists beside me.

I exhale because the explosion of flavors in my mouth is divine. "It's amaz—"

"I'll be right back." Massi strides away.

What the hell is going on? He left so quickly, I don't even know which way to follow him.

"Massi?" I call after him, but there is no answer.

I'm torn and oddly deflated, but I try to tell myself there must be a reasonable explanation. There is only one hallway leading out of this room. On each side there are two doors, but they're closed. The double doors at the end of the hallway are slightly ajar.

I peek in, confronted with the most beautiful bedroom I've ever seen. Everything is white with deep brown accents, but most of the colors come to the room from Central Park through the glass walls.

"Massi?" I whisper, but I don't see him anywhere. A soft groan comes from behind the door and I step in tentatively, my feet sinking into thick carpet.

There is another door by the side of the bed, behind it a luxurious master bathroom. But I don't have time to take in the decor because my eyes land on Massi.

He sits on the tub, his head between his knees, wheezing.

I don't understand what I'm seeing, but instinct

pushes me forward. I kneel and touch the sides of his thighs gently. "I'm here, baby. What's going on?"

He pants, gripping his hair. I place my hand over his and lean into him in an awkward hug. "Massi, talk to me, please."

"Go back and eat. I'll be right there." He shakes his head, but shifts his weight slightly toward me, accepting the embrace.

I pull at his shoulders and he slides down to the floor, where I finally can wrap my arms around him properly, holding him while his breath slows to its regular rhythm.

I came today expecting intimacy, but not at this level. Yet I wouldn't want to be anywhere else. Holding Massi in my arms when he's vulnerable—even if I don't understand the trigger—feels right.

It feels like home. Like I've wandered the world escaping him only to end up here, right now.

"Fuck," he growls. He pulls away, avoiding my eyes and standing up before holding a hand out for me. Still without eye contact, he walks to the sink and rinses his face, then runs his wet hands through his hair. He turns off the water and leans on his arms, bowing his head. "Fuck."

I step closer and lace my arms around his waist, resting my cheek on his back. He squeezes my hand. "I'm sorry," he rasps.

"Don't. I'm not sure what has just happened, but I'm here if you want to talk about it."

"I'd rather not," he says, but squeezes my hand tighter.

"Remember how we agreed on honesty?" My lips are so close to his skin, only the thin fabric of his shirt preventing me from tasting him. Aching need overwhelms me.

"I've been having panic attacks. I had them under control for a while, but ever since you've come back they've been sneaking up on me."

"Massi." I'm his trigger? I cause him to panic? My arms fall slack and I back away, but he turns around and cups my face.

"Honesty, we said, so don't you retreat on me now, Blue."

Tears burn my eyes. "But if I'm causing you to panic... how could we ever... I mean... I-I..." I trip over my words, unwilling, unable to articulate what that would mean.

I'm poison to him. I've always been the bane of his existence, and I can't even contemplate our second chance because it would only be a second chance for more heartbreak, more suffering, more pain.

"Blue, baby, you got it all wrong. It's the idea of you leaving again that spirals me into panic."

His words flow into my bloodstream, finding every

secret corner of any resistance I might have still harbored. My breath hitches and tears stream down my cheeks, but I laugh. And cry and laugh.

Our lips meet in a sloppy kiss that tastes salty and slimy, but I don't care. Here and now in the arms of this man I'm complete for the first time in as long as I can remember.

We keep hugging and kissing, not a passionate, desire-driven make-out session, but a connection of pure relief. Of reclamation and rehabilitation.

My stomach growls and we both giggle.

"Okay, let me feed you now," he says.

"Yes, please."

We walk out of the bathroom, his arms around my shoulders, mine around his waist.

"I guess you got a sneak peek of the bedroom before dinner after all." He kisses the top of my head.

"And what a bedroom. Seriously, this is too much."

He laughs. "Baby, it's not enough until you scream my name here."

Chapter Seventeen

Gina

"If you tell anyone I fed you warmed-up food, I'll deny it, fire you, and probably punish you." Massi watches me with hooded eyes, sending tingles into parts of me that haven't been this alive in years.

"I'll keep your secret, master chef, but you may need to motivate me. What kind of punishment do you have in mind?" I bat my eyelashes. Before we were too young and awkward, but our flirting skills have matured and I'm enjoying the innuendo.

"Spanking, obviously," he deadpans and my cheeks heat up, but my entire body pops open the celebratory champagne.

I lick my lips, trailing them with languid luxury. His eyes follow the move with dark promise sparkling in his irises as his tongue darts out and mimics mine, giving me a needed confidence boost. "It might be hard to keep that secret…"

He jumps from his seat and hauls me to standing, laughing at my squeals and half-hearted protests. Scooping me up, he carries me to the middle of the room and puts me down.

I wasn't expecting this destination. We're standing in the center of his foyer/living room, the park providing a perfect backdrop as the light outside has dimmed to emphasize the romance this city forges.

Massi pulls his phone from the back pocket and taps the screen. The lights in the room fade. He taps the screen a few more times and throws the phone on to the sofa.

Before I ask what's going on, the mood is set and sensuous violins fill the room. I recognize the beat immediately and I smile at Massi, whose eyes are sparkling with joy and desire. He plants his hand firmly on my waist and pulls me closer.

We move in basic tango steps at first, more enthralled by our closeness and the anticipation than the milonga. But the music takes over quickly, and we glide around the room in a harmony so rare in our turbulent relationship.

It's different from the ballroom last week. Alone, without prying eyes, we sink deeper into the passionate steps. The song he's chosen is slow, allowing me to slide my leg down his calf with luxurious sensuality, almost stopping us, completing the move with leisurely decadence.

Our pelvises and thighs are practically attached as he leads me through the dance, and I slide around him. Massi's eyes ignite me with need and want, burning me like hot coals. He lowers his forehead to mine and I inhale his breath, wanting to consume so much more of him. Let him consume me.

I cross my legs, my hip grazing his as I twirl around to step back. Our eyes locked, the communication between us is filled with desire, promise, anticipation. As I rock my hips to get back in front of him, his erection twitches against my thigh.

He lunges back, leaving me no choice but to go with him, his body hard and warm against mine. Through the fabric of my dress, his touch scorches me. His scent intoxicates me like the most potent drug as my heartbeat sinks down to my core.

I want to run to the bedroom right this minute, but Massi continues to guide me into moves that are no longer pure tango. He halts us for a moment, savoring the closeness. His breath continues sending shivers down my spine, tugging at my center. As soon as I almost succumb to the connection, he pushes us back into the staccato.

It's like standing at the precipice of a mountain with a parachute, but pulling back every time just before the wind would take us sailing through the air.

Our bodies blend into the melody, and my core tingles with a need so strong I want to cry. Yet, I can't interrupt our dancing because the build-up is strangely rewarding.

And so new to us. We used to jump at each other like rabbits, burying our frustration in carnal acts, hiding, escaping, chasing solace.

Tonight we don't rush things, and my heart hopes that perhaps this time we have a chance. My body, on the other hand, is so wound up, I fear I might just explode.

"Massi," I whisper, but it comes out as a whimper.

His eyes darken and he gives me a slow, satisfied smile. "I know, baby."

I moan and lower my head to his shoulder. Got, I've never been this needy. But Massi swirls me again and increases the tempo, so I let him lead us into another song until my head gives up and my body and soul take over, completely surrendering to his lead.

And lead he does.

* * *

Massi

I've never found a woman who can simultaneously undo and complete me like Blue does. I wanted tonight to be perfect and the episode before the dinner almost spoiled it. But it didn't in the end. I went to hide with my little issue and she found me. And instead of the judgment that I so freely bestow on myself, she provided silent support.

The realization that I must keep her by my side at any cost rocked me to the core, but it really seems a question of survival.

When we finally stumble into my bedroom, Blue is quivering with need and yearning. I fear that just a touch would set us both off, but I'm determined to savor her slowly. To deliver pleasure to her that might —at least momentarily—erase all the suffering I caused her.

I stand behind her and unzip her dress and she shimmies it off her shoulders. She wears a strapless bra and the sight of it gets me even harder, if that's possible. I don't want to rush things, but shit, I'm ready to pounce.

As my lips touch her shoulder, her tremor sends electric waves through me. She tilts her head forward, allowing me access to her neck. My hands graze her ribcage down to her round hips where her dress is pooled. I yank and it floats to the ground.

"Massi," she moans, and I hold her tight because if I move, I won't last. Her voice is innocent and wanton at the same time, the devil and angel morphed into perfection.

I stroll around her, taking my time, admiring every inch of her silk skin, trailing it with my fingers as I go. When I get in front of her, our eyes lock and time stops. It only takes a few heartbeats of complete stillness before we get desperate.

Blue finds the hem of my T-shirt and drags it over my head. Her eyes widen, giving me an indecent amount of satisfaction. I flex my pecs and she smiles, mischief in her eyes. She rasps her nails down my torso as if it was a string instrument. It might as well be given how taut I am, ready to snap.

She unbuttons and unzips my jeans and sinks to her knees, pulling my pants with her. When she looks up at me, the angle is too much to take.

She is too beautiful. Too perfect. Too much.

Even on her knees, she holds complete power over me. When I feel her fingers in my waistband, just exploring slowly, toying with me while drawing out the satisfaction that is evident in her hooded eyes and lingering smile, I lose my patience and pull my briefs down.

My cock springs free, almost hitting her in the face and she gasps. I pull her up.

"Sorry, Blue, I can't wait anymore." I throw her onto the bed and follow her.

"Finally." She laughs and unhooks her bra. Her full round breasts spill out and I bury my face in them, finding a nipple with my mouth.

She moans and bucks her hips, seeking friction. Her reaction aches in my cock and I can no longer deny her anything.

I could never deny her anything.

I don't want to deny her anything.

Ever again.

I get to my knees and pull down her panties, throwing them to the floor. I take in the beauty before she stretches her arms and beckons me to her.

I reach to my nightstand, throw a pack of condoms on the bed and tear one wrapper with my teeth. As soon as I'm sheathed, I yank her legs apart, dragging her into position, and she laughs.

"Now you're full of urgency." Her tease elicits a groan from me.

"I can slow down." *I can't.* I lower myself, my elbows bracketing her head.

"Oh, God, don't you dare." She fists my hair and pulls me to her mouth. *Thank God.*

I balance on one elbow, never disconnecting the

kiss while I guide my cock to her entrance. She's wet, rolling her pelvis with need and want. My Blue.

I push in and it's like nothing has changed, yet everything is different. She stills for a moment, as if surprised by the invasion. I raise my head and find her eyes filled with tears.

"Welcome home," she whispers, her voice broken with emotion.

What those words do to me is close to resurrection. I move in and out slowly, relishing every sensation, every moan, every reaction Blue is expressing so liberally.

When I watched her earlier eating the dinner, I thought it was the best reward a chef could receive. It's one thing to be praised for a well-prepared meal and its presentation, but watching Blue consume every bite with all her senses was a completely new level of satisfaction.

Until I got her in my bed. The woman, so shielded and often unreadable in everyday life, is completely open and free in this act of surrender. She takes me without hesitation and it encourages me, draining away all the reason and care.

I pound into her, chasing release for both of us, and she accepts me with an eagerness that expands in my chest. Her walls contract around me and I smile at her.

"Come for me, Blue," I whisper as I feel the tingling at the base of my back. She clenches, screaming my name. The sound sends me over the edge, and we both ride the wave until we're spent and absolutely elevated at the same time.

I roll on to my back and discard the condom into a tissue on my nightstand, not wanting to leave her for a second. I pull her to me. She shivers with aftershocks, clinging to me with such ferocity I want to hold her for the rest of my days, to provide her with the safety she deserves.

If I had ever thought we could casually explore a second chance, I was mistaken. There is nothing casual about this moment.

We lie there, our limbs tangled, slowly returning to Earth.

"This was—"

"Careful with your words. I'm a sensitive man," I tease.

Her chest heaves against my ribcage with silent laughter. "I'll be sure to tiptoe around you. It was different, I wanted to say." She places a lazy kiss on my shoulder.

"Different good?" For some reason my head needs confirmation of what my body and soul have just experienced.

"Different wonderful. Your ability to satisfy me matured like a fine wine. You're an excellent vintage, Mr. Cassinetti."

She yelps as I roll her on to her back, clasping her wrists above her head. "Are you calling me old?"

She giggles and tries to free herself, but it's a lost cause.

"You're just the right age." She cranes her neck to kiss me. I lower my head to meet her and our tongues dance lazily, exploring and playing.

"May I invite you to my dazzling bathroom?"

She laughs. "And what would we do there?"

I nuzzle her throat and move down to her collarbone, grazing with my teeth and lips. "First, we could fuck against the sink, so I can watch you in the mirror."

She moans in what sounds like agreement. I find one of her nipples with my mouth and the other with my fingers, pinching hard and biting at the same time. She gasps and her back arches. Oh, how I like these reactions.

"Then I would get down on my knees and eat you as my dessert before we take a bath." I continue kissing her down to her belly button and then I look up.

"That sounds like an intense itinerary. Are you sure you can keep up, given your vintage?" She bites her lip and I growl, jump up and grab her foot to drag her to the edge of the bed.

"Vintage has only ever improved the quality, Blue." I haul her over my shoulder, her squeals pleasing me ridiculously.

Gina

Massi delivered on his promises and more. Oh, but this bathroom is meant for that. We fucked against the sleek vanity with the double sink lining the wall of the mirror. Our eyes locked in the reflection before us.

I've never felt so ravished and cherished at the same time. It was raw, it was real, and it was beyond intimate. We reached a level of ecstasy that left us spent and energized equally.

And something has shifted between us for me. The tender trust bolstered. Not yet fully restored because I don't even know if we ever held each other's complete trust, but for the first time in years I feel like I can tell him the truth.

I didn't get the chance immediately, because Massi dragged me into a large glass cubicle that I hadn't noticed before. The floor was wood and pebbles in neat square sectors, with a large shower head above us and a bonsai tree planted in the corner.

As soon as the water rained on us, Massi got to his

knees and enjoyed his dessert. And he wasn't the only one enjoying. I'm still trembling from my third orgasm.

"You have a plant in your shower?"

Holding his hand in mine, I kiss his knuckles. We are luxuriously relaxing in the frothy warmth of the corner bathtub. My back against his chest, we've been drifting in and out of conversation for I don't know how long.

The mood is set with soft glowing floor lamps flickering like candles around us. The tub is across from the shower, and as with all the important rooms in this apartment it's set against a glass wall. I'm taking a bath overlooking Central Park. I might never leave.

"Blame it on my sister. Paris designed this place." He nuzzles my neck and I tilt my head, granting him better access. "But I'm hoping your favorite memories of this bathroom go beyond the freaking plant." He nibbles on my earlobe.

I laugh. "Let me think. I might need more memories to override the impressive design."

"Have mercy, woman," he pleads, but his hand travels to my nipple, and my breath catches in a pleasant sigh.

"Paris is very talented, though. As are you."

"Why, thank you. Are you talking about my tongue?" He accentuates his point and turns my head to reach my mouth. We both moan into a kiss that is deep and decadent.

"Your mouth, your tongue, your hands, the little mister down there—"

"Little?" He pinches my nipple and I scoot away, sloshing water to the floor.

"I was talking about your work, your craft, your kitchen. I didn't know how it all connected to your father. I wish I knew. I wish I understood your motivation back then."

We stay silent. Massi draws mindless circles on my forearm as his heart hammers against my back. Mentioning the past may have destroyed the tender thread of affection we'd woven. But I wanted him to know I needed that missing piece back then.

I need him to understand how sorry I am I didn't stick around. For the better, but mostly for the worst. I want him to know that before I kill our current joy with the rest of our story. The part he doesn't know about.

"You would have left anyway." He doesn't sound bitter, but he speaks with conviction. Would I have? I don't know, and we'll never find out. If only I had the courage, even now, to tell him how I felt back then. Explain some of my motivations. But I'm a coward, so I turn to my side and kiss him instead.

He hugs me tighter, and somehow this connection feels even deeper than lovemaking.

"Blue, it was the initial draw for sure. But oh, I enjoyed it so much. Creating dishes from scratch, experimenting, trying to become the best, the competition, the friendly or less friendly rivalry. I was good at it, but when my mother gave me that check... I didn't know it then, but I was so scared I'd fail that I found any reason to blame everyone else... mostly you, which I've regretted ever since.

"By the time you mailed me the divorce papers, I recognized the mistake I made and I was determined to fix it, but you sent a proxy to the proceedings and... I destroyed us. And when you married Frederick so fast, I understood I'd missed my chance. Or perhaps I'd never had one."

I shiver, goosebumps covering my skin. I have to tell him what happened.

"Let's go to bed, Blue, because you're about to turn blue." He kisses my temple and pushes himself up to sit. Water drips everywhere as he gets out and wraps a fluffy white towel around his waist. Then he offers me his hand and helps me stand up.

The fatigue dragging at me is too much, and it has nothing to do with the late hour or the physical exertion. It has all to do with a confession I need to make. One that might bring this night to an abrupt halt.

He effortlessly lifts me and sets me down like a fragile flower, with care and love. He dries me, taking care of me as if I was a princess or a child, but I let him because it might be the last time he does it. The last time he worships me.

He carries me to the bedroom and puts me down on the edge of his bed as he draws the covers back. "In you go, Blue." He winks, the shadows of tiredness lining his beautiful eyes now.

I climb into the bed and he follows me, tucking the covers around us and gathering me into a tight embrace. His heat melts my worries a little. For a moment, before he speaks again.

"I broke us because I couldn't see through my ambition. I was a stubborn prick. I wanted to claim you, so I forced the marriage. And when you in return expected me to grow up and compromise, I could only smell sacrifice. My stubbornness killed all the good in our relationship.

"All the good in both of us. Or at least in me. You were right—the restaurant could have waited. When you lost the baby, I demonstrated my grief by washing my hands of any responsibility. The biggest regret of my life is I didn't focus on starting the family with you back then."

The oxygen leaves my lungs. I jump out of bed, tripping over the duvet. His deep voice calls my name, but I can't make out the words. The only thing I know is that I have to leave.

Chapter Eighteen

Massi

I've replayed last night's events in my head a hundred times, falling asleep briefly only to jerk awake with a ball of dread in my stomach. She made some lame excuse about her mom's early morning doctor appointment she'd forgotten about, but the way she bolted suggested there was more to it.

Was my honesty too much, too soon? After the way she held me through my panic attack and the emotions roused by our lovemaking, I was sure we were on the right track to recover what we had lost, and possibly find something more and better.

I'm not fucking giving up easily this time. If Gina Accardi thinks she can run away again, she is mistaken.

Something pushed her to panic last night and I'll make her explain, and then I'll fix it.

I'll make her fall in love with me again. I'll make her trust me again, so she stops keeping things bottled up.

My phone beeps as the car weaves at a snail's pace through a stupid traffic jam. I check the message my mother has sent and dial the number immediately.

"Ms. Scalding, it's Massimo Cassinetti. My mother has spoken to you about my friend's mom."

I hear the keyboard on the other end of the line, the woman multitasking.

"Yes, of course, I told Bianca we have a long waiting list, but your generous donation could go a long way. We should be able to accommodate your friend's mother within the next few weeks. Tell her to get in touch with me so we can set up the time for them to visit us."

I make a mental note to find out what sort of donation my mother promised. But I don't care about the money, as long as I can help Blue.

"Thank you, Ms. Scalding, I appreciate your flexibility. Could you send all the paperwork to me? I don't want to burden Ms. Accardi." I doubt Blue would accept my support without a fight, but I'll figure out a way.

"No problem, and please thank Bianca again for

the spot in the club. I really appreciate her support in getting my membership."

So it's not just my money that got things moving; but it doesn't matter. This is the best senior home in Riverdale and a large proportion of its clients are of Italian descent, which should suit Gina's mom well.

I hang up and dial the restaurant to debrief with Lena. She's still in shock that I took a day off, but I know she has everything under control.

The car pulls to the curb in front of Gina's house and I ask the driver to wait. I don't even know if she's at home, but my worries evaporate when she yanks the door open before I reach the porch.

"Good morning." I smile at her, but her expression is stern as she studies me with narrowed eyes.

"What are you doing here?" She steps back when I reach the door. Distancing herself? Sometimes my stubbornness pays off and this is going to be one of those times. I need to tread carefully. I bullied her into a commitment once already.

"I'm taking you on a date. Since you cut the last one short, I demand a re-do." I lean against the door frame, the picture of nonchalance while my stomach twists in knots.

She folds her arms over her chest. "You could have *demanded* over the phone."

"As much as phone sex would be fun, Blue, I want

to take you on a date. Hence I'm here." I keep my cocky grin. Fake it until you make it.

"Now?" She frowns. "You have to work today."

"You called to take a day off and I thought it was a great idea." I shrug.

"*You* took a day off?" She snaps her head back.

"Affirmative."

"To spend it with me?" Her lips quiver slightly, but she recovers quickly and puts the strict mask back on.

"That's the plan." I wink again and she rolls her eyes, which I take as a win. "We don't have to talk about the past or why you ran yesterday, but you need to give me a chance to woo you."

"To woo me?" Her lips curl up now.

"Yes, Blue. No need to repeat everything I say." I push off the door frame and dare to reach out and tuck a strand of her hair behind her ear. Doing so I brush her cheek, and my stomach relaxes slightly.

The reaction to the contact is not one-sided, as much as she wants to pretend. She swallows and looks away as if a plausible excuse was written on the porch.

"My mom is at the community center for an art class. I have to pick her up. I can't leave her alone for too long. The nurse comes later in the afternoon for a few hours only."

"My mother is coming over to keep her company. Maybe to take her shopping. She'll organize someone to pick up your mom from her class." I better call Mom quickly. She was quite willing to help Gina's mom, but she didn't know it would be a full-time job. I plan to spend at least twenty-four hours with this woman.

"Bianca is coming to babysit my mom?" She puts her hands on her hips, cocking her head.

"Yes, and to tell her about an amazing senior home where there is an opening. But I'll explain more in the car. Let's go."

The internal struggle is clear on her face. I'm not sure if I'm losing or winning, but I can see the struggle is real. Whatever happened last night has left her distant and conflicted.

"Where are we going?" she asks, and if I was an idio I'd pound my chest in victory. But I'm not an idiot, so I do so only in my head.

"It's a surprise."

"I need to know what to wear," she deadpans.

"Something blue, baby." I wiggle my eyebrows.

She shakes her head. "Give me five minutes." Blue shuts the door in my face. Not the warmest behavior, but she is coming and that's what matters.

I walk to the car and lean against it to type a quick message to my mom. I can't call her. The first call this morning was already full of inquiry, warning and hidden glee. I love her, but talking to her once a day is enough.

I get a quick reply: *You owe me.*

I snort. My mother's unconditional, limitless love.

The door opens and I look up, and a wave of heat radiates through my chest. She is wearing jeans and a blue blouse that hugs her under her breasts and fans out.

Her hair is loose, falling just down to her shoulders, and the good man in me is dazzled by her natural beauty.

The depraved bastard imagines fisting her hair as I ride her from behind, spread on my kitchen counter. Both men are idiots, judging from Blue's frown.

"Close your mouth, master chef," she quips.

"My lady." I bow and open the door for her.

Gina

I climb into the black sedan and greet the driver whom I recognize from yesterday. The shadows under Massi's eyes suggest he slept about as little as me. How we're going to spend a day exhausted and raw with unanswered questions is beyond me. But here I am, weak and needy, unable to refuse him.

I was thrilled and horrified when he showed up. I called Phillip and Mila earlier to let them know I needed to stay home today. A reckless choice since we're only a week from the private dining event. A point Mila graciously didn't make.

I needed a day away from Massi. To regroup. To think. To decide what to do next. I shouldn't have run last night, but after he confessed his deepest regret was not having a family with me, all the alarm bells screamed inside me.

I based my entire life on the knowledge that Massimo Cassinetti, the love of my life, didn't want to have children with me. How does one recover from such a misconception? How can I look back at my decisions and find a sliver of reason if the only reason evaporated with his honest, heartbreaking admission?

I didn't get a chance to regroup, to think or to decide how to talk to him. I spent the rest of the night, or rather early morning, tossing and turning in my bed. Luckily Mom was having a good morning and decided to go to a class she sometimes attended.

In the silence of the empty house I sat on the sofa, staring, imagining how my next conversation with Massi would go and coming up naked, hurt and destroyed.

When he showed up, my initial impulse was to hide, but part of me, perhaps the nineteen-year-old girl who really wanted a chance for a do-over, ran to the door. That girl couldn't let him leave. And that girl needs to tell him the truth now. The whole truth.

"Massi, I need to tell you—"

He turns and puts a finger on my lips. "No, Blue, you don't. Not today. I don't understand what I did yesterday to spook you and we will talk about it, but let's pretend for one day that this is not a second chance. That we are just two people enjoying each other's company, having a date, unburdened by our past."

I open my mouth to protest, but he leans over and seizes my lips. Oh, how I love his kisses. They make my soul glow with joy. They make every cell of my body tingle. They make everything better.

"One date, Blue," he mumbles against my lips and continues exploring with his tongue.

Oh, and how his kisses rob me of reason. I know I shouldn't agree to this because it will only make things worse, but I push that aside. What's one more day after seventeen years? A day that promises joy and love.

Once I explain why I married Frederick, the clouds will eliminate the sunshine and God knows if we'll survive the storm.

I lean into the kiss, getting as close as possible, consumed by everything this man is offering. Lost in the world of Massimo Cassinetti. Where I belong. But perhaps don't deserve to be anymore.

We kiss like teenagers until the driver clears this throat. "We are almost there, Mr. Cassinetti."

Massi pulls away and looks down. "I might need a minute before I can get out without traumatizing seniors."

I glance at the bulge in his crotch and giggle, unreasonably pleased I have this effect on him.

"Don't you laugh at me, it's all your fault." We both grin like idiots.

We get out in front of the iconic Carlyle Hotel and I search Massi's face. "You booked us a room in a fancy hotel? Is that your idea of a date?"

He throws his head back and laughs, the sound of it lacing my heart with joy. "You dirty girl." He fakes outrage but winks. "It would have been the perfect plan, but I figured we need to rest and relax a bit."

"So you booked us a room to take a nap?"

"No, Blue, I got us a day, or a few hours, at a spa here, starting with a couple's massage."

If he offered me a marathon of orgasms, I couldn't be happier. I can't imagine a better way to spend my day than melting away all the stress that's built since I arrived to bury my father.

"Your face says I wasn't wrong booking us here." Kissing my temple, he slides his hand into mine and we enter the luxurious hotel.

On the third floor we are greeted by a young

woman whose white dress looks more expensive than my outfit. The place is beautiful, an oasis of dark wood walls, sparkling chandeliers and marble countertops everywhere.

It feels very different from a regular spa, more private. As if we stepped from the buzzing city into a calm refuge that doesn't even belong to the cosmopolitan life.

The next several hours are spent being pampered and lounging around, touching gently, not even speaking, just being together. We even nap, for I don't know how long, which re-energizes us.

"Is it wrong that I want to purr like a kitten?" I drawl.

We are lying on the most comfortable loungers in a private room.

"Any sound you make, Blue, makes me want to lock you in a cage so no one else has the joy and privilege to hear you."

Why that threat makes me feel like a goddess I'll never know. I slide down from my recliner and join Massi, sliding my hand under his fluffy robe, scraping the muscles of his chest. He turns to face me and our lips meet.

We barely fit together on his bed and I almost fall to the floor, but he rolls me on top of him. I straddle him, our chests pressed together, never disconnecting the kiss that is getting more and more heated.

I know we should stop before things get out of hand, but somehow the grand, lavish environment and the idea of a forbidden, off-limits affair set my heart racing and my core craving.

I straighten up and pull at the sash of my robe. As the sides fall open, Massi hisses and immediately cups my breasts.

His erection throbs, plush fabric the only barrier between us. He gives my nipples a tug that sends shivers down my spine, though I'm too hot in the warm robe. Burning, really.

I spread my palms to expose his chest and lean down to graze those beautiful muscles and his glistening skin with kisses.

"We shouldn't," I whisper, I'm not even sure why since I won't stop now. God, the idea of getting caught arouses me almost as much as his touch.

Massi slides his hands down my ribcage, gripping my hipbones and circling my hips. The friction makes me gasp. He pulls me by my hair and my lips are crushed against his. My nipples pebble as they connect with his warm body.

"You have to be quiet, Blue," he rasps and tugs at my lower lip with his teeth. My eyes widen because until now it was a playful game for me, but his command sets my heart racing and my center on fire.

I'm so wet I probably soaked the slice of fabric still between us. Massi moves that fabric, opening his robe. He rearranges the sides of my robe to cover us, as if this act of decency would overwrite what we are engaging in.

"What if someone comes?" My whispers hitch as he pinches my clit.

"I paid enough for the private experience for them to dare." He nuzzles my neck.

"For us to *nap* privately," I protest, and immediately contradict myself when I graze my fingertips over his head, already slick with pre-cum.

He inhales sharply. "Let's hope there are no cameras here then."

This should arouse my sense of reason—instead it awakens desires I didn't even know were hidden in me. But it's the realization that I trust Massi that gives me the green light. I trust him in this risqué situation, but I trust him beyond that.

With my life.

With my future.

However complicated the path to that might be.

It's that trust that leads my hand to grab his erection and guide him to my entrance. No condom. No protection. Just faith. For better or worse.

He fills me to the hilt and swallows my gasps with kisses that are desperate and decadent. We are both sweaty, so it's like indulging in salty caramel. Only a thousand times better. I'm beyond the ability to find words for the sensations that are washing through me.

We ride together to the place where all the worry of the outside world no longer exists, where harmony resides and I know without a doubt in my mind, in my heart, that I love this man. That I've never stopped loving Massi.

Chapter Nineteen

Massi

The forbidden lovemaking at the spa unlocked a new level in our journey of reconnection. It was hushed, illicit and—likely because of that—more intense. It was an act of trust and mutual understanding.

And while I know it was just sex, I also know it wasn't. The intimacy was off the charts. Our hearts communicated there, and although we're not putting it into words, the feelings are palpable. I saw it in her eyes, and I accept that for now. It was the best sex we've ever had.

And the most expensive because there *were* cameras. I didn't mind paying the exorbitant fine, relieved they didn't call the police, but I felt bad for Blue who was mortified. Still is.

"I can't believe they were watching us. I mean, they didn't interrupt, so they must have watched." She marches down the path in Central Park.

"They were discreet." I try not to laugh.

"More like pervs." She turns to face me and it might be my expression or just the nerves rebelling, but her lips quiver and then she bursts into laughter. The sound is contagious and we both erupt into howls.

"I can't believe—" She tries to catch her breath, wiping her cheeks. "I can't believe we did that." Her chest heaves and I grab her hand and tug her closer.

"There are bushes around here, Blue. Now that we know how public indecency tastes..." I lick my lip, but the memory of us on the playground all those years ago when she accepted my proposal flashes through my mind.

I'd forgotten about that. Somehow, over the years, my mind focused on all the bad stuff, but I guess my heart remembered the good things as well. Why else would I have cared for this woman for all those years?

I let go of her and put my hands in my pockets because otherwise I might just show everyone around us how I feel about her. In the middle of the day. In a park full of tourists and families. That's how strongly I feel about claiming her. Making her mine.

The intention is as strong as seventeen years ago, but I plan to be smarter about the execution. Yeah, hands in the pockets, but I still give her a mischievous smile.

"You can't be serious." But she smiles, as if considering it. "That was enough indecency for one day."

"Oh, for one day. Good. As long as you didn't say lifetime."

She swats at me, but her eyes sparkle. "I think I need a drink."

"Let's get hot dogs and then I'll find you a good cocktail."

I spot a vendor and chance a touch, grabbing her hand and dragging her across the lawn.

"I haven't seen you drink," Blue says.

And here we go, there is no way we could avoid the past.

"It's because I don't drink." I turn to place the order.

I put mustard and sauerkraut in my bun while Blue tops hers with all the condiments available.

"You're still doing that? Those flavors don't go together."

She laughs. "I've been told."

"Because it's a criminal act." We say the last two words together and our eyes meet for a moment before we look away, each taking a bite to cope with the memories.

As much as I wanted this day not to be about the past, it's impossible. We can try to form fresh memories, but the old ones—good and bad—linger. I might as well tell her everything.

We sit on a bench. Blue is leaning forward because, of course, her over-adorned hot dog is a mess to eat.

Since she's not looking at me, I find it easier to confess.

"After you left, I wasn't doing well. I started drinking a lot. Somehow I still opened my first restaurant, but I was sloppy. First, there was a health director warning. I got into a fight with a customer. I drank even more, and then there was a fire."

All the misfortune is connected to Blue, but as I speak, I realize I don't blame her. I don't know when it happened, because I'd charged her with responsibility for all of that for as long as I remember.

"Fire? What happened?" She turns to me, ketchup and relish dripping to the ground.

"I don't know. It was a shitty week, we had cancellations, and well after everyone left I got really drunk. Luckily my sous-chef at the time forgot something and came back. He saved my life. The insurance company concluded foul play. I don't know if I burned the place down, but my negligence was undeniable."

"Massi," she breathes. I don't want her pity, but when I look at her, her eyes are full of compassion. "I didn't know. Is that why you said you would have had an easy start with your mom's money?"

"Yep. My mom's investment went up in the flames. Literally." I wipe my hand and stand to throw away the napkin. When I turn back, tears roll down Blue's cheeks. Her hand is outstretched, the leftover atrocity dribbling down.

Despite the heaviness of my recollection of past events, I can't help but chuckle. I take the messy food from her and dump it. I pull her up and take each of her fingers, licking her hand clean, all the while watching her face contorted by emotion. She is breathtaking.

I gather her in my arms and kiss the tears off her cheeks. "Don't cry, Blue, that hot dog was horrible to begin with." Her shoulders shake with tears and suppressed laughter.

But then she shudders. "I destroyed us." She shakes with swallowed sobs.

"Jesus, woman, if we're to entertain the citizens of New York, I'd rather fuck in the bushes here. Stop the waterworks." I try to lighten the mood.

She shakes her head and then drops her forehead to my chest. We stand there, a statue of lovers ridden with regret and fragile hope.

"Blue, I destroyed what we had, and then I destroyed the only good thing left in my life. But let's leave the past in the past. Let's get you that cocktail now."

I take her to a popular rooftop bar only a few blocks from my apartment. Against the backdrop of the cosmopolitan buzz that has been my home, Blue enjoys a mojito while I sip a sparkling water with lemon. We have spoken little since the park, slowly digesting the missing pieces of the past.

"I think we need to stop blaming ourselves for what happened. We both played a role and we can't change it anymore." She watches the skyline of the city, the breeze playing with her hair.

"I don't blame you. Not anymore." My words hold a conviction and an atonement.

"But you blame yourself." She looks at me now, her eyes directed to spot the truth.

I nod.

"Don't. Someone told me recently I need to forgive myself in order to move forward. Can you?"

I swallow, a lump sprouting out of nowhere in my throat. A loud party of businesspeople stumbles in, cheering and ordering champagne. The city bustles below us. The sun offers a few shy rays that reflect in Blue's hair.

A snapshot of stillness in our relationship that I

would like to remember as the time we buried the past, but I don't think I can do that yet.

"I will always blame myself, Blue, just like I will always love you."

She lowers her drink, her jaw slack. She swallows several times. "Why, Massi? Why do you love me?"

I watch her while I'm trying to find the right words. It doesn't take me long, the feelings are complex, but still easy on my tongue.

"When I'm with you, my world expands. I feel like I can achieve everything, be anyone I want to be. I'm an angry bastard, but you calm me down. You make me feel other things, not just that built-up anger. When you smile, my life is better. I'm a better man because you took a chance on my grumpy ass. When you smiled at me that first day in high school, I knew there was light to all the darkness in my soul."

She clasps her hands over her mouth, tears rolling down her cheeks, but I'm not done.

"Even during this past month, when I still foolishly believed you were my enemy, my days were already brighter. You bring peace to my life, Blue. I don't know how or why, but you do. The breathing is easier. I loved you then, and I love you now."

She stares at me, a war raging in her eyes, and suddenly I fear I might lose her again. That I might be too late. That she loves her second husband. Or she isn't ready to step into this same river again. Was I too soon? Too vehement?

She stands up and a heavy ball of disappointment sinks to my stomach. But she steps around the table and sits in my lap. I almost drop her, stunned. She takes my cheeks in her hands, her eyes glistening with tears.

"No matter what happens, Massi, remember, always remember that I love you too. I loved you with the heart of the silly girl in high school. I loved you with the insecure heart of your young wife. I loved you all those years we were apart. And I love you now."

The warmth that spreads in my chest is love and relief wrapped in velvet and decadence.

With her lips she brushes my eyelids, my temple, my cheeks, my jaw, and at last my lips. We kiss, not a desperate kiss of lust and desire, but one of deep commitment and love.

"I will disappoint you, Massi, but I will always love you." The words bring me joy and fear, but I don't think she's ready to explain, and frankly I'm a coward who prefers to keep the moment on the loving note.

I pull her closer, holding her tight, her head resting on my shoulder. The loud cheers and commotion in the corner and the honking of the relentless traffic disperse, practically inaudible in the intimacy of the moment.

"I wanted to take you out to eat and dancing, but let's go home, baby." I revel in the scent of her hair.

"I happen to know your cooking is the best in the country and your living room is the largest dance floor, so I guess home is perfect for your plans."

We walk the few blocks to my building, hand in hand, drunk on the newly rediscovered love.

"I know you didn't want to talk about the past today, but I'm glad you shared with me. That you told me about your troubles after I left," Blue says as we wait for the elevator.

"I'm glad to. I wanted to stay away from the past because I feel it's something big you didn't want to share last night. I wanted us to spend time together, so you can see how good we could be together. Better than before. Happier. And then you will hopefully trust me enough to share. Do you trust me, Blue?"

She licks her lips, that internal fight brewing again. "I trust you, but I don't yet trust that you won't run away."

I raise my eyebrows. Fuck. What is she hiding? Part of me thinks she must be taking something out of proportion, because we've experienced so much shit already I can't imagine what could shock me or make me give up on her. On us.

"That bad?"

Both our phones ring at the same time. Blue looks a

bit disoriented, but then she checks her phone, frowning. She answers and I look at my screen, finding several desperate messages from my mother.

"It's my mom." Blue hangs up and dashes toward the front door.

Chapter Twenty

Gina

"Wake up, baby." Massi's voice penetrates the darkness. He glides his strong, warm hand up my thigh and peppers my shoulder with kisses.

"It's dark," I groan, but I turn to him. The man has an insatiable appetite. Well, he's not the only one. It's as if we are trying to make up for lost time.

"You don't have to come with me, Blue, but I need to shower and get going in half an hour." He kisses my forehead.

I force my eyes open. The room is dim, but I still have to blink to fight the sleep. My lids are too heavy, but I remember it's the day of the event and I promised I'd go to the market with him.

"No, no, I want to come." I yawn.

"Join me in the shower, but hurry." He leaves and I shiver, immediately feeling the loss of his warmth.

We've had the craziest week in history. My mother got lost, forgetting where she was going, interrupting the potential moment of truth during our do-over date. With the help of Bianca and the police we found her. Seeing her ashamed for her brief lapse in memory was one of the hardest things I've ever experienced.

It was apparent she can't stay alone. And it's insane what money can achieve. I've spent weeks looking for a place for my mom… yet Massi made a few calls and my mother is soon moving to a wonderful home.

A hefty donation was involved, but I'm pretending I don't know about it because at this point I can't deal with another money issue. One more problem to file for later. For after the event.

For now, I accepted Massi's offer to pay for a twenty-four-hour nurse, under the condition I'll pay him back. My mom is pretending to hate "strangers" in her house, but I suspect it's for show as I caught her laughing a few times this past week. It's so much easier to leave her now, knowing someone is there all the time to support her.

I'm speeding headfirst into disaster, but the constant support and the loving arms of the generous man—who, for now, I can call mine—softens all the sharp edges and thorns in my life.

Massi has been supportive on all fronts while getting ready for the event. This is the area where I clearly see how he's matured, dividing his attention and love between his private and professional life. The lines are blurred since we have been working together, but still, this is a new version of Massi that I love even more.

Me, on the other hand, I'm still the lost girl. With more wrinkles and pounds. I still haven't told him why I married Frederick and stayed on the West Coast.

I push myself up, resting against the pillow and taking in the beauty of my surroundings, trying to wake up. It's still dark outside, the lights of the city not yet ready to say good morning to its citizens.

The view of the park is gently interrupted with the light fabric of curtains that hang like pillars, giving the room a slightly Mediterranean feel. I've spent every night here this past week, and every time I admire the view I fear it may be the last time I see it.

I drag myself out of bed and join Massi in the shower. I wrap my arms around him and let us stand there under the hot water. He then washes me like a child, which is oddly arousing as evident by his erection.

He looks at the clock above the door and startles

me when he spins me around, plants my hands on the tiled wall and spreads my legs. I guess we have time for a quickie.

"I have something for you," I say as we finish dressing.

Pulling his watch from the drawer in his closet he looks at me, smiling. "Yeah? I don't think we have time for another orgasm, Blue."

I shake my head, laughing, and open my carry-on suitcase that has been lying in the corner. I pull out the box. I brought it when I was in LA the last time, finally ready to give it to him, but now I'm oddly nervous about it.

"What is it, Blue?" He tries to tame the urgency. Perhaps I should have waited for tonight, but it's too late.

"Here." I hand him the box.

He eyes it before he lays it on the bed. "What is it?" He lifts the lid. "Blue..." Emotions color his voice and tug at my chest. He lifts one watch from the box and admires it. "This-this is..."

"I got one on your birthday every year since I left. For your collection." My voice is softened by the bout of vulnerability I feel. "I got each of them to remember something I wanted to share with you that year. They aren't expensive, not like your own pieces—"

He crushes his lips to mine, swallowing my words

and worries, holding me so tight I can barely breathe. "Thank you, baby." He lowers his forehead to mine.

"Don't get sappy with me, Massi. We need to go get the fish." I fail to bring lightness to my words as we reluctantly pull apart, both of us wiping tears. Happy tears. Hopeful tears.

He takes a watch and replaces the one on his wrist with it. "What is the memory of this one?"

Fuck, did he have to choose that one? I can't tell him that. Not now. We have to focus on the event.

"We better go. We'll talk about the memories after the event." I hate that I can't be open with him. I hate that I've let things go unsaid for this long.

Massi admires the watch, and then grabs my hand and kisses my knuckles.

We arrive at the market quickly at this ungodly hour when the city still sleeps. Kind of, because we spot drunken parties, early morning runners and delivery trucks everywhere. Yet the traffic is at its lightest, so it's not even five in the morning when Massi drags me through a large warehouse toward a fishmonger who's been his supplier for years.

By the sight of it, the man is packing up for the day. Already? Massi squeezes my hand before he drops it and walks over to the stall. I watch the interaction, not really hearing what's said, but the man shakes his head and Massi runs his fingers through his hair, pacing around like a caged animal.

Something is wrong. I walk to join them.

"But you knew I'd come to select the best tuna today. We talked about it several times this week." Massi's words are sharp.

"Sorry, man, but I got a large order at four this morning that I couldn't refuse." The fishmonger wipes his hands on his apron and moves a crate.

"After all these years you fuck me over." Several vendors stop what they were doing and turn our way.

"I still have tilapia left." The man shrugs. "I'm really sorry."

"I don't want fucking tilapia." Massi's voice carries as he lunges forward.

I step in front of him and place my palm on his chest. He blinks a few times and looks at me, the god of vengeance, as if he's just remembered I was there. His heart pounds against my palm. From the corner of my eye I see him clenching his fist.

"Massi," I breathe. He's looking at me, but he doesn't seem to see me. "Breathe, baby. Fuck him. Let's not waste the time. You can come up with a new menu."

His chests rises and falls rapidly, but his gaze refocuses on me. "I'd have to redo the entire menu and get new wine. It's too late for that."

The onlookers slowly return to their previous tasks. I press my palm firmer against his heaving muscles and rub his arm with my other hand.

"If anyone can change and adapt the menu, it's you. Let's look around and get steaks..." I scrunch my face, hoping my ideas won't set him off again. "Lamb?" I try.

He puffs out the air from his cheeks and drops his head. "Okay, let's look around."

And so we do. Massi finds veal that seems to satisfy his expectations and calls Lena who is at the vegetable market. They consult and change the menu on the fly. The next call goes to Phillip, who promises to source the wine.

By six thirty in the morning we are at Casa Cassi. The kitchen is silent and the deliveries won't be here for another hour, but Massi wanted to come straight here.

He unrolls his knife pouch on the shiny surface of the prep table. He runs his fingers over the sharp blades and I feel like I'm interrupting some kind of ritual I shouldn't witness.

I tiptoe to the front to turn the espresso machine on, letting Massi have his moment.

"Blue," he rasps.

"Yes, baby, I was just going to make coffee. Do you want some?" I wish I could take away the tension gripping his shoulders.

He walks to me and gathers me in an embrace, kissing the crown of my head. "Thank you. I lost it there and you helped me. Thank you." With his finger, he nudges my chin up and kisses me. "Let me make you breakfast."

"Are you sure? You should focus on work today, baby. Don't worry about me."

"I still have time before Lena and the deliveries arrive. Let me feed you. Watching you eat is the best motivation for me." He plants a kiss on my forehead. I didn't know it was possible, but I've just fallen deeper.

He pivots and grabs a pan before he heads to the cold room. "You're still in charge of coffees, Blue," he calls over his shoulder and I laugh, shaking my head.

We eat poached eggs with salmon and drink our coffees, discussing the new menu. "I'll type it up and have Mila do a rush print of everything. By the end of the lunch hour we'll be all ready, as if nothing happened."

"Thank you." He squeezes my hand. "What would I do without you?"

Massi

The morning fiasco at the market was only the beginning of the disaster.

"Where the hell are they?" I yell at Lena, as if it's her fault one of the line cooks and our dishwasher didn't show up.

"I don't know, but let me get someone to fill in." She walks to the board where we have the number of the temp agency.

"To fill in? To fill in on a night like this? Are you out of your mind?" If I don't get my heart rate under control, we won't need anyone filling in. We'll close.

"I'll call the temp agency, and when you have any other suggestions we'll try that."

It's only the beginning of the lunch hour and the kitchen is a mess. The orders are coming in, and if I ever needed a drink in the past sixteen years, it's right now.

"Oh my god, oh my god, oh my god..." Sharon, the new floor manager selected by Blue, comes running, almost colliding with a server carrying three plates. "Two of my staff called in sick. They won't be coming tonight."

"Fuuuuuuck!" I yell and throw a bowl of gravy across the kitchen. It sprays the tiles and drops with a loud clank, but it only creates a mess. No relief.

Mila and Blue dash in from the dining room.

"What's going on?" Blue asks, and Sharon whine-repeats what she's just told me.

My eyes dart to Blue. She's good under pressure. She nods to Mila, who immediately drags Sharon out of the kitchen. "We'll get backups, no worries," Mila chirps with a smile before the door closes.

Blue returns her eyes to me. "Mila takes care of the front. If she doesn't find anyone, Sharon will serve and I'll be at the door while Mila schmoozes with the media."

It's not only her words, but also the composed way she takes control. Everything about her in this moment, and all the other moments leading to tonight, regulates my breathing. I need this woman in my life.

She removes the distance between us, her heels clicking loudly as everyone stops what they're doing to stare. We are half an inch apart, but it feels like she consumed the entire room with the sole purpose of getting me refocused.

"Sharon made a mistake by running in here. I'll talk to her so she understands it's her responsibility to come to you with solutions, not problems. The veal smells divine. I think the new menu is better than the tuna one." She squeezes my hand and turns to Lena. "Have we filled the missing staff here?"

How she knows what's happening here is beyond me, but fuck I'm grateful.

"I got a dishwasher coming in half an hour, but I think we'll have to do with one man down here"—she gestures toward the range with her head, not a sign of stress in her voice—"and I'm sure we can manage." She raises her eyebrows and all the other cooks nod. "Can't we?" she challenges and they yay in unison, returning to work promptly.

This finally snaps me from my anger-induced stupor and I start shouting commands, reassigning duties, so we can manage the evening without a hitch.

I catch Blue's smile before she leaves the kitchen, and I know everything is going to be all right.

But I'm wrong. So wrong.

Several hours later, I stand in the middle of a silent kitchen. It's my biggest fear and failure all wrapped in one. The first seating was half an hour ago and the restaurant has remained deserted.

No one dares to speak. I could hear my breathing, that's how pronounced the silence is. The kitchen has never been this silent, even when I'm here alone in the morning.

I don't want to go up front and face Blue, whose idea this event was. But as the clock ticks, drilling a hole in my brain, I have no other choice but to venture out, taking with me my murdered dignity and pride.

Blue stands at the entrance with her back to me, tapping her heel nervously. Phillip sits at the bar and Mila paces in circles, typing on her phone. The staff waits in the shadows, avoiding my eyes as soon as I enter.

If things were different, I would just yell at the two women and fire them and then yell some more. But I don't want to yell at Blue. I don't want to accuse her of whatever has happened here tonight. We have just rekindled our relationship, and I don't want our work to loom over it like a thunderous cloud.

But it always will. My work will *always* be a part of me, and as much as I've tried to find balance over the past few weeks, this place matters to me. Not as much as Blue, but I'm not complete without it either.

The door chimes and Blue steps back.

"Oh, hey Gina, are we early?" My brother, Gio, with his long-legged, platinum blond with fake boobs and unnaturally puffed-up lips companion enters. He takes in the room and the mood. "Shit."

Everyone stills for a moment and then I bark, "Seat the guests." It's Blue's responsibility tonight, but I don't look at her when I speak. She doesn't move, but Sharon finds her groove finally and rushes to take care of my brother and his guest.

"Open for the walk-ins right now. Stand someone outside to offer a free drink or something," I say to

Phillip, and then I turn to Mila. "You better fucking hope the place fills up," I hiss, but she seems distracted, staring at Gio. For once, her phone is not in front of her face. What the fuck?

I almost turn around to get back to my kitchen, but I feel Blue's scent behind me. I step to the side, but then it hits me.

It's just one night of business for me. For Blue, it's her first project on this side of the country, and I know for a fact she's been working her ass off to make it a success. I don't fucking know what went wrong, but I want to support her.

I place my hand on the small of her back and she tenses. Our eyes meet and I nod slightly to encourage her, and I can feel her exhale.

"If they are not responding to your messages, start calling the guest list now," Blue commands, and Mila hesitates for a brief moment before she dials the first number.

Blue looks at me, her eyes full of remorse. She bites her lip and keeps tapping her foot.

Sharon rushes to the kitchen to take care of Gio's order, I suppose. Phillip removes the "closed for private event" sign from the door.

I weave my fingers through Gina's and squeeze. Her eyes are now on Mila, trying to eavesdrop on her conversation, but she squeezes back. Fuck, she's crushing my bones.

I hate seeing her this stressed out. And it's because of my stupid need to get the fucking star. I want to pull her into a hug and tell her everything will be okay.

"Oh, well, of course, enjoy your evening and we'll let you know about the new date. We look forward to having you dine with us soon," Mila chirps into her phone. She hangs up, and for the first time since I've known her, she is pale and her face only a ghost of the usual sunshine. Her eyes find Blue's with an expression that might be either shock or horror.

She swallows a few times and I want to snap at her. It feels like we've grown gray hair by the time she speaks again.

"All the guests were alerted earlier today that the event has been moved to another restaurant." She swallows again, tears filling her eyes as she shakes her head as if she could shake off the information she's just learned. "They are all dining at Modigliani's."

Frederick's place?

I think the gasp I hear comes from Gina. I drop her hand and stumble backward, the information twisting in my gut.

The floor moves slightly and I grab the edge of the bar, searching for balance. The man stole from me again.

This isn't even déjà vu—this is much worse.

"Massi." I hear the voice of the woman I love.

The one that this time found an even sharper knife to slice through my heart.

"Get the fuck out of here," I roar.

Chapter Twenty-One

Gina

I run.

The street blurs in front of my eyes.

I don't even know where I'm running. It only occurs to me about five blocks from the restaurant. I try to hail a cab. I fail.

I keep going.

I destroyed him.

Yet again.

My feet hurt and my chest heaves with exertion and imprisoned sobs. I slow down to walking. And I walk and walk until exhaustion hits me and I stop in the middle of the sidewalk. New Yorkers swim around me in flowing lanes.

At first many bump into me, but slowly the stream

diverts on both sides of me as if I was standing on an island in the middle of all the commotion.

Isolated. Outcast.

On this street. And in my life.

"Are you okay?" A voice penetrates my mind and I snap back to reality, disoriented by the stillness I suffered in the middle of the pulsing city. A young woman with a stroller searches my face.

"I couldn't get a cab," I sob, uttering the most outlandish reason for standing there.

"Oh, honey, you're not from here, are you?" Neither is she, based on her southern accent and kindness. "You need to be persistent. Do you have Uber?"

I look at her as if she's speaking Martian. Then I look down at myself. I left everything at the restaurant.

"I forgot my phone." The idea of returning to the restaurant draws another loud sob from me.

The woman squints at me, probably assessing the level of crazy she's dealing with, and then pulls out her phone.

"Let me get you an Uber. Where are you going?" She clicks on the screen.

"I can't accept that. I live in the Bronx, it's too expensive. How will I pay you back?"

"Just give me your address and consider it my good deed for the day." She beams at me, and her kindness hits me so hard I burst into tears again. "Oh, come on, it's not a big deal. Why don't you do something nice for someone tomorrow and we'll start a chain of goodness." She winks at me.

There is no amount of altruism that can undo the damage I've caused.

The car, paid for by a stranger, gets me home finally. The house feels empty, large and cold. A perfect dwelling for someone like me. I sit on the sofa. That's all I'm capable of doing. The television drones in Mom's room, but I suspect she's asleep.

I sit there for a lifetime, the ticking clock counting down my demise. What the hell have I done? The question crosses my mind along with the other thousand unanswered questions freely roaming in my head, trying to anchor themselves in some sort of logic, welcoming the darkness.

I drop to my side, my legs dangling from the sofa and I close my eyes.

Shivers pull me back into reality. God, I need a blanket. I pat around myself, realizing I'm still on the couch. I must have fallen asleep. I sit up, with a vague aim to move to my bedroom.

What have I done? The question returns, and that's when the reality hits me and I spring up.

Hushed voices sound somewhere in the house and the change of light confirms I must have slept all night.

I stand up and join my mom and Clarissa, her nurse, in the kitchen.

"Did we wake you up? You must have been exhausted, you didn't even make it upstairs. I thought you'd sleep in the city," my mom says as she digs in her purse.

I probably no longer have anywhere to sleep in the city. Tears burn at that realization. I blink them away and try to sound normal.

"Are you leaving? What time is it?" I take a mug from the cupboard and pour coffee.

"I'm spending a day in that facility you want me to move into."

I don't even have the energy to argue the need for her to move there.

"Now, now, don't make trouble, Mrs. Accardi, you'll love it there," Clarissa says and winks at me.

"Clarissa, could I borrow your phone? I left mine at work."

She hands me her phone and starts arguing with my mother about wearing a more comfortable pair of shoes.

I'm exhausted, but my mission propels me into action. I abandon my coffee and rush upstairs. I sit on my bed while I log into my account to find the phone number, but as soon as I dial, I pace.

The phone rings and rings and I'm about to hang

up when the voice I know so well comes alive on the other side of the line. The other side of the country. With no remorse or regret.

"What have you done?" Bile is bitter on my tongue when I spit the question at him.

I half expect him to deny it, but he doesn't. Frederick launches into a detailed recounting of the extent of his sabotage and I listen, stunned by the satisfaction in his voice. He talks as if it was his right to wrong Massi.

Shocked, I sit silent, listening. Because that's how it's always been—he talked, sweet-talked, lied, and I listened. But back then I listened because my wounded soul was grateful for any attention. This time, I listen because I need all the details of his evil, so I can hopefully start repairing what he destroyed.

I severed all ties with him after the divorce. When he called me to offer his condolences after my father's death, I didn't think about it much. I just assumed he'd moved on and I appreciated he was thoughtful. But there he was, always with an ulterior motive.

"You used me for years," he dares to accuse me. "I was good to you when you were a coward and ran away to California. And I helped you. I took care of you, and after all these years you go back to him?"

I almost drop the phone. This was a jealousy stunt? Catira's inquiry that I foolishly assumed was gossip comes to my mind. But this time its shape is much more severe than just rumors.

There was gossip before Beaufort moved to LA that he'd been purposely jeopardizing their careers. Probably just jealousy rumors.

I shudder at the idea that I've been enabling this man. Rage licks my core.

"What's wrong with you? Why do you fucking care who I'm with? *We* are not together anymore."

"Oh, darling Gina, think about your motivations to be with me in the first place. You're not Mother Teresa in this scenario."

"I'll go to the media. I'll expose what you've done. It took me years to realize how you manipulated me, and stupid me, I still trusted you. No more." My throat is sore with the words.

"You do that, darling, and it will cost you the most important relationship in your life." He hangs up.

I lower my head against the cold wall, the phone dropping to the floor. How did I let this happen?

I need to stand up for myself, and for Massi. Finally, I have to do that. Sebastien is coming in a week to stay here with me until I sell the house. I had hoped we might look at schools for him here, but I can't see Massi accepting me, us, anymore.

Still, I need to fix the situation. For him, if not for us.

I take the phone downstairs and say goodbye when my mother leaves with Clarissa. I summon all my willpower to act like a reasonable human, but I'm relieved when they're finally gone.

I trudge back upstairs and slide under the covers, not even bothering to get undressed. And I stare at the ceiling, drawing an imaginary balance sheet.

Who called the employees and paid them to stay home? Frederick.

Who bought all the fish for an exorbitant sum? Frederick.

Who called all the patrons, explaining unforeseen technical issues and moved the event to his place? Frederick.

Whose fault is it Massi's big moment was ruined? Mine.

Only mine.

* * *

The sound drills into my brain. What is it? It My mind hovers on the verge of wakefulness, not yet ready to function. But the sound... It keeps up with its short, screaming detonation in my poor aching head.

Oh God, the headache is brutal. My stomach churns as I pry my eyes open.

As the room comes into focus, I finally identify the

source of my torture. Someone is at the door. Down-stairs. So far away. An unsurmountable distance.

When the banging joins the ringing, I slide my legs over the edge of the bed and push myself to sitting.

I stagger, patting the bedside table to find my glasses. I somehow reach the door of my room, then the landing, then one step after another, progressively making my way to the front door. Before I turn the doorknob, I freeze.

What if it's Massi? The thought, irrationally, almost makes me laugh. I can't be sure of many things in my life right now, but I know Massimo Cassinetti never wants to see me again.

I don't even bother to check before I pull the door open and exhale. Mila, minus her signature smile, stands there with a cup of coffee in one hand and my purse in the other.

I reach for the coffee and turn. The door closes and her heels click, following me to the kitchen. I sag onto the bench at the breakfast nook.

"You look like shit." Mila puts my purse on the counter and slides into the seat across from me.

"Not half as bad as I feel I'm sure." I must have fallen asleep just minutes before she arrived and I'm still struggling to climb out of the depth of my slumber, slightly disoriented. As if my mind wanted to protect me from the ordeal, so it refuses to fully wake up.

"Since you didn't defend yourself last night, I'm going to take a guess and assume Frederick's involvement is not a coincidence. What were you thinking?" Mila asks the million-dollar question.

I take a sip of my coffee, wishing it was liquor. Or poison.

"How is he?" I blink away the tears. Fuck. My mind is numb, but the stupid tears work overtime.

Mila sighs and I don't need her to answer, her somber expression and the lack of any emotion on her beautiful face are confirmation enough. Massi either burned the house down or scared everyone away yelling.

"He's oddly silent. They had a decent number of walk-ins last night, so it wasn't a complete write-off. Massi left as soon as the last guests, thanking the staff for a job well done."

This concerns me way more than the opposite scenario. Outbursts are his natural coping mechanism. I numbed his ability to cope. Him not exploding is worse than him burning the house down. I don't even want to think of the ways he'll let out that stress.

I also notice Mila said "they." Of course, it's no longer "us."

Fuck. Fuck. Fuck.

"Phillip agreed to pay for half of our agreed-upon

fees and asked me if I want to continue to liaise with the media for them."

"That's good. I'll transfer the money to you as soon as it clears my account. You deserve the whole fee. I'll be selling the house, so my financial problems are over soon. I'll put the house on the market, introduce Sebastien to my mother and go back to LA." The numbness spreads from my mind to my limbs and I feel like I'm floating above us, just watching the shell of a woman going through the motions.

Mila doesn't protest. She just stares at me, waiting. We sit in silence for a bit until, for the first time in our friendship, we reach a point where she pushes for answers. "What happened? Why? How did he get the guest list?"

She deserves the answer, regardless of how ashamed I am. I close my eyes, summoning the strength to speak. I owe it to her, to everyone really, to explain. But Mila is the only person who would listen at this point.

"I gave it to him." Perhaps she deserves the truth, but speaking it out loud guts me. Admitting to my friend what has happened, how stupidly I acted, only confirms for me how I might never recover from this.

Mila doesn't react immediately. She waits for more, or maybe she's trying to process the magnitude of my colossal fuck-up.

"Fuck me." She stands up and walks around the kitchen, stops a few times, turns to me and opens her mouth, but then she shakes her head and paces more. When she repeats the confused routine for the third time, she finally finds her voice. "Why?"

"Over the years he'd call occasionally. I cared little for his calls, but when he called to offer his condolences, I was so down, I somehow opened up. I told him about the financial issues and why I'm staying here longer. He called again, wanted to make sure I was doing okay." I roll my eyes at my stupidity.

"He realized I was happy, so in his sneaky way, he got me talking, being all supportive and pleased I'm doing so well. I don't even know why I was talking to him. I told him about the event and he suggested I share the guest list with him, so he could add some of his contacts to help."

"To help his competitor?" Mila asks, pushing me to a new level of realization of how useless and stupid I've been. This level is even bleaker than the previous one. A swamp of worthlessness.

"I didn't think of it like that. I only thought about taking any help to make the event a success for Massi."

"The man only ever helps himself. Oh my God, Gina. How are we going to fix this?" Mila leans back, her eyes trailing to the garden beyond the window. I've never seen her this down. This dejected.

Another victim of my stupid decisions to add to the list.

"We? You have nothing to fix. I'm glad Phillip still wants to work with you. If I can't fix this I'll just run back to LA, yet again."

"No, no, no, you can't just let them blame you. I mean, yes, it was stupid to give the list to a competitor, but they would see you didn't think of him like that. He's your ex-husband and well respected in the industry, so you gave it to him as your former mentor. If you're guilty of anything, it's your naivete and your shortsighted trust in Frederick."

"Mila, stop making excuses for me! I fucked up. I lost my credibility, but more importantly I lost the love of my life. Again. For the second fucking time. And by default he lost his opportunity because of my *naivete* and *shortsighted* trust."

The self-loathing still lingers in the pit of my stomach, but it's now joined by growing anger.

"What opportunity are you talking about?" Mila stares at me, her eyes wide at first, and then she narrows them, observing me as if I was a foreign object she needs to approach with care. "He doesn't know, does he?"

"I'm talking about the business."

She shakes her head and her expression screams of disappointment and disapproval. Another first in our friendship. "Gina, it was one night, and frankly not so much damage was done, if we don't count hurt egos. It's not like Frederick's cuisine is so much better to charm everyone over forever. Those people will be more than happy to come for another schmoozing and dining at Casa Cassi."

Despite my exhausted half-functioning brain, it dawns on me that she's right. Frederick's despicable tactics didn't destroy the competitor. It hurt me and Massi, it hurt us, our relationship.

It wasn't a shitty business attack. It was personal. Many past moments between them—starting with Frederick's behavior at our wedding—flash through my mind. It has always been personal.

I stand up and rummage through my bag to find my phone. "Get your phone ready, Mila."

"What are we doing?" Her fingers already sliding on her screen.

"Getting personal."

Chapter Twenty-Two

Massi

"Are you drunk?" Phillip's concern seeps through the line after I dropped the phone and had to pick it back up.

"Does it matter?" I lose my balance and grip the counter to offset the swirling floor. My kitchen is a mess, which is a new low for me. The worst kind of low. "I'm at home, not a threat to anyone." My tongue won't work properly. Perhaps I had a bit too much.

I haven't left the apartment for a week. Since the night that the woman of my dreams stomped all over me. Again. History does indeed repeat itself, and I'm the fucker who willingly stepped—jumped—into the same river that already tried to drown him once.

"Okay, asshole, you need to get your shit together.

Just because one night exploded in our faces, I'm not folding my investment and calling it quits. I've never seen you drink like this and I'm worried, frankly. Also, I'm not postponing my wedding because you keep my fiancée too busy. Get your ass back here."

I stay silent. The poor bastard thinks I caved out of my business because of one failure. And the restaurant wasn't even empty at the end. It's the personal betrayal that keeps me here hiding.

The last time this happened, *I destroyed* my business in the aftermath of betrayal, so Phillip should be fucking grateful for me taking pre-prec-caution. Precaution is a hard word to pronounce even in my mind. Hm.

I grab a bottle of Chateau Palmer and turn it around to pour. Because I'm the prick who drinks five-hundred-dollar wine to drown his sorrow. A drop dangles on the edge of the bottle's neck and slowly slides into my glass, mocking me. Fuck.

And to think I was blaming myself for all that happened, and the whole time it was just a scheme my lovely ex-wife and her former husband plotted all along?

"Your ex-wife? What are you talking about?" Phillip's irritation startles me.

Shit. I didn't even realize I said the last part out loud.

"Gina. Gina used to be my wife."

"Fuck me."

"Oh, yeah, she did. Fuck me, I mean. Fuck me over." I hold the phone between my shoulder and my ear as I open the wine fridge and pull a random bottle out.

"I should have fucking known there was a history between the two of you. Fuck."

"Yeah, and you know who she married before the ink on our divorce papers dried? Frederick fucking Beaufort." I fidget with a knife to get the wrapper off the cork. It slides right into my fingertip. "Fuck." I drop the knife and the bottle onto the counter and turn to the sink. "I cut myself."

Phillip sighs. "You said you're not a threat to anyone. Do I need to come over?"

"No, it's just a scratch." I watch the blood mingle with the cold water, whirling down the drain, wishing the other wound was this superficial. Easy to flush down.

"Listen, man, clearly I don't know what the fuck happened between the two of you this time—or the last time—but I don't think this was intentional. I'm sending you an email with media coverage. Read it and call me back."

"Why would I want to read news summaries?" I stop the water and return to my bottle.

"Because I'm asking you to, asshole. Read the email and call me right back." He hangs up.

I open the bottle and top up my glass, sloshing some—well, enough—on the counter. I try and fail to climb on to the stool, so I move the party to the sofa. The phone chimes with an incoming email.

I close my eyes, and I might have dozed off because the phone rings and it's Phillip again. Fuck. I disconnect the call and open the email.

Renowned restaurateur's "success" built on shady tactics.

Frederick Beaufort, culinary villain.

Former cook comes forward claiming Beaufort poisoned him.

I scan through the links and scans of several articles, many of them exposing Frederick's shady practices. I'd always sensed the bastard was scheming behind my back. Behind everybody's back. There were rumors back then, but I didn't pay attention, buried in my misery.

The articles are not helpful. They don't make me feel better. He succeeded because *she* helped him.

Phillip calls again and this time I answer.

"So what? Mila did a good job, I guess," I start without a preamble.

"Yeah, we're booked solid again for weeks to come.

However, according to Mila, Gina spearheaded the campaign."

Fuck. "Why would she?"

"Look, I don't have the details. You need to talk to her, but from my understanding that fucker Frederick tricked her."

Hence the smear campaign. Well played. "I'm not interested in Gina's public quarrel with her ex-husband. I don't give a flying fuck about her."

"Yeah, it sure sounds and looks like that, man." The sarcasm isn't lost on me, loud and clear even over the line. "Are you coming back soon?"

"Not likely." I can't go back yet.

Partially because my ego needs more wound licking, and partially because I've lost interest. All my life I've been chasing that star, and it has always cost me my heart and soul. The star isn't worth it. I need a new dream.

"If you don't come tomorrow, I'll close the restaurant." Phillip hangs up on me again. The fucker thinks he can threaten me.

I tilt my head back, the cushion of the backrest soft on my nape. I close my eyes, willing to stabilize the floating feeling in my brain. I spent the last few days in the gym or sleeping. I'd work out to the point of exhaustion, sleep, and then go back to the exercise.

The routine did nothing to make me feel better.

The pain expanded from my heart to my body, and when I collapsed on the treadmill yesterday I realized I need to change my numbing strategies.

I've only finished one bottle of wine, but I guess after years of abstinence a glass is all it takes. Here I am, though, feeling like shit.

The elevator bings open and Gio saunters in. He's followed by Sydney. Fuck me. My mother and my siblings are on the list of my guests with access privileges. I need to change that.

My brother—clad in a tailored navy suit, including a vest as if it wasn't over eighty degrees outside already—doesn't lift his head from his phone. Whatever he came for is not as important as his business.

Sydney takes in the takeout boxes scattered on the coffee table and in the kitchen and starts cleaning up, as if a tidy environment is a prerequisite to whatever intervention they're planning.

Because I'm sure as hell the two of them didn't just hang out together—they never do—or run into each other and decided the three of us would be merrier.

Gio puts his phone back into his pocket and looks me up and down, unimpressed. And then his eyes lands on the bottle and he whistles. Asshole.

"Lafite Rothschild." He nods his head a few times. "What does it go for? Three, four thousand?"

Syd stops what she was doing, her eyes wide. Then

she shakes her head and violently squashes a noodle box.

Sydney chose to become a teacher, not touching her trust fund. That was until her husband died, leaving her with mounting debts. I don't judge her choices and she has no right to judge mine.

"The last time she fucked you over you burned down a restaurant, so I guess this time you're more frugal." Gio ambles to the kitchen and gets his own glass.

I get along with Gio just fine, but right now I want to fucking strangle him. He's lucky that standing up is too cumbersome right now. I glare him to death instead.

He unbuttons his suit jacket and sits down across from me on the second sofa. He looks beyond me, pretending to admire the view. Then he takes a sip and purses his lips, nodding his appreciation. "This is good stuff, bro."

"I'm pretty sure you could afford a bottle or ten of your own, so I'm guessing this is not a sommelier experience visit. And thank you, Syd, but I have a cleaning lady."

I set my glass down, worried I may be worshiping my toilet with the expensive wine soon. I wish the kitchen wasn't so far, or that I'd have brought a glass of water with me before I sat down.

"So..." Gio starts, and I wonder how long it's going to take before he checks the markets on his phone. "Mother is worried."

Even Syd stops what she was doing and looks at him as if he was an idiot. Bringing mom into this is neither motivating nor threatening. Unless she'd shown up herself. Oh shit, I hope she's not on her way.

"Look, Massi." Sydney gives up and throws a hand towel on a still-cluttered counter. She walks over to sit beside me. "Gio told me it appears Gina jeopardized an important event."

"It doesn't appear to have happened. It happened. She screwed me over. Yet again."

Sydney puts her hand on my thigh, but her touch carries none of the calming properties of... the woman I refuse to think about.

"Don't be dramatic. The whole fiasco caused very little damage. You'll be opening a new location soon enough." Always the businessman, Gio nonchalantly sips from his glass as if we're having a casual conversation at his club. I mean, I assume he has a membership or two.

Sydney looks at me with almost a smile, waiting for my reaction. Gio pulls out his phone and scrolls down and my sister shakes her head.

"What can we do?" Sydney decides, by the sound

of it, that well-meant advice won't land on fertile ground.

"Leave," I say. One can hope, after all.

She lets the air out through pursed lips and Gio puts his phone away.

"Look, bro," he says. "Do you want to go out and get laid?"

"What?" Sydney gasps.

"Exclusive escort." Gio shrugs and looks back at me for support.

"That sounds good," I say, not sure why, because I've been to Gio's gentlemen's club many times before I learned—by experience—that I can't fuck Gina out of my system.

"You two are idiots. Can we focus on something actually productive? I think you should talk to her, Massi. There must be a reasonable explanation. Maybe you can't forgive her for what she's done, but at least you should hear her out. It would help you get closure."

"If you knew what your husband did with all your money, would you get closure?" It's a low blow, but I'll do anything to shift the attention to someone else's shit show.

Sydney sucks in a breath but shakes off the attack. "It's not about forgiveness—though that would be the most productive way to move forward—but about understanding. She was your wife once, you loved her."

"Not once," I admit automatically. Suddenly it feels like keeping it all in would be suicidal.

"You're still in love with her? Dude, it's been what, twenty years?" Gio huffs.

"Seventeen. It's been seventeen years and yes, I fucking love her. We got back together a couple of weeks ago." The anger boils in the marrow of my bones and I jump up to pace. "I gave her my heart on a platter and she carved a hole in it again."

"But why?" Sydney asks.

"I wish I knew," I holler. Syd winces and sits up straighter while Gio raises his eyebrows.

"Listen, asshole, she is no longer with Frederick, and if she got back together with you she really has nothing to gain from this."

"Not everything is about fucking gains and profits, you dickhead." I'm losing it, all the signs are there. My heart rate is through the roof, my chest heaves, but there is no oxygen coming in. The dry mouth and nausea might relate to my hangover, but I recognize them for what they more likely are. "Just get out of here. Get the fuck out of here."

Sydney stands up. "Massi."

Gio follows. "What the fuck?"

"Get out of here. Get the fuck out of here!"

I can hear their voices, but they echo, incomprehensible, in my mind. I storm into my bedroom, Sydney's shocked face the last picture I register.

I slam my door closed and collapse to the floor. I'm on all fours, unable to draw air in. I try to calm my breathing, counting. Thinking positive thoughts usually helps, but I can't access any.

I remember the three-three-three technique. Name three things you see, then three sounds you hear and move three of your body parts. I should be able to do that. I look around, scrambling to name three things, and my eyes land on the box with the watches Gina collected for me over the years. Definitely not helping.

I squeeze my eyes shut when the door clicks. "I said get out!" The words come out a wheeze.

Light blue heels blur in front of me. My elbows buckle and I drop my head to the carpet. A warm hand touches me between my shoulder blades. It works, so I don't snarl. Slowly, my breathing regulates to its normal levels.

As I stop hyperventilating, I become hyper-aware of my surroundings. The scent of the meadow hits my nose, awakening a picture in my head. One that I can't see right now. Not yet. Not ever.

But she is here, and again her presence is the calming element missing from my life. Regardless of how much I don't want her here.

I fucking need to change the guest list downstairs.

I turn to sit, my back against the bed. I hear a sigh. I don't have the energy to open my eyes or fight with her right now. Water runs in the bathroom and then she taps my shoulder. I pry my eyes open, but don't look up. She hands me a glass. I take it and drink, the glue in my mouth dissolving.

I push myself off the floor. My head swims slightly but I stand upright, and when I finally look at her, my heart squeezes with pain. Blue's face is bloated with tears. Small red lines weave through her eyes.

God, I want to hug her and make everything better for her. It's an instinct. But then I remember it's hate I feel for her. Is it always going to be like this for us? Bouncing between soaring happiness and complete desolation?

"You have no right to be here," I snarl.

The sob that originates somewhere deep inside her shocks me. It's savage, desperate, full of something I don't recognize. But it doesn't stop me.

"If you fucking came to apologize, you can just go. I trusted you! I trusted you and again you marched into my life and screwed me over. Get the hell out of here, Gina. And leave me alone. Alone! This time forever."

"Sebastien." Her shoulders and voice shake. "He-he-he ran away."

I frown, thrown by her words, not really understanding who or what she is talking about, but it hits me quickly. Her son?

I shrug, shaking my head.

"He's coming to look for you." Her face scrunches with new tears and remorse.

"Why?" I start toward the door, but her words stop me dead.

"Because you're his father."

Chapter Twenty-Three

Massi

Traffic is so thick, the car barely moves. The past half hour in the closed space with Blue has been an ordeal of epic proportions.

"How did he find out?" I asked before my car arrived.

"Frederick told him," she whispered, staring at the ground.

"So everyone knew," I said flatly, and that was the last time I looked at her.

We are driving to JFK because Gina's credit card statement gave us the information about his flight.

I have a son.

I have a son.

I gave up on having children a long time ago, after I

tried and failed finding a woman who would measure up to my expectations. I was looking for Blue's clone. What a waste of time that was.

Perhaps I sabotaged my dating endeavors because I was too afraid that living with someone would be a catastrophe like the one that scarred me for life.

And now I'm a father.

Sixteen years too late.

A teenager.

Poor kid.

How is he coping with all of this? I don't even know the boy and I feel strangely protective of him. Mad as a bull at the world that put him in this situation. At the people who put him in this situation.

I look at Gina.

Tears roll down her cheeks as she watches the flow of vehicles outside. Her leg bounces, but otherwise she is completely still. Her hands are folded in her lap, and she is... she is... Fuck, how can I love this woman? She doesn't deserve all these feelings I harbor and can't ever unload.

"Why did he tell him? Why now?" I bark and she flinches.

"The media coverage." She swallows. "He threatened that if I exposed him, he'd hurt me back."

And she did it anyway. She encouraged the bad

press, knowing this might happen? What was she thinking?

"So you have a quarrel with your former husband, and me and my..." I don't know why I stop myself from saying *my son*. "And Sebastien are caught in the crossfire?"

"I..." She sighs, the burden of the world heavy in the sound. A lump forms in my throat, but I ignore it. The only way for me to remain civil is to ignore all my reactions to this situation.

"I wanted to tell you... both... to tell you both, but... Can we talk about everything once we find him?" She is so worried about the boy it breaks my heart. Fucking instincts.

"I hate everything about this. I hate that you didn't tell me, that you robbed me of so many years with him. I hate that I lost all that time. I hate that fucking Frederick got to experience him growing up, his first steps, his first words, his first everything."

"Frederick never cared. He was the shittiest stepfather. They have never had a good relationship. He was an absent father. An absent husband."

I don't know why she feels the need to add the husband part, but I hate her for that even more.

"And I hate that through Sebastien—if he even accepts me—I'll be forever connected to you."

She winces, but accepts my anger without a retort,

which pisses me off even more. Why doesn't she fight? Why doesn't she try to explain? To make her point? Why doesn't she argue? We used to know how to do that really well. Too well.

"The watch you wore the night of the event. I bought it when Sebastien was born."

And now I hate that watch as well. I hid the box under my bed and I don't need her reminding me of it now. The touching gesture seems obscene in the light of current information.

For the rest of the longest trip of my life we sit in silence, the air bursting with anxiety, anger and regret. If there ever was a chance to forgive her for what happened with the private dining event, that chance has been murdered.

The dreadful death of any possibility hurts me all over again. Because before I was mad at her, but now... now I despise her so much, I don't think I can ever look at her again. But unlike before, this time she will stay in my life. A painful reminder of what we could have been. Of all she destroyed. How will I survive her this time?

She's the woman who stomped on my dreams. Twice. She's the woman who strangled my heart with barbed wire.

She causes my panic attacks.

She is the bane of my existence.

She is the mother of my son.

Fuck. What am I going to say to Sebastien? Having no time to process the enormity of this new reality, new responsibility, new role in my life, how am I going to react? Should I hug him? What will we talk about?

Suddenly I have another thing to add to my Gina hate list—I wish I could ask her about him, ask her what I should do. And she took that away from me as well.

Fuck. I hope he's okay. I hope we intercept him at the airport. He's coming to look for me, she said. My boy. The conflicted feelings mingle with my disjointed thoughts.

The most fucked up thing is that in this prison of a car, sitting so close to her and having just discovered I have a child I didn't know about, I've never felt lonelier in my life.

"Fuck!" I yell, and the driver's eyes dart to the mirror and back to the traffic. Gina angles her shoulders closer to the window, turning her face away from me. Distancing? Or hiding?

We finally arrive at the airport. Gina consults the screen. His flight landed twenty minutes ago.

"Try to call him again," I snarl.

Gina looks at me through her eyelashes and utters another sob. Her glasses, fogged by tears, are sliding down her nose. A few people look our way with raised eyebrows and judgment all over their faces.

What must we look like? I feel like a deranged tyrant. Inhaling, I close my eyes briefly and shove my hands into my back pockets.

Gina dials and stands there, tears rolling down her cheeks. I want to wipe them away. I want to hold her while she lives through this nightmare, but I keep my hands in my pockets.

"He's not answering." She lowers the phone.

I turn to watch the monitors above our heads, as if memorizing flight numbers could get him here faster, sooner, safer.

"Let's go to the police. There is a boy missing. He was smart enough to find an airline that accepts kids of sixteen without adult company, but we don't even know if he got on that flight." I use all my willpower to stay grounded, literally and figuratively. I'm so close to pouncing that only the last shred of rational thinking keeps me leashed.

"Let's wait a minute longer. He might come through any moment." Panic laces her voice. "God, he doesn't even know New York. Frederick has never allowed us to visit."

I whip my head around to look at her, the suggestion preposterous in my mind, but her expression sends chills down my spine.

Conviction boils in the depth of her eyes. Frederick, the selfish, sleazy prick. She, and my son, lived with that fucker for years. Fuck.

And I don't even need confirmation, facts or proof —her somber expression holds not a hint of exaggeration. That man threatened her before. I fear not allowing a trip to New York might be only a drop in the ocean of manipulation my former mentor is capable of.

Our eyes lock, and bitter regret coils around my bones, stripping me momentarily of my anger and hatred and replacing it with compassion, with a need to protect her.

The hustle and bustle of the airport moves to the background, rendering Blue's broken stature in sharper colors. Her remorse radiates grimly and I want to make everything better for her. I pull my hands from my pockets.

A loose strand of hair is glued to her tear-stricken cheeks. Her nose is red, her eyes a new shade of blue that I haven't seen before.

Somewhere deep inside me, empathy tries to break free and capture my heart. We stare at each other, our eyes communicating without words.

I step closer and her chest heaves with a sob and a hint of relief. I brush the damp hair from her face and she leans into my palm ever so slightly. A sound somewhere between a sigh of solace and a sob of regret escapes her.

I lean in, our noses almost touching, her breath warm on my skin. The war raging within me is a losing battle. On all fronts. I can't be with her and I can't stay away. I want to punish her and protect her at the same time. I want to make her feel better and throw her under the bus. I hate her so much, and I love her even more.

I drop my forehead the last inch, connecting with her skin, the scent of her equally intoxicating and repelling.

"Why?" I rasp, the loaded one-word question scratching my throat.

Blue's shoulders shake. Hesitantly, she places her palm over my heart and the simple, yet significant touch almost unravels me.

Her phone rings and we jump apart as if an electric current ran through us.

"It's Mila." She answers, listens and gasps. "Oh my God, thank you. We'll be right there."

Relief jolts through me before she even speaks, because her body relaxes so visibly I know Mila called with good news.

"He's at Casa Cassi."

* * *

Gina

From the moment I realized Sebastien bought a plane ticket and sneaked out to come over here, I ran to Massi. Without thinking, considering the miserable state of our relationship, the betrayal, the lie, I was pulled to find him. Because in this dark moment, no one can make me feel better. Even hating me, he is still my rock.

We spend an eternity driving to the restaurant. An eternity filled with relief. And something else. The moment we shared at the airport had a thorny hope swelling inside me. One that will probably cause me more pain soon. But that's the thing about wounded, damaged people, we know we'll survive.

So here I am, fighting atrocious New York traffic, letting the hope glow inside me. Massi probably pitied me, but still I don't think a man full of hate would look at me like that.

I know all his looks. By now I believe I know all his darkest corners. And many of the bright ones. And that look at the airport seemed too real to pretend it didn't happen. But pretend we do. And there is nothing I'm going to do about it because the wounds I inflicted are too raw.

If I released the arrow, can I also be the one tending the wound? Is that possible? Do I have any right to stand by this man? He hates me, he said. I robbed him. And I did. But I believed I did it for him.

We don't speak anymore, the moment at the airport replaced by the relief and anticipation, and it hits me suddenly. It hits me hard. My mother's instinct pulls me out of my internal quarrel with a fresh jolt of worry spreading through my mind, seeping into my limbs.

I have to face my son and his father reuniting under the worst circumstances. Just thrown into a sea of complicated feelings without a lifeguard in sight. Oh, that role should be mine. But even I, with my heart hardened by the ordeals of the past, know that I've lost that privilege.

I thought I was protecting them. Instead I hurt them both. And now they'll face each other, lost, vulnerable, without a chart to navigate these waters.

Over the years, I've imagined this moment many times. When things were really difficult with Frederick and I was forced to tackle motherhood by myself, I'd often fantasized that when we returned from the park or movies, Massi would magically be waiting for us.

The fantasy grew so strong over the years that at times I thought I might be slipping into a delusional world. And yet I believe that fantasy helped me survive. Helped me cope.

No matter how much I endured, nothing prepared me for this scenario. A scenario where the two most important men in my life face the truth about their connection without the benefit of a supportive environment, without guidance. And it's my choices that have led us here.

Spreading pain seems to be my specialty.

Fuck. I could kill Frederick for this. I often wished I'd never met him. His manipulating, conniving persona that ruled my mind and life for way too long. But never before have I wished him dead.

The violent thought startles me, but it's planted firmly. I let him destroy my life and the collateral damage is too big. Too dear to my heart.

I wish I could have a moment with Sebastien before he meets his father. But I know I don't have the right to ask for that. What must he think? What was going through his head when Frederick told him?

The minor consolation is that my beautiful, smart boy chose to come here. Chose to find his father. I hang on to that thin thread of optimism with all my might as the clock ticks backward in this stupid, unmoving car.

Massi is a ball of nerves beside me. His muscles taut, his jaw rigid, I worry he will snap any minute. I can't help it and reach out gingerly, placing my palm on his thigh. His quad tenses, but then he relaxes. Dropping his shoulders, he sighs.

There is so much said with that soft sound. The relief and annoyance mingled. I know I still have an effect on him and it guts him. Forever we'll stand on the opposite sides of the river, attracted by the beauty and the peace of the other bank. The bridge between us always missing planks or crumbling into the wild rapids.

"Stop here," Massi orders the driver. "We can walk faster, for fuck's sake."

We trot down the busy street, almost running. By the time we reach the restaurant I'm drenched in sweat, and half-dead with worry.

Massi halts in front of the entrance but I dash past him, unable to wait a second longer. I enter, startled by the activity. In my mind's eye I was picturing Sebastien standing in the middle of an empty diner.

But of course it's lunchtime and everyone is running around in a hectic, but well-performed choreography. Sharon greets me, but doesn't stop to talk to me. It takes me a few moments to focus and sort through all the movements and sounds before I locate him.

God, I spent the weekend with him two short weeks ago and he looks taller, older, more mature. He's sitting at the corner table, his profile to me, eating and talking to Mila and Phillip. Rely on a teenager to stuff his face with a spoonful of something while I'm losing my mind with fear.

Mila spots me and waves. I dash toward them, my

heart hammering inside my chest. But it's when Sebastien raises his head that all the joy dies in me.

He stands up and I pause briefly, but then, despite the contempt written all over his face, I gather him in my arms and hold his uncooperative, stiff body in my embrace.

"You have every right to be mad at me, Seb, but let me have this moment. I was worried sick."

I feel—or imagine, most probably—him lean into me briefly before he pushes away. "Is he here?" The defiance in his eyes disappears, replaced by hope, expectation, trepidation.

I look over my shoulder, surprised Massi is not right behind. My eyes find him quickly.

Watching our interaction, Massi is frozen in the door, blocking the entrance. He doesn't look at me, his eyes focused on his son.

I look at my boy. Jesus. I've always known that in Sebastien I had a younger version of Massi, but seeing the startling resemblance firsthand shocks me.

Both of them too stunned to move, they assess each other across the floor. The moment is filled with recognition, even though they have never met or even known about each other before now.

Sharon pulls Massi inside to allow patrons to leave, but no one else seems to notice this life-changing moment happening. It occurs unobserved in the background of a busy lunch hour, and yet it will forever stay engraved in my mind.

Snapped out of his hesitation, Massi marches toward us. I step aside, suddenly sure that I'm disturbing the air, the creation of a memory. Nothing about this moment matches my fantasy. Nothing about this moment screams happy family. Everything about this moment is my fault.

Both men, father and son, stare at each other and then simultaneously look at me with expectation. Lost for words and void of any action, I sag into the seat beside Mila.

"Why don't the two of you join Sebastien for lunch? When was the last time you ordered at your own place, Massi?" Mila saves us and everyone seems relieved.

Phillip excuses himself, but Mila stays and I'm grateful for her willingness to pose as a buffer in this weirdly stalled situation.

"What are you having?" Massi asks, eying Sebastien's bowl.

"Chicken soup. Mila said it's good for my soul." He rolls his eyes but continues assessing Massi.

"Do you want a burger?" Massi asks, and Seb nods enthusiastically.

The waitress comes and hesitates, not sure if we're customers or just having a meeting. I save her and ask for a pitcher of water, and a soda for Seb, and she rushes away.

"Do you want to help me make it?" Massi stands up.

"Really?" Sebastien looks back, as if assessing the path to the kitchen.

Massi gives him a lopsided smile and nods. My son glances at me, but then he remembers he's mad at me. After a beat of hesitation, he pushes his chair back.

"Cool." He smiles at his father.

Chapter Twenty-Four

Gina

"They'll both come around." Mila pushes the bowl of uneaten soup away.

I keep watching the swinging door. The sight of my son and his father disappearing there lingers heavily in my stomach. It's a mixture of pride and jealousy, relief and fear, awe and disbelief. Love and, well... love. The conflicting emotions spread through my veins, lacing my nerves with poison.

I feel lonely, discarded, abandoned. And I know I led myself down this path, which only makes me feel more desperate.

"Do you think they will make a burger for me?" I look at Mila, begging her to nod in agreement.

I return my focus to the kitchen door. I don't even

like burgers, but somehow getting one now is paramount. As if my entire future, my relationship with my child and with Massi, is dependent on this one thing. Them making a burger for me. Them walking through that door and sharing a meal with me.

A meal they prepared together. Seb practically grew up in Frederick's restaurant before I started my own business, when I finally found the courage and clarity to save myself from that marriage. But for his first ten years, the restaurant was his home. He knows more about the business than any kid his age.

And he would have known more if Frederick cared. He was always distant with him, and I wondered over the years why he had offered to marry me and be his stepfather. He marveled in the fact that Massi didn't know and he took something this important from him. I understand that now. Too late.

"I don't know." Mila doesn't sugarcoat reality.

I keep staring at the damn door.

"I was financially dependent on him." The need for the truth is so strong suddenly. It's as if I need to bury the past by making it resurface completely. I don't know if I'll ever get an opportunity to explain my actions to Massi, so I speak now.

Mila leans forward, her attention on me.

"On Frederick. After I moved to take the job at his new place in LA, I found out I was carrying Massi's baby. But Massi made it clear he didn't want a child. Deep down, I knew he regretted marrying me so quickly and so young, and Frederick became an answer to all our problems.

"Frederick went to talk to Massi and came back confirming he wasn't interested. I was devastated, and Frederick proposed. In my state back then, I agreed. That marriage solved my financial problems, and I also set Massi free from any obligation. And we all paid a price."

Mila squeezes my hand. "But Frederick has never loved you. I've seen the two of you. So why did he agree to it?"

"For some outlandish reason he wanted to harm Massi, and stealing his wife was a great opportunity. I was scared back then. My father practically disowned me for my failure to save my marriage. I was heartbroken over the separation, overcome by grief over the baby we'd lost. I was nineteen, pregnant, with a failed marriage... not a confidence-building situation.

"I was grateful for Frederick's attention. He seemed like a new beginning for me, but I guess he always knew my heart was elsewhere. He was good. He fed my insecurities and made me feel more and more dependent on him, blackmailing me really."

"God, I've always known he was an asshole, but...

I'm so sorry, Gina." Mila's voice surprises me. I almost forgot she was there.

"Don't be. Your friendship and your support helped me to find a way out of that doomed relationship. Seeing you freely dive into so many weird adventures showed me how I'm barely existing instead of living. Having you admire me, learn from me, assist me in building my business, helped me pick up the shards of my confidence and start therapy. That led to me recognizing the failure of my second marriage wasn't my fault. And the failure of the first one was a shared responsibility. Both realizations were key to setting me free." I chuckle sadly. "Well, with shackles of betrayal attached."

We fall silent. My mind, fatigued by the confession and the stress of the past hours and days, stills, interrupted only by the hum of the conversations, clang of dishes, thumps of footsteps and the lounge music.

Several times the kitchen door opens and sends my heart into overdrive, but it's only the servers with lunch orders.

Mila folds her hands in her lap as she digests what she's just learned. I might have lost my son, my livelihood, my love, and now probably my best friend. Loneliness sucks.

The door swings open and Massi appears with two plates. Seb walks behind and I can't see if he's carrying anything. It takes an indecent amount of time for them to reach us. Well, in my mind at least.

Massi nods and greets some patrons, not looking at me. When they reach the table, they both slide to their seats. It's unnerving to see how they move with similar cadence.

Sebastien places a bowl of salad in front of me and one in front of Mila.

"Mom, I made my burger medium rare." He picks up the bun. "Oh, we made you a salad because you don't eat burgers." He takes a bite, some of the garnish and sauce dripping down to his plate.

I look at the salad. It's beautiful, all ingredients I like. I'm touched and gutted at the same time. An outsider at a burger party. I pick up my fork.

"Would you be okay if Sebastien stayed with me for a day or two?" Massi asks, and I spear a tomato slice.

Mila chokes and excuses herself, rushing to the bathroom. Sebastien is looking at me with expectation and I can't find words. I can't agree with this. I know, rationally, this is a reasonable suggestion, but I can't agree.

Even though our relationship is rocky—or rather frozen at this point—I trust Massimo with my life. And Sebastien deserves to get to know his father. Yet I can't.

This feels like it's them against me. "Don't you

have to work?" I try to sound casual, but my voice is combative, failing to hide my frenzy.

"I can split duties with Lena, and Sebastien would like to watch the rush hour. But if you're not comfortable—"

"Seb, you've just arrived. I was looking forward to spending time with you. I missed you." I sound whiny and needy. Why do the words come out as a plea?

"You also lied to me." He drops his burger, lifts his chin and crosses his arms. "You made me spend a big part of my life with a stepfather who hates me. You told me my father was gone, never once explaining more. How could you? The least you can do is let me spend time with my *real* father."

Massi stretches his arm and squeezes Seb's shoulder. "Easy." It's an intervention of sorts, but it doesn't feel like he's on my side. Why would he be?

"Give me a moment." I stand up and stumble away, before they can manipulate me. To make me into a villain here, the inflexible mother. I barge into the bathroom and find Mila leaning against the sink, her back to the mirrors.

"Shit, I had to leave, sorry. I didn't feel like I should interfere," she says, and I slump against the wall, the cold tiles failing to cool me down.

"I can't let that happen, Mila. Five minutes in and

I'm an outcast already. Discarded." I swallow tears of despair. "And Sebastien is so mad at me."

"Gina, stop it right now. Stop making yourself a fucking victim here. You let fucking Frederick care for Seb—you can't deny Massi time with his son. You've done that already and look where it got you. I love you, Gina, but you need to own this mistake. Now."

"I lost Massi twice already. And now I'm going to lose my son. I'm not strong enough to let that happen."

"You're not thinking straight right now. Sebastien will cool down. He has the right to be mad at you. It's all too recent. But I can guarantee you *will* lose them both if you don't allow them to spend time together."

"Jesus. I've been so focused on the shit show of the grand revelation, I didn't have time to think about the next steps." I tilt my head and close my eyes, pathetically hoping I can reopen them in a new reality.

"I know, sweetie." Mila steps closer and rubs my arm. "But you need to do the right thing now."

I drop my head and count the patterns on the floor for a moment, hoping to calm my racing mind.

"Are you free tonight?" I ask Mila finally, looking at her in the mirror's reflection.

She raises her eyebrows and cocks her head.

"I have *custody* to negotiate, and then I need to get drunk with my best friend."

Mila gives me a hug and I find the courage to return to our table.

"Perhaps we can arrange for some time, but we need to talk, Sebastien. I know you're mad at me right now and you have legitimate reasons to be, but I'd like to explain." I try to focus on Sebastien, but I'm so painfully aware of Massi's eyes on me, it's hard. The mother and the lover in me fight for attention. Both men here deserve an explanation.

"I'll leave you to it, then." Massi starts to stand up.

"No, stay. Mom, I'm not ready to listen to you yet. I want to get to know Massi." He stands up as well, and when I see the two of them side by side I have to look away because it's too much.

Two people I disappointed. Two men I love. Two men who aren't ready to accept my apology.

Mila is right, they need time to cool down. "Okay."

"Yes." Sebastien pumps a fist in the air and I close my eyes, already feeling lonely.

"Where are your things?" Massi asks.

We find out Seb didn't really bring anything, but Massi immediately offers to take him shopping. With every new plan their enthusiasm grows, and my walls get thicker, isolating me further.

I remind myself it's only temporary, and that deep down I'm happy they are reunited. But the deep down is cluttered with the growing hysteria I struggle to hide.

As much as I'm trying to hold myself together, I burst into tears when the time to say goodbye comes.

"Jesus, Mom, it's two days." Sebastien rolls his eyes and hugs me briefly. Part of me knows this is his typical I-am-embarrassed-by-my-mother behavior that started two years ago, but part of me still blames Massi.

"I'll take good care of him," Massi says.

"I know. I just missed him so much and... anyway, have fun, and call me if you need anything." I pivot on my heel, almost losing my balance, and stumble away, leaving them at the table.

Mila joins me at the door. "It's early afternoon, but I'm happy to get started on those drinks."

* * *

We order cocktails in a small bistro near Casa Cassi, but not even the ever-positive Mila can lift my melancholy.

"You should focus on good news." Mila plays with her straw, stirring the ice in her mojito.

"And what would that be?" I wrap my arms around my shoulders and slouch deeper on the upholstered bench.

"The two of them hit it off. It could have been all kinds of awkward, but they took to each other well. And Sebastien has never had a father figure in his life aside from the ignorant and absent Frederick, so having one now is good." Mila takes a sip.

She is right. Absorbed by my jealousy, I haven't appreciated that Sebastien didn't fixate on not knowing his father for years, but rather dove right into it. And Massi put his anger aside and focused on the relationship with his newly discovered offspring.

Well, his anger was probably still aimed at me. And for all the right reasons. While I was consumed by fear and then jealousy, the two of them effortlessly started exploring the new dynamics of our family. *Our* family?

"Yet I still feel like an outcast. Like everyone has gained something today and I've lost." I hate how defeated I am.

"You'll feel better tomorrow. Today is tainted. I know it's not ideal that Frederick broke the news to Seb and that Massi had to find out this way—"

"That's my point though. I lost control over the situation and by default the right to demand their time, their forgiveness."

"Oh, please, stop with the fucking drama already. Do you really think, they will cast you out forever? You're Seb's mother, and Massi will get over himself, eventually. Shitty timing will not derail the future."

"It's my betrayal that will. Or already has. Mila, I've never felt this isolated, and I've been lonely most of my adult life."

"Okay, let's stop whining. We'll order another round and figure out how you can show them you love them. We'll fix everything." She gestures for the server to get us more drinks and looks at me with expectations.

I can't stop Massi and Seb from spending time with each other. It hurts I'm not with them, but I see how that is my fault. I know Seb will hear me eventually and hopefully understand why I acted the way I did. Hopefully even forgive me. But will Massi? Not only did I keep him from his son, but I also sabotaged his business.

And then it hits me. I can show him I didn't do that on purpose.

"I need to go." I grab my purse, throw two twenties on the table and kiss Mila's cheek before I shuffle out of the booth.

"What's going on?" She watches me with wide eyes.

"Sorry, we'll go out together soon, but I need to start fixing things."

"Gina? I didn't expect you," Bianca says and turns on her heel, so I follow her.

"I'm sorry I came unannounced, but I wanted to

talk to you."

When we enter her spacious kitchen she leans against the countertop and studies me for a moment. Under her scrutiny, I momentarily forget what I came for. But this woman practically supported my decision to leave Massi all those years ago, and I feel a strange need to explain everything to her.

I swallow hard. "You have a grandson."

She raises an eyebrow, but otherwise stays eerily still for what seems like the longest seconds of my life.

"May I offer you anything to drink? Coffee or lemonade?"

I was so ready to pour my heart out that her formal hospitality throws me off. "I-I'll have a glass of water. Thank you."

Click. Click. Click. Her heels echo through the large room as she steps around the island to get two glasses and fill them. She gestures toward the large glass door and I follow her to the deck.

We sit down, and relief swamps me at the realization that, with no drama, she's created a space for me to say my piece. Bianca Cassinetti is scary, but she isn't a bad person.

In what feels like a single breath, I tell her everything. How we lost the baby, how Massi reacted to it, how I escaped my grief to California and what happened afterward.

I explain what transpired with the dinner event, how Frederick tricked me and how stupidly I believed he was trying to help while all the evidence of my life with him spoke against it.

And I tell her about Sebastien finding his father.

Bianca listens to me in complete silence. Not asking questions, not interrupting with any gesture of shock, disgust or support. I don't expect her to forward my words to Massi. That's not why I came. I don't even know why I felt the need to confess to her, but now I'm happy I'm here. I feel lighter after letting it all out.

"So my grandson is with Massi now?" she asks. "Are you going to stay on the East Coast?"

Her question shocks me. In my mind I haven't considered anything beyond the next two days when Seb returns from his father's. What if Massi demands shared custody? In two years Sebastien will be eighteen, but in the meantime do I have a right to keep them apart?

"I haven't thought that far." The lightness I felt a moment ago evaporates.

"I'd love it if you stayed. I'm looking forward to meeting my grandson. I always thought you were going to trap my son, but I see now you set him free back then."

I'm so relieved she grasped my motivation, tears push into my eyes.

"That's not the way Massi sees things. I screwed up."

"But your intentions were good and he will recognize that in time. But if you leave again, there is no chance for the two of you. I mean, this might be a very selfish request on my part, but stay for the summer."

"I have to sell the house to settle my parents' debt. I can't pay for my condo in LA and for the house here. Let alone the fees for Mom's assisted living facility. I don't have any work here anymore." I explain my situation.

"Is the financial consideration the only barrier?" she asks. I recall Massi's donation to the senior home and a bout of apprehension sweeps through me. I can't financially depend on this family.

"It's quite a barrier." I try to sound firm.

"Why, of course it is, but I ask if that's the only one. I think my son loves you, and you're the mother of his son. There are layers upon layers of history between the two of you. Where is your heart, Gina? Is the financial barrier the only reason you can't stay here?"

I came here to be honest. I blink away my tears. "Yes."

Her smile is warm and conspiratorial and I don't know what to think about it, but somehow I know that after nearly two decades, I might have found a true ally in the Cassinetti family.

Chapter Twenty-Five

Gina

After a sleepless night, I wake up to a sunny day and want to get a head start on packing the house. But as I drink my coffee Sebastien calls and my plans screech to a halt.

"Mom, I was thinking, why don't we stay here for the summer? Massi said I can work with him at the restaurant. My first summer job. Isn't that cool?" If I wasn't sitting I would have sunk into the chair.

I hear Massi's voice in the background and then hushed words, and Massi's voice comes in.

"Sorry, Blue, I wanted to discuss the idea with you first. Make sure you're okay with it."

He called me Blue. My heart expands in my chest,

but then I remember he's probably just being nice to get me to agree.

"Can we talk about this tomorrow when you drop him off?" I will my voice to be level, but it comes out as if someone's strangling me. Something is. I'm dying here alone, missing my son who I haven't seen properly in the longest time, and yearning for his father who is being *nice* to me.

And my stupid heart aside, I don't want to tell Massi over the phone that I can't afford two households, not even for another week, let alone two months.

"Sure, of course, I'll bring him after the lunch rush hour so I can get back to the restaurant before dinner." He sounds distant, business-like.

Why is this so hard? Why can't I simply enjoy them bonding? Perhaps I'm just used to not sharing him at all, so it's an adjustment. It was so hard to leave him with Danielle and see him only a couple of times these past few weeks, and now when he's finally here... I don't know. What's wrong with me?

Having Sebastien spending time with a man who hates me while I love him is difficult.

"Seb wants to talk to you." Massi passes the phone without saying goodbye, and Sebastien launches into recounting his day with such excitement my heart is bursting. I'm happy for him and so sad at the same time. But the sadness is purely selfish, so I try to file it away.

After I hang up, I sit. And sit. Motionless seems to be the best way to absorb everything. Of course I won't refuse Sebastien working with Massi this summer. What I don't know is how I'll pay for it. I have to find clients here.

Energized by the idea I pick up my phone, eager to call my former clients on the West Coast who have restaurants here to see if they may need an assessment, or perhaps if they can recommend me. Then I remember it's too early to call California, so I take a shower instead.

Sweatpants and a T-shirt are more appropriate for my mood, but I decide to fake it until I make it. After a long shower I blow dry my hair and pull a dress from my closet. I eye the jeans, but decide I have to be all business now.

Before I even get dressed, my phone rings. An unknown number?

"Gina Accardi speaking."

"Hello, Ms. Accardi, this is Lionel Brown. I own a small bistro in Brooklyn and I plan to open a new location soon. I hear you're currently on the East Coast and I was wondering if we can meet. I need someone with your experience to set everything up. The new location is much larger. And if you could coordinate the opening that would be great, if you're available of course."

"Mr. Brown, I happen to be available. May I ask where you heard about me?"

"Oh, from Bianca Cassinetti. She spoke so highly of you, and knowing her son is the best in the city I'm assuming I can get some good counsel from you."

I smile to myself. Of course, Bianca was smart enough not to offer me money, but a business opportunity? I can't refuse that. I ask Mr. Brown to send me his website and tell him I need a couple of days to scout his business before we meet. We talk for a few minutes, so I can get a better understanding of his needs and explain to him what my focus is.

I shoot a text to Mila and get several dancing emojis back. I open my laptop and type Mr. Brown's bistro's website into the browser, but before it loads, my phone rings again.

Another restaurant. This one is a big fish.

And then another.

And two more.

Bianca Cassinetti has been busy raising my profile. Or perhaps a lot of people owe her a favor. This may be a very unorthodox word of mouth campaign, but I know I can prove myself, and none of these businesses will regret hiring me.

I call Mila and we agree to meet later that afternoon.

Sebastien sent me a few pictures from Central Park, and then of a dish he made himself. Through his pictures, I see how important Massi could be in his life. I've not seen my son so excited for the longest time. And I can't help but feel grateful that the two most important men in my life are bonding.

Mila was right—things look different the next day. Though I do still feel a little sorry for myself. Sorry I'm not there sharing those moments with them. But at least it seems Seb is no longer pissed at me. Or maybe he's just trying to placate me so we stay here longer.

As I get ready to meet with Mila, my phone beeps with a message. She has changed the location of our meeting. The address is vaguely familiar, but my mind is too distracted by all new clients and the new reality of my family life. And the almost extinguished flame of hope that Massi and I might work things out.

As my Uber comes to a stop, all my thoughts halt. What the hell is Mila doing here? What was she thinking?

The driver clears his throat to remind me I haven't exited his car in a timely fashion. As I set my foot to the ground on a familiar street in Tribeca, I can't figure out what's going on.

Why would Mila suggest we meet at Modigliani's?

The place looks deserted. Perhaps they haven't opened yet for the evening? Did I mistake the address? I step closer and pull out my phone to call Mila when the door opens.

I look up and flinch when my eyes meet with the icy look on Frederick's face. "Come in, Gina, we're waiting for you." He steps aside.

We?

The room is dim and I have to blink a few times. With the blinds drawn, no daylight enters the premises. During all the years I spent with Frederick, I was never physically scared of him.

Until now.

He always had me where he needed me. Doubting myself. But right this minute, there is no doubt in my mind that he has the ability to hurt me. Though he has said nothing, nor has he made any threatening moves. It's pure instinct.

Then I see Mila.

She has duct tape over her mouth, her eyes wild with horror. Her arms are behind her. The bastard must have bound her.

A thousand thoughts scream for attention in my head, and the only words that come out are: "What's going on?"

"What's going on, my dear Gina? I don't like the turn our relationship took. The negative coverage impacted me as expected, so I need you to correct it. Isn't crisis management one of your specialties, my dear?" His tone sends goosebumps down my spine.

He locks the door and ambles casually to sit across from Mila. Crossing one leg over the other, he smiles at me, waiting. Dressed smartly in a dark three-piece suit, including a handkerchief in his breast pocket, he's the picture of a gentleman. A soul of evil.

"Let Mila go. She has nothing to do with this." I find my voice. Just barely.

"Don't worry, I won't harm Mila. I will take care of her, feed her—mind you, feed her very well, given my talents in the kitchen—nothing will happen to her. But, as you can see, the place is deserted. I've had no reservations for a week now. Thanks to you and your pitiful little scheme to save Massimo fucking Cassinetti."

I always attributed my inability to think rationally and this man's complete domination over my thoughts and feelings to my own lack of self-confidence. Suddenly, in the barely lit room, listening to his cold, calculated, entitled voice, I discover that I've spent a big part of my life with a psychopath.

The realization shivers through me, leaving me oddly confident. As if, in this moment, all my self-doubt is erased.

"What do you want from me, Frederick? Haven't you caused enough problems already?"

The bastard chuckles. "I don't cause problems, Gina. I only work to get what is rightfully mine. It's my duty in life—my vocation—to forge perfection, to create the best flavors. I've dedicated my life to searching for the best culinary experience. I'm the best chef in the world. It's not about feeding people, it's not about getting the fucking star. It's about the ultimate experience that only I can facilitate. It's my purpose. *My* purpose.

"Not one of those wannabes like Massimo. Or the other assholes. It was easy to get rid of some of them. I poisoned one, I scared most of them. Here a sleeve caught on fire, there someone slipped and broke their hip. Eliminating potential competition used to be easy. But people got suspicious, so I had to work harder, be smarter. Over the years, you helped me many times. All the mishaps happening at your client's places? You should be grateful. You developed the crisis management capability thanks to me.

"But Massimo always rises from the ashes like a fucking phoenix. I stole his SoHo location all those years ago, I sent health inspectors to his place, I paid a cook to set it on fire."

With every word, my newly-found confidence weakens. The poison of his words, of his actions, is almost impossible to accept. The realization of what he's truly capable of squeezes at my stomach like a merciless vise.

I glance at Mila, who is frowning and wiggling her shoulders as if she is trying to shake off whatever is tying her. It doesn't seem to disturb Frederick.

"Yet, the man doesn't scare easily. I fucking stole his wife and son. And you ran back to him, to help him achieve even more than he managed before. I endured life with you, you frigid ice queen. You owe me. You will help me get back on top." His nostrils flare.

Mila has stilled. The man is deranged, and while I'm shaking all over, a clear thought penetrates my terrified mind. I have to cooperate to increase our chances of getting out of here.

"What do you want me to do?" I don't know if it's my trembling voice or the words themselves, but he smiles. It's his usual smile, and I don't understand how I'm only now seeing the true menace behind it.

Something glistens in his hands and I realize he's holding a cleaver knife. I gasp and Mila whimpers.

"I want you to call all the bloggers and media and tell them you made up all that shit about me."

I stare at him, understanding the ugly despair behind his actions. Unlike all the vile, coldly calculated actions he's just recounted, desperation drives him now.

In a brief moment that follows, I think about Massi

and Seb, about all the decisions I've made out of fear, or because I misjudged the circumstances. I think of all this man has taken from me, regardless of how much I let him. And while I'm scared for Mila, and for myself, I push my fear aside, and an odd sense of empowerment settles over me.

"Can I sit down?" I ask. I clench my fists a few times. My palms are damp and a trickle of sweat runs down my spine, but I will not let him win. Not this time. Not anymore.

"Of course, Gina. Forgive my lack of hospitality." He speaks sweetly, and I'm not sure if he's mocking me or if he has lost his mind completely. He walks around and stands behind Mila.

I take a seat where I can see her, and one glance confirms she is tied to the chair at her waist and her ankles.

Frederick fidgets behind her back and releases her hands, but before either of us can react he grips her wrist, pushes it against the table and smoothly slices the cleaver over it.

I scream. Mila goes pale, but when I look down there is no blood. He feigned the cut, sweeping the blade barely above her skin. My heart pounds in my temples as my eyes meet his. I'm flooded with so much hatred right now I can barely see straight.

He stands between me and Mila, the knife over her

trembling hand. "You better start dialing, and make it believable."

Does he really think this would work? As if he could hear my thought, he adds, "Or you can leave and take care of the business while I wait here with Mila. How long is it going to take? Perhaps a pretty little finger for each day?"

"I'll start calling now." I pull out my phone with shaking hands. "I need to use my laptop where I have a spreadsheet with all the contacts and social media handles."

I lift my bag, waiting for his consent. I don't need the laptop, but I'm trying to buy time. For what, I'm not sure.

What if he kills us? Mila doesn't deserve this. At least my son has a father now.

A mother bear awakens within me. I left my son with this lunatic so many times. Thoughts scramble wildly in my mind, not helping the situation.

"Okay, get your laptop out, but don't try anything funny."

I pull my computer out and open it. I will my fingers to stop trembling and somehow I type.

"What's taking so long? Do you need an incentive?" Frederick asks casually and Mila weeps.

I look over my laptop and see that he is holding the knife over her pinky.

With shaking hands, I put an ear bud in and start a call while keeping my eyes on his. How have I never seen the malice in those eyes? Was I so focused on my own inner struggles I missed what was right in front of me?

I talk, at first tripping over my words, but then getting the hang of it, leaving a voicemail where I even at the end offer a free dining experience with Frederick himself. This seems to placate him enough and he walks around to sit across from me.

But there is no reprieve as he grabs Mila's other hand, holding it like a piece of meat he's ready to carve. Her shoulders shake violently.

But he moved away from me, and I should try to take advantage of his comfortable belief that I'm not a worthy opponent.

"Okay, most of my contacts prefer a text communication. Let me shoot a message to foodiegoddess as she is the one trending currently and she usually responds immediately. She would also get something out within minutes, and it would get the others more intrigued."

He narrows his eyes and I'm certain he sees through my bullshit, but then he nods. "What are you waiting for, text her." At least Frederick has never cared about social media enough to get my game.

I run my fingers over the screen as quickly as possible. "And now we wait," I say, but he swings his cleaver and hits so hard the table cracks. Mila screams through the tape and I jump up, yelling.

I want to help her, but when my gaze lands on her hand, I realize there are only wooden splinters, no blood. Again, Frederick toyed with us. Thank God. He hit the table, splitting it and scaring us to keep me in line.

"I'll keep contacting the others." I lift my phone. By the third call, my story is reasonably believable. With the appropriate amount of remorse and apology, I tell them the *true story,* including an invitation for a free lunch at Frederick's for them or their followers.

As I'm about to attempt the fourth call, the police burst into the restaurant. Everything happens so fast that I barely register the action, but minutes later Mila is free and we hug and cry hysterically.

Frederick is taken away as I speak to a couple of officers, giving my statement, and Mila sits at a table where a young paramedic tries to assess her, but is failing miserably as she insists she is okay. Neither of us is okay, but we are holding up.

Even as I automatically recount the events, I feel strangely detached. As if all this was happening to someone else. As if I was the person watching while my life with a psychopath unraveled on a screen. Just an audience, not a willing—fuck, *willing*—participant.

I answer the questions on autopilot. And when it's

finally over I realize that a normal person would call their loved ones. But who do I call? I don't think Massi wants my emergency call, and I don't want to worry Seb.

As the new level of loneliness descends on me, Mila finishes speaking to her officer and dashes over.

"We need to make the calls to stop that story." Only Mila can survive an ordeal like this and immediately think of damage control.

"There is no story. I pretend dialed the whole time." I shrug. My body shakes and I stumble and sit down.

"I thought something was amiss when you messaged foodiegoddess. I've never heard of them." While I'm boneless in the chair, Mila is bouncing around like the Duracell Bunny. We both might need medical attention after all.

I smile at her wearily. "I texted 911."

Chapter Twenty-Six

Massi

We reach the open entrance to Modigliani's, several uniformed men milling around the place. I spot Blue and Mila, embracing. My knees almost give out as a wave of relief washes through me. Fuck, when Mila texted I immediately jumped into a cab.

For a moment I regretted that Seb was with me because I wanted to shield him from this, but even with only twenty-four hours of parenting under my belt I know I can't protect him from everything, and I can't set him aside when it's inconvenient having him around.

"Mom." He rushes to her. I see the surprise in her eyes as she embraces our son.

Mila smiles at me and walks over. She looks disheveled and fatigued, but buzzes with enough energy to light up the city. Adrenaline probably.

"I didn't want her to be alone," she says.

"You're a good friend. What the hell happened? Why were you even here?" I look around the place that holds so many memories from my first years of apprenticeship. Not much has changed here. The place is still heavy with fucked-up feelings.

Mila tells me what happened and I want to kill the fucker. He's hurt my family so many times. My family. This is the first time I think of Blue and Seb as my family.

"Mom, let go." Sebastien wiggles out of Blue's embrace. Her face is awash with tears, but she releases him and our eyes meet.

Fuck, I wish I could hug her. Hold her and tell her everything will be all right, but I can't. Our look stirs up all the feelings in me, all the love I don't want to feel for her anymore. So I glance at Seb again.

"She was very brave. She saved my life," Mila says and steps away.

Frederick is a sick bastard. I've known that since I met him. Since he first laid eyes on Blue, he was trouble. And she trusted him. She trusted him more than she did me. I'm so conflicted right now.

A part of me wants to take my family home, but the

much louder part reminds me she chose him over me. Even after she knew she was having my child, she divorced me and married him. Fuck. I count my breathing a few times before I approach them.

"I'm glad you're okay." I sound like a robot. It's not that I'm not honest. I am glad. It's just having a normal, civil conversation is so hard when so many unresolved issues hang over our heads.

"I was hoping Seb could come home with me. I don't want to be alone." Her voice breaks and she sniffles.

Seeing her this vulnerable makes me physically sick. Again, my need to protect her, to help, is stronger than my own hurt over her actions. But then I spot the corner table where we dined with Frederick all those years ago, and a wave of regret washes over me. Blue was pregnant that night. And I didn't like that. Fuck.

"But Massi and I have plans," Seb protests. "You robbed me of sixteen years with him. I'll be back with you tomorrow."

"Seb, I just had a really shitty day. I'd really appreciate your support and your company. And we need to talk."

"Well, I'm not ready to talk. You can't force me to go with you. You kept things from me." Sebastien rakes his fingers through his hair.

"Don't talk to your mother like that." Instinctively I

step closer to Blue, as if protecting her physically. I'm an asshole here because I'm mad at Seb for not giving Blue what I'm unwilling to offer. While wishing the whole time that I could take her home.

Fuck.

"Whoa, you've been a father for one day and you're bossing me around already?" Sebastien turns and walks out.

"Sebastien," we both say at the same time.

He turns, unimpressed. "I'll wait for you outside, Mom."

"Ha, teenagers." Mila snorts.

Blue exhales what sounds like years of tension and I find myself at a loss here. I don't know what right I have to reprimand Sebastien because I don't really know him. I don't know how to parent a child, and I'm expected to parent a teenager. Shit.

I'm mad at him for not wanting to do what I'm not willing to offer. But as much as I still harbor resentment for Blue's decision to never tell me about Seb, I don't want him to feel the same.

She has raised a fine young man, based on my impression of him over the last day, and she doesn't deserve this. Or perhaps she does. I need to get away from her as quickly as possible. She is confusing me.

"Thank you for standing up for me," she whispers. We're both staring at the door where Seb disappeared.

"Have you decided about the summer?" I say, again sounding like a robot. The colder I treat her, the easier it is to focus on the fact that she chose Frederick.

She sighs. "Massi, Frederick just threatened to cut off Mila's fingers. Could we talk about this tomorrow?"

"Sebastien is really looking forward to it." I can't let her take him away from me.

"Well, for future reference, if your plans impact me, it would be nice and respectful to discuss them with me before you fucking get him all excited."

She turns and walks away, leaving me feeling like an asshole. And I can't even blame her.

Gina

The drive home is fast but feels much longer, filled with tension and Sebastien's resentment. Unlike other occasions when he acted up, this time is filled with lost time I can't give him back. But I don't have it in me to explain to him why I made choices that impacted him this negatively. God, I wish I could rewind and take it all back.

Frederick keeps spreading pain even when he's not around. Weariness covers me with a heavy blanket even before we arrive home. It's when we step out of the car that I realize Sebastien has never met his grandmother.

Fuck. I was going to prepare my mom, but there was no time. And in his current mood, the timing can't be shittier. *My life* can't be shittier.

"Sebastien, could we sit on the porch and talk for a minute?"

He looks at me, and even though he doesn't roll his eyes I know he's doing it internally. He flops down on the top step, resting his elbows on his knees.

I take a seat beside him. I want to wrap my arm around his shoulder and pull him closer. Hell, I need him to hug me. He's *the man* in my life and I crave his support after the ordeal with Frederick today. I don't deserve it, I get that, but God I need a break.

"I have several leads for new clients here in New York." Hopefully starting with the good news will make him happy. Selfishly, I also hope it gets me a better starting point for the conversation I wish we didn't need to have. One I wish I didn't have to put him through.

He doesn't react at first. How long will it take to truly mend our relationship?

But then he faces me, a sparkle of excitement in his eyes. "We're staying?"

"Well, you got that summer job here, so we should stay until your school starts again."

He smiles and hugs me. Oh, how I needed this connection. I know I'm the parent, the protector, but having his arms around me makes me feel safe. It's the calmest moment I've had in days and my eyes well up.

Even as I try to maintain my composure, the tension snaps and I start to cry. "I'm so sorry, Seb. I really am sorry." My words are swallowed by my tears and Sebastien stiffens, probably unsure how he should react in this new dynamic between us.

"Geez, Mom, chillax," he says finally, and my cry turns into laughter. A sniffly laugh, but it feels good that he's opened up the door to reconciliation. I never thought *geez, Mom* could sound so sweet. But in this fucked up situation I'll take it.

We sit there in silence, my head on his shoulders. I want to explain my actions to him, but it takes me a few long moments to find the words.

"Massi and I were very young when we got married, and we didn't do a good job of it. When I moved to LA, I found out I was pregnant, but I had reasons to believe Massi didn't want a family. I wanted to protect you from having a father who didn't want you.

"I was in a terrible place back then and as much as I hate to admit it, Frederick took advantage. I know that now, but back then it felt like he was saving me. I believed I was setting your father free. He was about to open his first restaurant."

"But you didn't give him a chance to reject me." Sebastien jumps up, and losing his support I almost topple over. He grabs the railing and stares at me. "It wasn't only your decision. He would have been a great father."

I almost snap we don't know that but stop myself. It would be a low blow, and I haven't sunk that far yet.

"I'm sorry. I thought I did what was best for everyone."

"You really thought a restaurant was more important to him? And frankly, child support would have been better than life with fucking Fred. I hate you so much right now."

I bite my lip and drop my head. What else can I do? I can't tell him about all the horrible things Massi and I said to each other after we lost the baby. I can't shed that light on his father.

"Remember how that boy in your school got arrested for stealing something and you were surprised because you'd have never thought he was capable of such a thing? And later we learned about his life and how his parents neglected him?" He stares at me with a frown, waiting to see where I'm going with the story. "We talked about it and I was so proud of you in the end, because do you remember what you said?"

He exhales, and his Adam's apple bobs. "I said that desperate people sometime make bad choices."

He is still very mad and disappointed, but his features soften. He looks around as if he wants to run away, and I realize he must feel trapped. In this situation, but also literally in this place because he's never been here and can't very well go hide.

"Seb, I love you. You can be mad as long as you need, but I can't turn back time and make different choices. I hope we can find a way to move forward."

He paces the length of the porch a few times and then he looks up. "I hate that I have no choice in this. I'm not forgiving you. Not yet, anyway."

A sliver of relief pierces through me. How a small word like *yet* can make such a tremendous difference, stop the bleeding, so the wounds can begin to heal. Or fester, but I'm hoping for the former. Even though I know hope can be harmful by itself.

"Thank you, son."

And as if the day wasn't eventful enough, we enter the house so my sixteen-year-old son can meet his grandmother for the first time.

Chapter Twenty-Seven

Massi

"Come on, buddy, we have to leave in twenty." I shake Seb's shoulder and he grunts. "You wanted to come with me, so get your lazy ass up."

Today, Sebastien is coming with me to the market for the first time. To my surprise he's been working really hard, but that doesn't mean he enjoys all of it. Sometimes I fear he's motivated by his need to please me. To get my approval. Fuck, it's shitty that he never got that from his stepfather.

It's been four weeks since Frederick was arrested. I don't know or care what the charges are, but it seems like evidence of foul play has been found to confirm he was instrumental in *accidents* at many restaurants, including the fire in mine.

I wake up at night sweating, images of Frederick threatening Gina and Mila causing me to panic. I don't care as much about him burning down my first restaurant, but him stealing my family is something I can't forget, or forgive.

From a few comments Sebastien has made here and there, life with that psycho was less than ideal. Warm and cold. Perfect and horrible. Unpredictable.

I'm tortured by the need to make it better for both of them. For her. To overcompensate for all they've been through. But resentment nags at me every time I want to make a move. Because despite it all, she chose to live with him. To raise my son with him.

One month ago, I became a father. I try to focus on that. Focus on the here and now and hesitantly on our future. Sebastien is a wonderful young man. He has my drive, talent and interest and luckily none of my temper. He's kind and pragmatic, like his mother.

His mother. Blue continues to be the bane of my existence. I'm stuck in a weird spot between hating her and yearning for her. I wish she was gone, but then that would mean Seb would be gone, too.

I can't stop thinking of her and hate that even more. Sebastien connects us forever. But there is no us. And forever is too long to hate her. Still, I don't seem capable of moving past that burning feeling of blame and disappointment.

I hit the button on the blender and the sound finally gets Seb out of his room. His hair is messy, his eyes still half closed, but he dragged himself out of bed.

"No shower?" I ask and pour the smoothies into portable cups.

He takes his drink from me, groans in response and shuffles to the elevator. I pat his shoulder, feeling equally proud he's doing it and sorry I didn't let him sleep.

Two hours later we're pulling to the curb at Casa Cassi. By the time we hit the market Sebastien woke up fully and enjoyed himself somewhat, but then he promptly fell asleep in the car on the way to the restaurant.

His head slid to my shoulder and I didn't want to wake him up, enjoying the silent connection. How was it to hold him when he was a baby? The thought propels a wave of anger. Fuck.

I ruffle his hair to wake him up and we enter the kitchen through the back door.

"Let me make us a second breakfast to get some energy." I pat his back.

"I'm having a coffee." He looks at me with teenage contempt and I bite the inside of my mouth to stop myself from laughing.

"Good morning," Lena greets us. "Let him have coffee, Massi, I doubt he'll like the taste. Phillip is up front. Why don't you get me an espresso too, Seb?"

I watch him leave, grinning. That seems to be the theme of the month. I either grin like an idiot, basking in the delight of this young man discovering life around me, or scowling, remembering his mother took away so many years with him. The pendulum is swinging, unable to level.

"Dad, look at this." Sebastien runs back, his face full of excitement. Phillip follows on his heels, grinning like a Cheshire cat.

Sebastien waves a newspaper in his hands. He drops it on the counter in front of me, but I can't make myself look there.

This is the first time he's called me dad.

The feeling that stirs in me is warm and new and so intense that tears build behind my eyes.

I'm not sure if in his excitement he even realized what he said because he's looking at me with expectation, tapping his finger on the paper. I realize Sebastien's is not the only pair of eyes on me, so I look down.

It's the *Sunday Times*.

Chef Cassinetti Perfects the Art of Fine Dining.

Under Catira Radamesh's byline, the article first gives an account of the day I cooked for her and then quotes several prominent New Yorkers praising my work. Lena cranes her neck to read. I only skim the words, unable to concentrate.

Sebastien bounces with excitement, scrolling on his phone. "It's already trending on several cool sites. The quotes are getting picked up."

"And I got a call from a producer who would like to include you in a documentary about iconic chefs in New York. He's coming to have dinner sometime this week." Phillip keeps grinning.

"Dad, say something. Mom did a great job. I mean, your reviews have always been amazing, but this shit is a real endorsement." He continues calling me Dad. And boasts with pride.

For me and for his mother. It makes me feel oddly conflicted. This is a moment we should enjoy as a family. But we don't because she took that away from us.

"Let me go and read it in peace." I grab the papers. "And get me that coffee before the deliveries pour in. Lena, give me five and let's confirm today's special." I hurry away, feeling like a bit of an asshole. Okay, a full-blown asshole, but Phillip and Lena are used to it.

I don't want Sebastien to see the contempt I harbor for his mother, so I'd rather show him this dickhead side of me.

I take a seat behind my desk and read the article. She did that. She did that for me.

I pull my phone and shoot her a message: *I read the Sunday Times. Thank you. Seb is very proud.*

The response comes back immediately: *The least I could do.*

A knock on the door saves me from spiraling into a place I'm not ready to access.

"Here is your coffee, boss." Lena places a small cup on my desk. "What fish did you get today?"

"Sea bass." I lean back in my chair, the newspaper haunting me.

"Mediterranean spicy pan-seared? With couscous?" Lena sits down on a chair across from me.

I nod. "Do we have enough eggplant for that?"

She makes a note. "Yes. It's too hot for a soup, but I got fennel, so we can have a nice light salad."

"Almonds, oranges and goat cheese?"

She scribbles down everything and stands up. "On it, boss."

I stare at the headline and fight the need to run and talk to Gina. Lena clears her throat. I didn't even realize she was still standing here.

"Remember how I mentioned my late husband and you asked if I loved him? I never did, but I married him and stayed with him for what I believed was an excellent reason. My daughter. I stayed with him because I wanted her to have a better life than what I could provide for her by myself. So I suffered and plowed through. What I did is the definition of being a gold digger."

"No, you wanted a good life for your child. Gold diggers are selfish," I say, already sensing where the story is going.

"I'm telling you the story because if Phillip only saw the surface value without giving me a chance to explain my faulty rationale, we wouldn't be together today. He would have assumed I'm a selfish gold digger because all the evidence pointed there.

"You loved that woman once. Follow your heart and give her a chance to explain, to uncover that invisible layer of her truth. One that might have been misguided but was probably the best she could have done at the time."

Lena's words hit my stomach, swimming there undigested. In all the sulking, blaming and regretting, I've never asked Blue why.

"What's the point? I still can't forgive her. I can't get back the lost time." The words are harsh in my throat, coming out around the lump that's been lodged there for weeks now.

"At least try to understand her point of view. You owe it to yourself and to your son."

I close my eyes and Lena sneaks out, but another knock prevents me from contemplating her words.

"Dad, I'm mad at her as well. I was, I mean. She made a mistake. A big one, but she wanted to protect you. And me."

I frown. Fuck, how have I never realized Seb might need to talk about this. I'm a selfish bastard.

"Sit down." I fold the paper and put it away. "Things are complicated between me and your mother."

"Really?" he deadpans. "Don't give me a speech about how it's not my fault and blah, blah, blah. I know it's not. Mom told me you didn't want children back then, or that's what she believed. Did you?"

I puff out the air in my cheeks. "I was only three years older than you are now, Seb. We lost a baby, and I was stupid and relieved I could focus on my work. But that didn't mean I would reject you if I knew about you."

"She didn't know that. She wanted to set you free of any obligation."

The fucking irony of it all. I pushed her to believe I didn't want him. I recall the night I told her how I regretted not starting a family with her and how she bolted with some silly excuse. She tried to tell me something and I told her to take time before she explained what bothered her. Never did I imagine it was this huge.

Would I have handled myself differently if she told me before the fiasco with the dining event? Would I have given her the benefit of the doubt if she told me while I wasn't mad and disappointed?

"Look, Dad, I have three more weeks of summer break left and then we go back to LA when school starts. I've always dreamed about having a cool dad like some of my friends have. One that cares about me and involves me in his life. But I'll stay with Mom. I can't leave her alone."

My son. Smarter than me, for sure. The realization that I only have three weeks left with him settles like spoiled milk in my stomach.

Avoiding a conversation with Gina is no longer an option. I'm not losing my child again.

"Thank you for talking to me, buddy. Let's go help Lena. We have work to do."

He smiles. "So you'll talk to Mom and figure this out with her?"

I nod and ruffle his hair. "Get to work now."

After the lunch rush we take the town car to my mother's for a quick visit. As we fight upstream against traffic, Seb challenges me to a mobile game he likes. I only started playing a few weeks ago and I must admit I'm getting hooked.

I win a round.

"Damn it, I never should have taught you," he grumbles. "You're screwing up my score."

"Language, young man." I nudge his shoulder.

He rolls his eyes, unimpressed.

"What are you going to do with the money you earn this summer?" I ask.

"I'll watch the flight prices and get a ticket to come and visit you." His fingers and eyes don't leave the screen, skillfully getting to the next level.

His words bring me joy but also emphasize our impossible situation. Or is it only impossible for me? "I'll pay for your flight any time you want."

"I wish we could live together."

His casual admission feels like a spear in my intestines. If I don't have an ulcer after this summer, I might live forever.

After Gina agreed to stay for the summer, I hoped... Well, I'm not exactly sure what I hoped for. But I certainly didn't let myself think as far as the beginning of the school year.

As we arrive at my mother's, the situation continues festering inside me.

"Here is my favorite grandson." Mom envelopes Seb in a hug and ignores me. Ever since he showed up in our lives I've been replaced, but I don't mind. She's always wanted a grandchild, and while the circumstances are not ideal I want her to enjoy her time with him as much as possible.

"Gran, I'm your only grandchild." He wiggles out of her strangling hold and strolls into the kitchen. Without waiting, he opens the fridge and pours himself a lemonade. Funny how quickly he became at home here.

"Get some for your father, Seb," Mom chirps. She actually fucking chirps her words. If the hospitality transgression was reversed, I'd have gotten a head smack.

"Would you like some as well, Gran?"

"No, I'm good. I only make that sweet stuff for my boys." She pats his back. He's already taller than she is. "I got something for you."

She leaves the kitchen for a moment and returns with a sheet of paper. "These are good high schools in New York. I made some preliminary calls and they would have you, should you decide to transfer."

He looks at the list and frowns. "But—"

"Mom, I don't think this is something we need your help with. The decision is Gina's and mine."

"Yeah, Gran, clearly *I* have nothing to say about it." Seb rolls his eyes and slides the list across the counter to read it.

"Darling, why don't you take the list and your lemonade out to the patio, we'll join you in a minute."

My mother's nostrils flare. It's almost imperceptible because her face is still composed, but I know her. She's about to voice an opinion I don't want to hear.

"Sure, Gran, I'll go outside so you can discuss my future and I'll pretend I don't know about it." His attitude falls just short of flipping my mom off as he leaves, shaking his head.

As soon as Seb slides the glass door closed, my mom whips around. This time, her nostrils throb. "What are you doing?"

"I can ask you the same thing, Mom. Stop getting involved. How do you think Gina would feel if she knew you're manipulating Seb behind her back?"

"That's beside the point right now. What have you been doing? I've organized clients for her so she stays the summer and we're only halfway through, and the for-sale sign went up again in front of her parents' house. I gave you two months to fix things with her. What have you done?"

Dumbfounded. That's me right now. "You got her clients?"

"That's what you focus on? How on Earth have I brought up a clueless man like you?" She stretches her arms upward and rolls her eyes. "Seriously, Massi, I've just gained a grandson and I'm not giving him up because of your stupid pride."

What the hell? "Mom, he has friends in LA. He grew up there. You can't meddle in their lives like this."

"So you want them to leave?" She puts her hands on her hips, her lips pursed.

"Of course not." I scratch my nape. "But this is not the way to go about it."

"No, the way to go about it would have been you using the time I bought for you trying to win the woman over again. Tell me one thing, Massi, and consider it carefully. If there wasn't a child involved, your son, would you be just perfectly happy if she left?"

I open my mouth. And close it. It's not a fair question because I can't imagine my life without Seb anymore, but at the same time, I know... deep down I know.

I can almost feel the regret just thinking about her leaving. I refuse to say it out loud, but my mother smiles as if she's just hit a jackpot.

Her eyes sparkle. "Exactly." She turns and joins Seb on the patio.

Chapter Twenty-Eight

Gina

The houses on either side of the road swim in my vision, so I close my eyes. The drilling pain weakened just slightly after I took the painkillers, but the headache is now joined by dizziness. Perhaps I've taken too many.

My days with Sebastien are so limited that I don't want to spend an evening in bed with a headache. I haven't had one in a while, but here I am in a cab on the way home, worried that bed is the only place I'll spend my evening.

Massi is dropping Seb off in ten minutes and I'm running late. My mom moved to the senior residence two weeks ago and I don't want Seb to wait for me, or Massi to arrive at the house before me. Somehow it makes me feel like Massi would win parenting points.

I wish he would talk to me. We need to discuss what happens next. It's quite clear Seb wants to stay involved with his father and his family.

"He texted me to say thank you." I told Mila earlier today as I folded the *Times* with the article I orchestrated.

"Stubborn prick," Mila muttered.

We were in a busy coffee shop, discussing our clients and sipping espresso. In the absence of an office, and since Mila has refused to commute to the Bronx for our meetings, we have been frequenting cafes to work.

"It's been a month and the extent of our interaction is related to the logistics of taking care of Sebastien. Mila, I'm dying inside. I lost him. He hasn't even given me a chance to explain."

"Then force him to listen. What about Sebastien? How is he coping?" Immersed in work, Mila simultaneously typed a message to someone and talked to me.

"At first, he accused me of dragging it out for too long and told me he hated me. He barely spoke to me for a week and then he hugged me and moved on. I'm glad he's handling it so well, but then he's so taken by his father and all the attention he's getting from Massi and Bianca, he has no time to hold grudges."

"I swear if the two of you don't discuss things within the next day or two, I'm locking you in a room and won't let you out until I hear you fucking."

Mila's plan might be the only possibility. I giggle at the memory of her expression when she said it and the driver raises his eyebrow, eyeing me in the rearview mirror. Jesus, my head is swimming.

The car finally reaches my house, and sure enough Massi is leaning against the luxury black sedan.

I stumble outside, but the ground shifts weirdly under my feet and I have to grab the car's door to steady myself.

"Are you okay?" Massi is by my side immediately.

I giggle. "I had a headache. I think I took too many painkillers. Is Seb inside?"

"Yes, I waited for you. Why are you smiling?"

"You're so handsome." I grin, my brain floating in my head, rational thought gone. Or not. I don't know. I'm sleepy.

"Okay, you definitely took too many. Let me help you in." He hoists me into his arms and I sigh, content.

I tilt my head, the muscles of his chest hard and yet the softest pillow. I close my eyes, engulfed by the scent of him. He's wearing a soft T-shirt. It's the softest fabric I've ever touched. So soft. Soft.

My back slumps into another softness. "It's my

bed." I sigh, not sure if the words are in my head or if I've spoken them.

"Yes, Blue. It's your bed. I'll get you water. Stay put."

As if I was going anywhere.

* * *

My head registers soft sounds coming from far, far away. The succulent smell of eggs and bacon follows from the same direction. Where am I?

Wait a minute? Images of my previous interaction with Massi flick through my head. Was I dreaming of his arms around me? No, he carried me to my bed. Events start slowly clicking into place.

I open my eyes. The curtains are drawn, but the sun is peeking through in a single ray of light. Sitting up, I realize I don't have a headache anymore.

It's eight o'clock and I'm in a T-shirt and my underwear. When did I undress? Did Massi do that? Jesus, as if there wasn't enough tension between us.

I recall the muscular arms putting me gently to my bed and my heart weeps. He was only being a gentleman, I know, but still. He cared.

Don't get ahead of yourself.

I follow the smell of bacon to the kitchen, assuming Seb is cooking.

The sight that confronts me when I get downstairs fills me with need and sadness. Massi is flipping pancakes. He's in the same T-shirt and a pair of jeans from last night, I think, but he's freshly showered. Did he sleep here?

With his back to me he doesn't see me, and I decide to enjoy the view, leaning against the door frame. I've never seen anyone sexier.

The picture is so domestic and happy, it's difficult to acknowledge this is not a regular situation.

"Good morning," I say eventually.

He turns and gives me a nod. "Feeling better?"

A nod, not a smile. He's here due to his sense of duty.

"Yes, thank you. Did you stay here last night?"

"After you fell asleep I went back to work. We had too many reservations to leave Lena there alone, but I came back."

I walk to the coffee pot to pour myself a cup. "You didn't have to."

"I know."

What does that mean? He knows, but he wanted to? Because of me? Or he didn't want to leave his son—our son, damn it—with an incapacitated mother?

I take my coffee to the breakfast nook.

"I guess we can leave the teenager asleep. Pancakes

or toast?" He dances around the kitchen as if he cooks here every day. But he never has.

"Pancakes, thank you."

Massi brings over two plates and sits across from me. It's amazing and weird at the same time. I've wished for a normal moment alone with him for weeks. And now it's here and I'm unprepared. I take a bite and smile at him. He wolfs down his eggs, watching me through his eyelashes.

We're like two people dancing on thin ice. If we don't speak, we may survive the cracks without plunging into the freezing lake. Our relationship died with words. Harsh words that were spoken, and honest thoughts that remained unsaid.

Those thoughts linger heavily above us as we pretend-enjoy our breakfast.

I straighten the mail on the table, just to relieve the awkwardness with something. A wrinkled paper catches my attention. I flip it to find a list. A list of schools. High schools in New York.

Massi puts his fork down and I take that as an admission of guilt. He's familiar with this piece of paper.

"What is this?" I ask, pushing away the breakfast.

He shakes his head in that way that says don't-make-it-a-big-deal, which only encourages me to make it an even bigger deal.

"My mother called a few schools to see if they would admit Seb. If he—"

"So the Cassinettis are now deciding the future of my son."

"If he wanted to transfer." Massi reins his tone into patient submission. Barely. "And it's *our* son."

"This is a shitty move to undermine me." I wiggle the paper in front of him and then ball it and throw it across the room.

How could they do this without involving me? How am I supposed to stay here and feel like a nuisance? Someone they tolerate because they have to. The feeling of isolation I've been fighting for the past few weeks grows, robbing me of any hope.

"I'm sorry. For what it's worth, she went behind my back and I don't approve of her meddling."

I bite my lip. "What did Seb say?"

"He'll stay where you are."

"Good." I cross my arms over my chest and turn to face the garden. It would have been such a pretty morning.

"So you're selling the house."

"I can't have two households." I look at him and see sadness in his eyes. I'm upset about the stupid list of schools, about what it represents. The idea of my future as someone standing on the sideline as my family thrives.

Massi nods and swallows, focused on circles he's drawing with his fingers on the table.

"I've been thinking about it and I can move to LA."

My mind misfires. What the fuck?

"But what about Casa Cassi?"

"I can open a new place out there."

"You'd give up your restaurant?" I'm having a stroke. Or maybe I took too many pills last night, and they're still skewing my perception of the world.

"Of course." He says it so matter-of-factly, as if it has never even been a point to consider.

I stare at him, unable to react or assess what's going on.

"I wouldn't be giving it up," he continues. "It's a well-established business now. Ideally I'd talk Lena into taking over, but if not I'll find someone else. And I can still host special weeks here. I like the challenge of opening a new concept somewhere else."

He has an entire plan figured out.

"Why?" I rasp. It's my heart asking. My stupid, needy heart would like to hear he wants to give everything up for me.

"What do you mean why? I don't want to miss any more time with Sebastien."

I swallow a sob of disappointment. So many sobs I've uttered or held back because of this man and he doesn't care. He transferred his attention to our son completely. It's not a family he would give his restaurant for. It's his son. Not me.

"Could you leave, please?" I stand up and grab the plates, marching to the counter and throwing them into the sink.

"Blue—"

"Don't you dare call me Blue. Just go, please." I control my voice, too aware of our sleeping child upstairs. A child I'm currently jealous of. The emotion rips my insides apart. I don't deserve this. I don't want to feel this way. It's too much. It's too hard.

The walls are closing in on me. I should be happy he's willing to make such a drastic change, and yet I'm furious and disappointed that I'm not part of his consideration.

Oh, the disappointment digs deep. Why can't he forgive me? Every time I see him it hurts me physically. I've yearned for him for years, but doing it from afar was survivable. This is just too painful.

I don't even realize how, but suddenly I'm pushing out the front door and running away. I can't stay in the same room with all these pent-up feelings. With the man who cast me aside.

I can't even blame him because I haven't forgiven myself. That thought punches me in the stomach and I pick up speed.

"Blue," Massi calls after me, which only makes me

run faster. My bare feet hurt, but that's a welcome break from all the other aches.

He catches up with me as I reach the grass of a playground at the end of the street.

"Blue, what the fuck is happening? Can we for once talk like reasonable people about everything? I offer to move and you get this upset?"

"But it's not about me, is it? You want Sebastien. You don't want me. You can't forgive me. And I don't know if I can survive staying close to you. It's killing me every single day. I can't change my decisions from almost two decades ago, but I deserve a sliver of happiness and I'll never find it with you looking at me like I'm the villain in this story. Even though I *am* the villain in this story."

He grabs my shoulders but I wiggle away, retreating farther into the playground. Déjà vu. This is where we argued until I agreed to marry him. The irony.

"I have so many flaws I can't even list them anymore. When I left here seventeen years ago, I was devastated. I felt worthless because I couldn't keep you interested in me enough."

"Blue—"

"Let me finish." I move around so a bench is between us. "I felt like a failure. But I still hoped that time and distance would give us a second chance. And then I found out I was pregnant. I was still grieving for you and the baby we lost, the one you never wanted. The one I *thought* you never wanted. I heard you were struggling, and the idea of waltzing back and announcing you have to postpone your dreams again shattered me.

"I didn't want to be the reason for your broken dreams, but I couldn't afford a child on my own. In my mind, if I kept the child I would forever be connected with you. Frederick came to New York, and when he returned he casually mentioned running into you and that you raved about how good it was that you were free to focus on your business.

"I should have seen through his lies, but I didn't. I couldn't do it alone and he seemed like such a simple solution. My relationship with him was doomed from the beginning. In bed, in life, in business. You can't fake loving someone if your heart is elsewhere. I know now that I was just a trophy in his war against you. Against anyone who he feared being better than him. I was a pawn on his chess board, but I'm not making excuses.

"Back then, I truly believed that by marrying and keeping my pregnancy from you I'd set you free of any obligation. And so I imprisoned myself in a loveless marriage with a man who is vile and vengeful."

"Blue—"

"I'm not done yet." I raise my voice, scaring away an approaching mother with a stroller who promptly pivots and walks away.

The words are setting me free and binding me tighter at the same time, but Massi is listening. Finally he's listening, and I'm not going to stop now.

"Everything I've ever done was to protect someone. With time, I could see I was hurting them. I believed I protected you by not telling you about your child. I thought I was protecting our son by not telling him the truth because I didn't want him to experience his father's rejection. All the while I was just scared. Hurt and stupid. But I'm done. I don't want you to move to LA."

A shadow passes over Massi's face and he clenches his fists but says nothing. The tension is almost audible.

"I don't want to be lonely anymore," I continue. "I put the house here and my condo in LA for sale. I wanted to talk to you and Seb, so we can find a new school—the three of us. Probably in Manhattan."

"So you aren't planning to return to LA?" He shakes his head, confused.

"Of course not. I wouldn't do that to Sebastien. To you. I love you, Massi. I will always love you. And it hurts that you can't forgive me, but I'll learn to accept that. I've never felt as lonely as I did in the past few weeks. I've never cried this much..." I'm sobbing now.

Ugly crying with mucus smearing my face. The deposits of the past years escaping with abandon.

Massi cuts the distance between us, jumps over the bench and wraps his arms around me. "Can I speak now?"

I cry into his T-shirt, loudly, unladylike. "I'd rather you leave."

"That's the one wish I will not grant you." He cups my face and looks at me. For the first time in weeks, he looks at me with that look that got me hooked on him all those years ago and I try to swallow a sob. He's too close. So close, I don't know if I'm breathing by myself anymore.

"Stop blaming yourself," he says, so gently that goosebumps sprout over my skin. I gasp or sob, or grunt, I'm not sure, but it's a sound of relief mixed with anxiety. "I pushed you away, Blue, and the only thing you're guilty of is that you stayed away. And then you came back and we got a glimpse of hope and it crumbled again too fast.

"Blue, being with you is the hardest thing in my life. I'm scared we'll keep hurting each other, but staying away from you hurts more. Staying away is so much harder."

"What are you saying?" The stupid hope blooms.

"I'd rather be consumed by love than by anger and

resentment. You didn't want to hurt me. We both need to forgive each other, but mostly forgive ourselves."

My face contorts as I try to stop the waterworks.

"I love you, Blue."

He crushes his lips against mine. Two wounded souls on the mend. Here at the playground where it all started, but without the adolescent angst and naïve urgency, we find harmony in that kiss.

New beginning.

Atonement.

Hope.

Love.

Epilogue

Massi

2 months later

I can't stop kissing her. I really can't. It's ridiculous. It's like I've been trying to cash out all the kisses I haven't gotten over the years.

"Get a room." Our son ambles into the kitchen and gets a soda from the fridge. "Seriously, the two of you, it's embarrassing."

We stand by the window, Blue's back against me, my arms around her. Just like that, because we can. Because we want to. Seb eyes us with all the teenage contempt he can muster and leaves.

"We should tell him before we tell the rest of the family today." I rub Blue's belly.

"I'm a bit scared. We've been so busy with the move and the new school, I'm worried his fragile hormones might not take the news the right way. Perhaps we should wait." She turns, wraps her arms around my waist, nuzzling the crook of my neck.

"Haven't we learned enough about postponing the truth," I whisper into her hair.

Her shoulders shake with a soft laughter. "Fair enough, but you tell him."

I pull her behind me and we go to Seb's room. We've remodeled the guest room for him. When I got this place seven years ago, it was meant as a bachelor pad, but the minute I saw it I thought how much Blue would love it. And she does. For now, we fit here.

"Hey, buddy, before we leave to see Granny and the clan, we wanted to tell you something." Suddenly I understand Blue's trepidation. Shit, this will be a major adjustment for him.

"Guessing by your faces, you're not getting me a car for Christmas or a Caribbean getaway with my friends for spring break." Lying on his bed, he peeks at us and then returns his attention to his screen.

"Sebastien, put away the phone."

He looks at me, sighs, swings his legs over and sits on his bed, waiting.

"You don't need a car in Manhattan and it's still a

long time until March." Fuck, I'm so going to get him both.

Blue clears her throat and raises her eyebrows. Thank God she keeps me grounded, or we would have the most spoiled child in the world.

I scratch the back of my neck. "Yes, right, we wanted to share joyful news with you. You're going to have a brother."

"Or a sister," Blue adds and squeezes my hand so hard I almost yelp.

Sebastien studies us, expressionless, or perhaps with contempt. I'm often confused by the mood swings. With all the changes in his life, he's been oscillating between a sweet child and an unbearable adolescent.

"Okay." He stands up and pushes past us. "Are we going to Gran's now?"

I stare at the open door as his footsteps recede. Blue lets out a deep breath of air.

"That went well?" I'm strangely defeated and relieved by his reaction.

"There will be a follow-up outburst or blackmail of some sort." She shrugs and walks out of the room. "Wanna bet which one?"

I chuckle. "Hundred bucks on blackmail."

She looks at me, unimpressed. "You were going to

pay for his Caribbean trip anyway, so if that's the subject of his extortion, the bet is off."

I grab her arm and pull her closer. "But March would be a perfect time to have a week to ourselves, before the baby comes. I'm looking forward to all the pregnancy sex," I whisper into her ear and she shivers, which sends a signal to my pants.

She hums. Actually purrs like a kitten. "I'm seeing spring break in a new, more positive light. Perhaps we should spoil our son a bit."

I capture her lips.

"For fuck's sake, the two of you. Can we just go finally?" Sebastien groans.

"Language," we say at the same time.

We arrive at my mother's in Riverdale and are greeted by Sydney at the door.

"Are we the last ones?" I ask her as we shed our coats. Blue and Seb go to the kitchen to talk to my mother while Sydney ushers me into the sitting room.

"You're not late, but you're the last ones. Baldo and Brooklyn are no-shows." She leans against the door frame in the large double door opening that connects the sitting room with the larger family room.

Of course they are. Our youngest siblings have been avoiding the family and traveling for years now.

Sydney's younger sisters, identical twins Paris and

London, sit on the sofa next to their father, flipping through some book or album.

"Gio hasn't stopped staring into his phone and Andrea seems utterly bored. What is concerning, however, is that Bianca dropped a few things on the floor and is talking in circles."

"My mother is nervous?" I raise my eyebrows and Sydney shrugs.

"Massi." Andrea walks over to me. "How are you, bro? I've been reading about you. I must make a reservation one of these days." He gives me a one arm hug.

"Yeah, stranger, that would be nice. Do it under your name, so I know to spit into your soup." I punch his arm.

"Asshole."

"Andrea." Our mother enters the room and we step away from each other as if we're still little boys caught doing something wrong.

Micah stands up with difficulty and joins her by the door. I haven't seen my stepfather in a while, but he seems to have aged rapidly. Mom smiles at him and takes his hand.

"We have something to tell you," Mom says and leads Micah to an armchair where he sits, but they keep holding hands.

Blue and Seb come over and something tells me we won't share our news today.

"We called you all here today—" My mom starts in a weird, detached voice.

"Let me speak, darling." Micah pats the top of her hand and I think that for the first time in my life I see my mother blinking away tears.

Blue weaves her fingers through mine. The room is heavy with impending news. I look at the somber faces of my brothers and stepsisters and I can see we're all expecting something we don't want to hear.

"We feel that life is short and we haven't been spending enough time together as a family. Now I know you all have busy lives, but Bianca and I would like to host a monthly lunch. You all are invited." Micah's words are met with a silence that stretches.

My mom clears her throat. "Not invited. You're expected. And someone needs to deliver the message to Baldo and Brooklyn."

We all stare at them. They are ordering us to have a family lunch?

"As someone who's missed out on years with my family," I say and pull Blue closer to me, "I think it's a fabulous idea."

"We got portable heaters for the deck, so today is a barbecue." My mom helps Micah stand up and they walk out of the room.

Paris slouches deeper into the sofa and London stares at the door where they left.

"I didn't expect that. Do you think Mom is okay?" Gio asks, his phone nowhere in sight.

"Yes, dickhead, she is fabulous. Something is wrong, but they are not telling us." Andrea shakes his head.

"Let's play happy families then." Sydney walks to the small bar in the room's corner.

"I'll have whiskey." Andrea ambles over and leans against the counter.

"Me too," Gio and Paris say at the same time.

"I'm not a bartender." Sydney rolls her eyes, but sets out four tumblers and pours from a bottle.

"Let's join them." I take Blue's hand and gesture to Seb to join us.

Eventually we all forget about the awkward invitation and the afternoon turns into a fun affair. Even London, who is usually pissed at the world, laughs a few times.

As Mom serves us dessert, my phone rings. I decline the call.

"Who was it?" Blue asks.

I've been trying to draw a line between work and family. Mostly failing, but I'm sure Phillip can handle whatever is happening.

Before I answer her, a message arrives. *CALL ME.* All caps. What the hell?

"I'm sorry. It's Phillip. It seems important." I leave to take the call.

Standing on the gravel path leading to the garden, I study the large oak tree in front of me as I listen to Phillip. I hang up and continue staring, unable to move.

"Is everything okay?" Blue comes from behind and touches my shoulder.

I whip around and seize her mouth. She loses balance for a second, surprised, but then she recovers and smiles against my lips. "Something good happened?"

"Michelin called."

"You got the star?" Her eyes wide, sparkling with excitement.

I shake my head. "No, Blue, I fucking got two."

Sydney

"Do you think one of them is dying?" I ask Massi as I take a plate from him and put it into the dishwasher.

We're alone in the kitchen, having been tasked with the clean-up. There really is no advantage in being the oldest in this family.

"What the fuck, Syd? Why would you say that?" Massi looks at me as if I'm deranged. Not the first time he's given me that look either.

"I'm just saying. It's weird they suddenly insist on a regular family get-together, and Dad used the life-is-too-short phrase." I continue loading the dishwasher.

Maybe I'm just being unnecessarily negative. Pessimism has been my virtue since my husband died. And it didn't improve with the current state of my relationship. If there is one. I groan inwardly.

"I don't know. I think it's a good idea to spend more time together regardless of the motivation. When they're ready to tell us, they will tell us."

"Tell you what?" Bianca walks in with a tray full of glasses.

"If either of you is dying," Massi deadpans.

She flinches. It's almost untraceable, but it's there. On the other hand, it's a statement any normal person would react to with disdain.

I glare at Massi. Asshole. Nobody in this family understands the word discretion.

"We all will die one day." Bianca leaves the tray on the counter and opens the fridge. I can't help but think she is trying to avoid us.

When she turns back she is all business, her typical pleasant, but strict, matriarchal countenance firmly in place. "Syd, why don't you see who else would like some coffee?"

I return to the deck. The men are talking on the side with Paris. London and Sebastien are on their phones, so I sit beside Gina.

"Your first big Cassinetti/Lowe event. How are you coping?" I pluck a grape from a plate in front of us.

"I was a bit worried at first. I've been practically alone most of my life and this is intimidating, but great at the same time." She smiles at me, her hands in her lap. No, no. Not in her lap.

I'll fish. "Your boobs look bigger." I vividly remember the night she lost the baby, and given the circumstances of her second pregnancy this would be such amazing news. Even a pessimistic skeptic like me would rejoice.

Her eyes widen, but she bites her lip. "Wow, subtle. We were planning to announce it today, but somehow we didn't get to it with everything else going on."

"So Massi getting the stars is more important?" I tease. I'm happy for them. And I try to push my own complicated situation to the side. Relationships like Massi and Gina are simply not meant for me.

"In this moment, yes." She beams. "And we might just enjoy this news"—she rubs her belly—"for a little longer between the two of us."

"My lips are sealed." I stand up. "I was sent to take your coffee orders," I announce to the group.

"It's not normal she's still alone." Bianca's voice reaches me as I approach the kitchen. They both have their backs to the door, so I stop and listen. I shouldn't, but I suspect they are talking about me and I can't help it.

"Stop meddling, Mom. You got me off your list, so now you're moving to your next victim," Massi says.

"Don't you give me that attitude, son. If I didn't drag you to Gina's father's wake or call Phillip to suggest he hire her to help you, you wouldn't be all settled and happy."

"You told Phillip to hire Gina?" The shock in Massi's voice is kind of amusing.

"I told him there was someone who could help you in your career." Bianca wipes the counter, speaking like Massi is still a boy. "There is a woman behind every successful man."

"Well, I guess, thank you, Mother, but I still think you should leave Sydney alone."

So they *were* talking about me.

"It's not normal to grieve her late husband for six years now."

My stomach squeezes.

If only she knew it's not my late husband I long for.

Who is Sydney longing for? Start reading Reckless Desire on the next page.

Thank you for reading Reckless Fate. Is Massi and Gina getting banned from other spas in Manhattan? Find out in this bonus epilogue at www.maxinehenri.com/fate or scan:

Reckless Desire

Sydney

"And then I watched him talking about himself with a full mouth or remains of seaweed between his teeth." I shudder internally at the memory.

London laughs. She sounds like a pack-a-day smoker despite a fairly healthy lifestyle—aside from the quarts of margaritas she consumes at times—and as much as I love her, I wish she wouldn't draw attention to us. I'm on my first cocktail, not yet relaxed enough.

"Oh my God, don't be so sour. One shitty date...so what? I'm sure there is someone on that app who clicks with you." She leans forward and winks, amusement tugging at her lips, which is concerning by itself. Lo cultivates a permanent scowl.

We're at the cocktail bar in the lobby of The Ritz-

Carlton, which isn't my normal social scene, and it feels like the whole place is staring at us when London cackles like that. And of course, my sister has maneuvered the conversation around to my unfortunate Tinder dates. I suspect she might have encouraged me to try dating apps for her own distraction, even though I don't really have any fun or exciting stories to share with her.

"Of course, I've chatted with several reasonably looking and intelligent men, but once we meet, it's a disaster. One guy called me seven times within an hour after our dinner. Just to check on me." I cringe. "Needy. Or the one who forgot to take off his wedding band."

Hmm. Maybe my dates are a cause for laughter. Why do I even bother? "Oh, wait, there was a guy who was so annoyed I was a few minutes late, he practically didn't talk to me for the first half of our dinner."

London snorts.

I take a sip of my drink. God, this strawberry margarita tastes good. The only good thing about this evening.

"And those who're the most interesting only want sex." Online dating is depressing.

"What's wrong with that?" London narrows her eyes and shakes her head like I've just said something ridiculous. She's not interested in love, but she doesn't shy away from a hook-up. Ruthless during the day and fun and loose at night. I envy her. Well, some of it.

"Not exactly the way I want to start a relationship. I'm not on that stupid app for one-night stands." This drink is delicious. I may need another cocktail.

I love hanging out with London. I'm closest to her of all my siblings. Perhaps because we have a similar, practical, realistic—some say pessimistic—outlook on life. We live in different circles because London manages her money more aggressively than I do, but we still spend time together regularly.

She is sensitive to my financial situation—not that she knows much about it—and we usually choose somewhere less posh, less ostentatious, and more comfortable for my budget.

Today, we're catching up on my birthday celebration—four months later—and London insisted we meet here since it's her treat and all. The location surprised me because Lo is the last person who wants to spend money on things. Experiences, yes, but things are a waste for her.

This being my birthday outing, I wish we were somewhere I'm not reminded of how ordinary I am. But knowing her, I bet there is some experience planned.

London is wearing a beautiful navy blue jumpsuit hugging her tall figure in all the right places. I'm pretty sure it's from a secondhand store, but she wears it as though it was tailored for her. She's not curvy like me, but still very feminine. Her dark hair is styled into effortless-looking waves and her makeup is perfection.

Me, on the other hand? My brown hair is in desperate need of a retouch and in a bun—*styled* by necessity because I didn't have time to wash it. In my green wrap dress, I'm acutely aware of how not glamorous, not attractive and very average I've become in the last three years.

Perhaps the margarita is not that good after all, just spiraling me into melancholy. This entire bar isn't good for my self-esteem. Why did she even bring me here?

"You need to loosen up. The whole point of signing you up on that site was to get your coochie serviced finally."

I roll my eyes and take another sip. No amount of alcohol can drown out London's well-meant and utterly annoying efforts to find me a man.

"I'm perfectly fine in that department." Not entirely true.

She throws her arms up. "Oh please, a vibrator wasn't invented to replace a man. Just to carry us over. But your dry spell is concerning. It's been three years since that asshole husband of yours died. Three years!" She raises her brows.

My stomach tightens at the mention of Jeremy.

How could you love someone so much only to discover you didn't know them at all? Yet, I'm offended on his behalf that she called him an asshole.

"Come on!" London shakes her head. "Enough with the sour face. Whatever happened to my fun and carefree sister? I want her back." She pouts like a spoiled child.

She is no child or spoiled. Lo was Bianca's—our stepmother's—sweetheart. Always willing to go shopping, get manicures and do all the other things daughters do with their mothers. Until she wasn't. She lost her spark and belief in love over several horrible months when she was seventeen and her darker side won over.

Frankly, she is the last one who should call me out on not being fun and carefree anymore.

"That girl is gone, Lo. I'm a deep-in-debt, responsible adult now."

She twists her lips, unimpressed. "Point taken. Still, you're an adult who needs her lady parts taken care of."

Two men, sitting at the table beside us, turn. Not with shock. With interest. One of them openly checks me out as if I was a piece of meat on display in his favorite steakhouse. What the hell? Heat rises in my cheeks, and I try to hide my reaction behind my drink, emptying it in one gulp.

"Sex is not a universal solution to all the world's problems." I put my glass down with a clunk.

"But we're not solving the world's problem, we're solving yours, Syd. And while you don't allow me to help with the financial disaster your dearly beloved late husband caused, I'm not giving up on other areas of your life. You've been stuck in some in between land of solitude. Not moving forward is the worst way to live your life. You have to start trusting people."

"You're one to talk." I frown at her.

"I'm living my life fully. Perhaps not to other people's expectations. Yes, I'm frustrated about the world's injustices, but I try to help where I can and I've been reasonably content for years now. And I'm not planning to change anything. Your trust issues sprouted three years ago and you need to move on."

She's right. I hate her for that. Well, not really, but I'm perfectly comfortable suspended between no longer having a husband and my next chapter. The next stage scares me, so I'm in no hurry to reach it.

I had my future planned. And it didn't involve anything that is a part of my life right now. So I'm not looking forward anymore. What for? Just to have my plans crushed?

"I don't have trust issues." I lean back and glare at Lo.

"You're right. You don't have trust issues." She

nods, her tone mocking. "And there are no protective walls. None at all. That's why you're a substitute teacher *by choice*. You're scared to get attached to a school, a class, those kids. You've arranged your life in a way that prevents any lasting relationships. You don't need to remember the names of your colleagues or the kids you teach because everywhere you go is temporary."

"And you're different? You don't even know your doorman's name and you see him daily." I'm defensive, which only proves how right she is. What nerve. She's preaching against the very life she lives.

Lo runs a charity and a palliative care center and is constantly pissed at the world for all the loss and pain that confronts her daily. To survive, she doesn't get attached. Ever.

"I'm not miserable as you are," she quips.

"I go to some schools more often. I know the names of other teachers." One or two. "I'm happy with my job. It's never boring, always changing." I wish I could raise my voice, but this place so deadened.

"Oh, that's the reason you haven't taken any of the permanent positions they've offered you? Because you *want* constant change instead of a better salary and stable position in a job you love?" She is baiting me, but I refuse to bite. "And when was the last time you hung out with any of our siblings?"

"I'm hanging out with you and you know how busy they all are." I spoke to Paris last... Has it been over two months now? Shit.

"Yes, but let's face it, I'm the only lasting relationship in your life and that's only because I force myself on you."

I'm not going to admit she is right. But London stuck around even after I refused to see anyone else. When I was sure I was going to die from grief and disappointment. In the darkest moments of my life, when I closed the door on her, she simply returned through the window.

"And having sex would help me regain trust in humanity, especially the male portion of it?" Why am I indulging her?

"Definitely not, but it's a start. It would snap you out of that ugly cocoon you wove around yourself as protection." She raises her glass. "Let's toast to burning down those fucking protective walls and enjoying life fully again."

I lift my glass by the stem and dip it toward hers. The crushed ice settles and I fake a smile. As luck would have it, I don't have any drink left to toast to fully enjoying my life. Because the Universe is too aware I don't know how.

London rolls her eyes and waves at the server.

The bar is half-empty. All the other guests look like

business people, still in the full swing of their work-week, having meetings probably. Come to think of it, there are mostly men here. Oh God, is this London's ploy to pick up men? Or, more specifically, hook me up with someone?

"I'm starving. Are you going to feed me anything but alcohol? Let's go have dinner." I try to get us out of there. "This birthday sucks, by the way."

The man at the next table is visibly watching at me now. He didn't even notice me before London shouted the comment about my lady parts needing servicing. And they do. Oh God help me, they do. But this douche is not my type.

Not that I have a specific type, but a man with a wedding ring is definitely not it.

"Don't be so impatient. Let's have a cocktail or two, so you're in a better mood before you get your present." She smiles and her eyes sparkle with mischief. I get an uncomfortable feeling she's planned something I won't like.

"You didn't need to worry about a present. You paying for an extravagant dinner here is more than enough."

She waves at the server and orders another pitcher of margaritas.

I can't stop her plans, so I better drink up to get into a more festive and receptive mood.

"I'm sorry I unloaded on you, Syd. I worry about you." She reaches over and squeezes my hand and then turns to the two men next to us. "And you stop drooling. It's not happening."

I laugh. She really does have my back. As the server brings our pitcher, the two ask for their bill and clear out, not giving us another glance. London rolls her eyes and we both burst into giggles.

The next hour is lighter on conversation and heavy on drinking. We laugh and I'm grateful she forces me to do these things because, as sad as my life is, she snaps me out of my funk occasionally.

I know it's her way of dealing with the darkness in her own life, but I let her work the magic on me as well.

A few men try to make a contact and join us or order a round for us, but London scares them off with her signature ice queen look that can freeze hell. That helps me relax even more. It's nice to have a girls' night out. Perhaps I should have more of those.

"So when will you give me my present?" I hunch my shoulders in glee, margaritas hugging my insides with a warm and fuzzy feeling.

She checks her watch. "In about half an hour."

I giggle. "What did you get me? Is it going to be delivered here? Are you going to embarrass me?"

"Excuse me." She pretends to be offended, but immediately smiles and wiggles her brows. She's having way too much fun with this. "You're having dinner with your present."

I frown. "You got me silverware?"

Her laughter gets attention around the lobby and perhaps on the other side of the street. "No, silly, but if you need silverware, I'm buying you some for Christmas."

We both snicker, more courtesy of our drinks than the conversation itself.

"My darling Sydney, I got you a dinner date and a room for the night here." She smiles, scanning me with expectation.

"What do you mean? You set me up with someone? On a blind date?" And it was shaping up to be such a great evening. The worst part is I realize I'm not as opposed to the idea as I should be. I've definitely had too much to drink.

"Kind of." She bites her bottom lip, the picture of innocence.

"And it's quite presumptuous to assume we would end up sleeping together. What if I like him?" I gulp down what's left in my glass because I can't possibly imagine dealing with this sober. Though I'm quite tipsy already. She got me drunk first on purpose. Oh, she's good. I frown at London, trying my best to imitate her stony stare.

"Oh, you *will* like him." She gives me such a

knowing look. Oh, for fuck's sake, has she set me up with someone she knows well?

"Cancel the room." I'm not hooking up with someone I've never met and especially not if she knows him. Oh God, has she slept with him as well?

"Whatever for? This date is for your coochie."

A woman passes by and turns to us, half appalled, half interested. She winks at me. What the hell?

"Don't be ridiculous, Lo. Oh my God, did you tell him I'll sleep with him? Is he coming assuming we would..." I think I just sobered up.

She smiles and shrugs nonchalantly.

"Oh my God, London, that is the worst birthday present ever. How could you? And why did you assume I'd even go along with that? A spa certificate would have been a reasonable gift. I'm not having sex with him."

"Don't be so dramatic. I'm not setting you up with your future husband. It's just to get you interested in men again. He has absolutely no expectation beyond tonight."

"What do you mean? He could like me." This evening is a nightmare.

"It's against the rules, I think. Or just unprofessional, so you can relax and enjoy a perfect night, no strings attached. No bullshit Tinder dates. He comes highly recommended."

"Highly recommended? Is he some sleazy player? Who recommended him?" Oh my God, a part of me wants to laugh, but I don't think this is a prank. And London seems perfectly pleased with her present.

"His other clients," she whispers, raising her brows, as if I'm the unreasonable one here.

I want to ask her to explain, but the words spring into comprehension and I freeze. I'm not even sure if I'm shocked or angry. Or a little bit curious.

"You got me a male prostitute?" I whisper, looking around to make sure nobody can so much as read my lips.

"Don't be ridiculous." London swats that idea out of the air. "I got you an exclusive male escort."

Also by Maxine Henri

Untamed Billionaires Series

Cinnamon Passion (A Fake Relationship Romance)

Caramel Obsession (A Secret Billionaire Romance)

Vanilla Flame (An Age Gap/Innocent Heroine Romance)

Chocolate Secret (A Forbidden Love Romance)

Reckless Billionaires Series

Reckless Fate (A Second Chance Billionaire Romance)

Coming soon:

Reckless Desire (A Single Dad Billionaire Romance)

Reckless Dare (A Fake Relationship Billionaire Romance)

Reckless Deal (A Bosshole Billionaire Romance)

If you loved Reckless Fate, please spread the word and leave a review here.

One sentence is enough to help other readers and make me very happy.

Acknowledgments

Thank you, dear reader, that you made it this far. I hope you enjoyed Massi and Gina's story. I loved writing it and it's always rewarding to find people who equally love reading it. My love for writing grows exponentially with every single one of you.

Thank you, Martin. You're my soulmate and best friend. You're probably a reason why I can't write dark heroes. You're my Prince Charming. Your support on this author journey means more than I can express with words (and I call myself a writer).

Editor Jess, you made this book readable and pointed out logical issues, but you also challenged the plot and pushed me to write a better story.

Jaycee DeLorenzo, I love the cover, both of them. You're amazing.

Thank you, Dan, for finding the typos and other mistakes. I really don't know how you spot them.

All the ladies in my author support group, you inspire me daily with your dedication, knowledge, wit and talent.

And I'm going to loop back and thank you, dear reader, again. Because none of this would be possible without YOU!

About the Author

Maxine Henri is a contemporary romance author who infuses her stories with steamy passion and complex characters. When she's not crafting stories that will have you swooning, she can usually be found sipping on a cup of black tea while reading a good book. Or traveling to new destinations.

Maxine believes that stories matter. They facilitate emotional journeys, inspire and entertain. And when it comes to books and fiction, stories are a great escape and probably the most beneficial addiction on this planet.

Her billionaire romances are the perfect escape, offering a taste of luxury and adventure. Maxine introduces heroes who may have a dark past, but are always balanced by a lighter side. And her leading ladies? They're strong, independent women who may be a little broken, but always find their way in life.

You can connect with her on any of these platforms: